Didn't I Say to Make My Abilities Average in the Next Life?!

VOLUME 5

Cherry

Devout Soldier Ogar

Beast King Marl

Didn't I Say
to Make My Abilities
Average in the
Next Life?!

Didn't I Say to Make My Abilities *Average* in the Next Life?!

VOLUME 5

BY

FUNA

ILLUSTRATED BY

Itsuki Akata

Seven Seas Entertainment

DIDN'T I SAY TO MAKE MY ABILITIES AVERAGE
IN THE NEXT LIFE?! VOLUME 5

© FUNA / Itsuki Akata 2017

Originally published in Japan in 2017 by EARTH STAR
Entertainment, Tokyo. English translation rights arranged
with EARTH STAR Entertainment, Tokyo, through TOHAN
CORPORATION, Tokyo.

Seven Seas books may be purchased in bulk for promotional,
educational, or business use. Please contact your local
bookseller or the Macmillan Corporate and Premium Sales
Department at 1-800-221-7945, extension 5442, or by
e-mail at MacmillanSpecialMarkets@macmillan.com.

Follow Seven Seas Entertainment online at
sevenseasentertainment.com.

TRANSLATION: Diana Taylor
ADAPTATION: Maggie Cooper
COVER DESIGN: Nicky Lim
INTERIOR LAYOUT & DESIGN: Clay Gardner
PROOFREADER: Jade Gardner, Kris Swanson
ASSISTANT EDITOR: Jenn Grunigen
LIGHT NOVEL EDITOR: Nibedita Sen
DIGITAL MANAGER: CK Russell
PRODUCTION DESIGNER: Lissa Pattillo
EDITOR-IN-CHIEF: Adam Arnold
PUBLISHER: Jason DeAngelis

ISBN: 978-1-64275-003-4
Printed in Canada
First Printing: March 2019
10 9 8 7 6 5 4 3 2 1

God bless me?

CONTENTS

The Kingdom of Tils

Mile

A girl who was granted "average" abilities in this fantasy world.

Reina

A rookie hunter. Specializes in combat magic.

Pauline

A rookie hunter. A timid girl, however...

Mavis

A swordswoman. Leader of the up-and-coming party, the Crimson Vow.

The Kingdom of Brandel

Eckland Academy

— Marcela —

Adele's friend. A magic user of noble birth.

— Aureana —

Adele's friend. A peasant girl.

— Veil —

A rookie hunter from the Hunters' Prep School. Looks after the orphans in the slums.

— Monika —

Adele's friend. The second daughter of a merchant.

Previously

When Adele von Ascham, the eldest daughter of Viscount Ascham, was ten years old, she was struck with a terrible headache and just like that, remembered everything.

She remembered how, in her previous life, she was an eighteen-year-old Japanese girl named Kurihara Misato who died while trying to save a young girl, and that she met God...

Misato had exceptional abilities, and the expectations of the people around her were high. As a result, she could never live her life the way she wanted. So when she met God, she made an impassioned plea:

"In my next life, please make my abilities average!"

Yet somehow, it all went awry.

In her new life, she can talk to nanomachines and, although her magical powers are technically average, it is the average between a human's and an elder dragon's...6,800 times that of a sorcerer!

At the first academy she attended, she made friends and rescued a little boy as well as a princess. She registered at the Hunters' Prep School under the name of Mile and at the graduation exam went head-to-head with an A-rank hunter.

The party she formed with her classmates, the Crimson Vow, made an impressive debut! But one problem after another has come hurtling their way—from golems, invading foreign soldiers, and fathers who are too protective of their daughters, to elder dragons, the strongest creatures in the world!

A lot has happened, but now Mile is going to live a normal life as a rookie hunter with her allies by her side.

Because she is a perfectly normal, *average* girl!

"A Fearsome Fight!" Doll Wrestling

THIS IS A STORY OF ONE PARTICULAR DAY, back while the Crimson Vow were still enjoying a carefree life as hunters in the capital of the Kingdom of Tils.

The four were walking the back streets of the capital together, as they always did, when they suddenly came upon a commotion. When they looked closer, they saw that it was a group of several children having a quarrel in the middle of the road.

"I'm tellin' you, *we're* the ones who always do that job! For you to just swoop in and... Anyway, that's *our* job!"

"And who decided that, huh? I'm pretty sure you guys are the only ones makin' that claim. Jobs go to whoever can finish 'em the cheapest and the best. It's the client who decides who's takin' on the job, not the ones taking it!"

"Well yeah, but *we're* the ones who always..."

Apparently, they were having a scuffle over a job. It was at least admirable that the disagreement was over a legitimate job and not pickpocketing or other thievery. Furthermore, the argument that the one side was making was a relatively sound one. That said, the Crimson Vow could also understand the feelings of the other side, who seemed to have been thrown into crisis mode by the first group intruding on a job in which they had a vested interest.

With this in mind, Mile moved to interject, but Reina was quicker.

"What are you all doing?! If you keep blocking up the road like that you're gonna cause a traffic jam! Step aside already!"

Hearing this, the children looked Reina's way and immediately replied as one: "Who d'you think *you* are, flat-chest?!"

"Burn, O flames of hell! Singe my enemies—"

"Gaaaaaaah! St-stoooooop!!"

The street had very nearly become the site of a massacre.

Seeing how not only Mile, but also Mavis and Pauline, who were clearly adults, moved desperately to interrupt Reina, the children finally comprehended the situation. The four were a hunting party, and Reina was wearing a mage's garb; the spell that she had been incanting was an incredibly dangerous one; and the children themselves had been only a hair's breadth from looking death straight in the face.

They all dropped to their knees, bowing their heads to the ground with a desperate apology:

"Please forgive uuuuuuuuuuuuuuuusss!!!"

Meanwhile, as per usual, a completely frivolous thought

flitted through Mile's mind: *I've been seeing a lot of dogeza-style apologies lately... I wonder if it's becoming a trend...?*

"W-well," said Reina, "Since you've shown some respect, I'll overlook this just this once... But let me make one thing clear: There will *not* be a next time. There. Will. *Not.*"

"Y-y-y-y-y-yes, ma'am!" the children answered in chorus.

By the looks of it, Reina had deemed that venting her anger further would be immature of her and had decided to spare the children. The matter was considered settled.

In reality, if Mavis and the others had not stepped in when they did, they would very likely have borne witness to a tragedy, so there probably was no such thing as "venting her anger further" here.

"What's with that look?!" Reina shouted, flustered, when she noticed the others eyeing her. "I wasn't really going to fire it!"

Liar! they all thought, totally unconvinced.

Well, thankfully, Mile already had a lattice-power barrier ready and waiting, so at least if the others had not stopped Reina in time, it would've been all right... Plus, even if she *had* fired the spell, she likely would have greatly limited the strength of it so that the children just felt a bit of heat. When it came down to it, Reina was not the sort of person who would murder children over a slight. Such a thing would see her executed, or sentenced to slavery at best.

However, for the children, who were aware of none of this, this seemed to be a grave exchange, and they began to tremble.

"Ah, they've wet themselves..."

Indeed, just as Mile had noted, several of the children appeared to have wet themselves out of fear.

"Guess that's to be expected..." Mile muttered, casting her cleaning magic over the children. The marks and smell vanished, and they were instantly dry, good as new—perhaps even *cleaner* than they had been before wetting themselves.

Now that they had involved themselves this far, the Crimson Vow couldn't just leave the situation unresolved.

Or rather, it was not that they *couldn't*...it might have been because they really wanted to help the children or merely because they thought the situation interesting and were sticking their noses in.

Either way, the children soon found themselves driven along to a nearby open area by an unforgiving Reina, unable to ignore her commands.

"Hm hm, I see, so that's when the conflict over the clients started..."

Reina, unfortunately, was a less-than-suitable candidate for extracting information about the situation from the children. It was not that she didn't know any tricks to make them talk, but rather, that the children were still utterly petrified of her. In order to get the full story out of them, Mile, who was closer to them in age and had an appearance that tended to put others at ease, was chosen as the interrogator.

These were Mile's findings:

One of the two groups of children, it would seem, hailed from an orphanage, and the other group lived on the streets.

The children from the orphanage wore clothing that was crude but free of stains and properly cleaned, and they were clearly a group. On the contrary, the children from the streets were generally unkempt, wearing filthy garb, riddled with lice, and lacking the mark of any guardian.

It was because of this that, when it came to odd jobs that were unworthy of the Guild's time, the children from the orphanage were the preferred hires for tasks that involved direct contact with other people or matters involving food or money rather than the scruffy street urchins. On the other hand, those urchins—who no one would care about should anything happen to them—were perfect for jobs that did not involve other people: dangerous jobs, unsanitary jobs, or even jobs that were borderline criminal.

Indeed, there was a clear caste system when it came to the world of temporary hires.

Lately, however, that dichotomy had apparently shifted.

There had been a transformation in the street urchins (who, in truth, lived in abandoned buildings or underneath bridges so were not so much "street" urchins as merely homeless children). Though their clothes were still ragged, the garments they wore were no longer dirty, and they were cleaning themselves up with water or dust baths. Thanks to a boost in confidence from registering and seeking promotions within the Guild, they were now refusing to take on jobs with criminal elements or otherwise unfavorable conditions,

SIDE STORY
"A FEARSOME FIGHT!" DOLL WRESTLING

and one after another, they had begun to encroach on jobs that were usually taken by the children of the orphanage.

They were clean, demanded lower rates than the children from the orphanage, and worked earnestly and diligently. Since they seemed to be concerned about winning brownie points with the Guild, they could be expected not to try anything funny while on a job. Because they knew it would cause trouble for all of their peers if they were to slip up, and because they knew that mistakes would result in penalties from the guild, these children could generally be relied on.

And then there were the children who were not yet ten years old themselves, whose eyes sparkled with the light of the futures they hoped to someday grasp and who were eternally grateful to be able to take on legitimate jobs without any underlying shadiness. Anyone who had hired them once would come to hire them every time they had an odd job needing doing thereafter; there were even times when people would invent odd jobs just to give them work.

Plus, the hunters who had grown up on the streets themselves, and those who were lifelong citizens from the capital, were strong backers of this movement.

The urchins were on the road to being promoted from "creatures no one would mistake for humans" to legitimate individuals, all thanks to one particular "idiot" somewhere out there...

Of course, there were some who were bearing the burden of this change. Specifically, the children of the orphanage.

Most children at the orphanage considered themselves unfortunate. They had no parents, they wore shabby clothes, and their rations could not be called anywhere near sufficient.

Besides helping in the fields that the orphanage tended, they often sought out odd jobs around the city and offered up a part of their pay to help supplement the institute's thoroughly insufficient operational budget. This way, they could have just a little bit more to eat.

Lately, however, the number of jobs available around town had dropped drastically. This was because of the street urchins—the street urchins who scrabbled around in such squalor that it made the children of the orphanage look like nobles and kings.

The orphans' livelihood was being stolen by those scoundrels.

The moment they became aware of this, the orphans panicked, plunging headlong into crisis mode.

The orphans, you see, could not register with the Hunters' Guild. Were they to do so, word would get around that the orphanage was letting orphans do dangerous work as hunters. Plus, if they were making money as hunters, then there was no reason for them to remain at the orphanage—or at least, no need for the Crown to continue providing them with funding.

Therefore, anyone who became a hunter had to leave the orphanage. In other words, none of the children who lived at the orphanage were hunters.

As for the urchins, those who were below the age of ten could register with the guild as G-rank errand boys, while those older than ten could join the guild properly at F-rank. Thus, the urchins, who could either work as hunters or take on odd jobs that did not make it to the guild, held the clear advantage.

All of which led to the present quarrel.

"Ah..." the Crimson Vow sighed.

The four came simultaneously to the same conclusion: there was nothing to be done for any of it.

"Well! We better be going!" they said, moving to make a hasty exit.

Suddenly, something seized on to Pauline's leg.

"Eeek!" she shrieked, looking down to see eyes swimming with tears.

"Don't leave us!"

Apparently, they were not getting away so easily.

A short distance away from the children, the four girls held a hushed discussion.

"So, what do we do?" asked Reina.

"What *do* we do?"

Even Mile was fresh out of ideas.

There was a shortage of jobs and an excess of workers, and they couldn't simply demand that the urchins only do the lesser jobs that they were originally allotted.

"Even if the orphans don't work outside of the orphanage, there's no risk of them dying of hunger. They receive subsidies

and donations, and they have their fields to work... The urchins,
on the other hand, will starve to death in just a few days if they
don't earn money themselves," Mavis mused.

"So, do we just tell the orphans to give it up?" asked Pauline.

"Hmmmmmm..."

The four of them pondered.

After hemming and hawing over the matter for some time,
Mile suddenly shouted, "I've got it: a conference!"

"A conference?" the other three repeated.

"Yes. See, the root of the problem isn't something that we'll be
able to do anything about in the short term. So instead, we just
have to get the orphans and the urchins to get along. If a sense of
solidarity forms between them, as fellow warriors fighting to secure
a promising future without anyone to care for them, then they'll
come to see one another as close friends, and they won't fight...

"Anyway, they need to empathize—or at least cultivate some
sympathy for one another. From there, they can make appeals to
their shared interests to form a bridge between them, which they
can cross together to seek the path toward a wonderful future for
them all."

As Mile wrapped up her explanation, the others looked
stunned.

"M-Mile, did... did you eat something strange?"

"Do you have a fever? Pauline, whip up some water..."

"O-of course! Right away!"

"Graaaaaaaah!! I keep telling you all, I'm not stupid! It's not
like this was some unexpected stroke of genius!"

And so, the First Annual Orphan-Urchin Solidarity Conference was established.

"Thank you and a warm welcome to all who have gathered here today! This marks the start of the First Annual Orphan-Urchin Solidarity Conference, here in the royal capital of the Kingdom of Tils!"

Hearing the grandiose title that Mile had given the event, the local hunters, who had heard the buzz and come in their free time to see what the whole thing was about, along with the other observers who had snuck into the crowd in disguise, pulled strange faces.

"There is plenty of food to go around so please eat your fill. Once your bellies are happy and full, please take a few moments to chat with your peers and see if you can't exchange information and forge new connections. Such bonds are sure to be of use to you all in the future!"

How exactly were the orphans and the urchins supposed to forge bonds with one another? And just what information did she expect them to exchange? Which restaurants had the most leftover food at the end of the day? What time they put out their trash?

The spectators suddenly felt as though they had headaches coming on and began kneading their temples.

The place they all currently occupied was a church within the capital. The orphanage, which was situated adjacent to the church, was under the church's administration as well.

Following the incident in the street, the Crimson Vow had accompanied the orphans back to the orphanage and explained their plans for a get-together to the administrators. Given the reason for the assembly, and in light of the fact that not only would the orphanage not have to pay a cent but that food would be provided for the children to eat all they wanted, the administrators gratefully accepted the girls' plan. They happily agreed to speak with the church regarding the use of the space, too.

The church, meanwhile, was not about to pass up a chance to have the orphans—who normally would not be expected to enter the church at all—visit the building of their free will, and readily assented.

Having secured a space that was even more spacious and stately than she had envisioned, Mile expanded the scope of her plans accordingly, calling on the orphans from the incident on the street to invite others with whom they might be acquainted with as well.

The other orphans needed little convincing. They needed neither to be told the aim of the gathering nor to be cajoled in the same way as the other children. All these orphans—who did not know what it was like to have plenty—needed to hear was that they would be able to eat their fill, and they were on board.

Anticipating the results of this invitation, the leaders of the orphanage and affiliates of the church began to spread word of the event around, hoping for donations or other contributions. This was not due to miserly tendencies on their part; they merely wished to rally the rest of the community for the sake of the orphans.

And finally, the day arrived, the venue so packed with children and spectators that it would have been little surprise to learn every orphan and urchin in the city was in attendance...

They ate.

All of the children ate and ate until they were close to bursting.

Somehow, no matter how much they ate, the food never seemed to run out. As soon as it seemed that the platters were beginning to go empty, a snap of the fingers brought out new plates, overflowing with fresh morsels seemingly out of nowhere.

There were some who might claim that the plates had "appeared out of thin air," but no one would believe that. Even with a reasonable amount of storage magic, producing plates overflowing with food without spilling anything—and moreover, without them going cold—would be patently impossible.

It was not only the quantity of the food that was astounding but the taste as well, with flavors that far surpassed even that which they had eaten on any festival day in their lives. Although they had been told to socialize in addition to eating, there was no stopping any of the children until they were stuffed to the brim.

"Say now, Chief of Finances... Is that rock lizard I spy?"

"Yes, so it would seem."

"And down there, is that a whole roasted deer...? Just how many tens of gold pieces do they intend to let these urchins gobble down?"

"They appear to be intent on using up more in a single day than the Crown allots to the orphanage in an entire year."

"........."

Once everyone had finally eaten all they could, and the children were stuffed and happy, Mile's voice rang out again:

"Now then, it's time for the games to begin!"

Naturally, just serving up food and compelling the children to talk to one another would not make for much of an event. Even Mile wouldn't overlook such a fundamental fact.

In fact, Mile, who had always been an outsider when it came to cultural festivals and other school events in her previous life, was not going to let a chance like this slip by her. No matter what, she was determined to take part in the games she had planned. That was the root of her motivation.

"Without further ado, we invite you to participate in our Doll Wrestling tournament—'DolWres,' for short."

At that, four small figures, each around thirty centimeters in height, appeared on the stage that had been erected.

According to Mile's explanation, sufficiently amplified throughout the venue using wind magic, the four were small-scale golems known as "Dolls." Those who aimed to utilize these techniques as a means of warfare disguised it as a game and planned an exhibition of skills, hoping to steal the Doll techniques of other countries for their own. In order to put a stop to that plan, one heroine who fought in the name of justice arose.

The Dolls were operated by their owners' verbal commands.

"Ogar, fight!"

A doll in the shape of an ogre, dressed in the trappings of an infantryman—the super heavy-weight, power-type fighter known as "Devout Soldier, Ogar"—stepped forward. The operator, playing the role of the ringleader of the evil organization, was Pauline.

"Go, Beast King Marl!"

The fighter controlled by Mile, the heroine of justice, was a speed-type Doll in the shape of a beastman, called "Beast King Marl."

Choosing to have the beastman be an ally of justice was just one facet of Mile's stealthy marketing scheme to promote the social standing of beastpeople, for the sake of young beast-eared girls the world around.

And then, to serve as assistants for both sides, two more fully automated Dolls appeared.

On the enemy side was Zenio, a Doll who had the looks of a secretary, with fox ears and a tail to match. On Marl's side was Marcy, a maid with feline features.

And then, the true battle began.

Power versus speed. Destructive blows versus skillful slashes. Both sides taking hit after hit, energy slowly dwindling.

During the breaks in the match, Zenio and Marcy stepped in to administer first aid to any damage done to the other Dolls and resupply them with power.

However, owing to his lightweight construction, the heavy damage soon began taking its toll on Beast King Marl, and he found himself in grave danger.

AVERAGE IN THE NEXT LIFE?!

Yet just when it looked as though it was the end for the champion, suddenly, riding atop her noble steed, appeared Cherry, the lightweight princess knight Doll. It appeared that she had no assistant, but the moment she dismounted, her steed stood upon its hind legs and transformed into the humanoid assistant Doll, Raging Speeder.

"I know much of your deeds, Beast King Marl. I've come to your aid!"

Naturally, the puppeteer behind Cherry was Mavis.

In truth, Reina had wanted to play the part as well, but Mavis had begged on her knees, so the role was hers. It was abundantly clear that one who aimed to be a knight, as she did, would never let such a chance slip through her fingers.

With Cherry bursting onto the scene, the match now became a three-sided battle royale.

The children were thrilled.

The adults were speechless.

This was hardly surprising—none of them had ever witnessed such a spectacle.

Also, there was that particular bit of Mile's patter about "those who aimed to utilize these techniques as a means of warfare."

They could not help but think about what might happen if these Dolls were constructed at human size. Or worse yet, larger still—the size of rock golems? And then if they really *were* used on the battlefield?

A cold sweat ran down the backs of all the invited guests' necks.

The Dolls before them moved only on command from their

human handlers, one action at a time, but in truth, their bodies were being moved independently via the nanomachines. Thanks to a prior discussion with Mile, a temporary contract of authority had been established so that, within permissible bounds, the nanomachines would obey and enact each of the Doll's user's directions. Naturally, this had only been accomplished through a detailed discussion with the nanomachines ahead of time.

Normally, Mile assiduously avoided calling upon the nanomachines in her everyday life or her work as a hunter for frivolous purposes, but she figured it was probably fine for a one-off occasion such as this.

She would never bring them into her work or private matters, but if it wasn't for work, but rather, for *charity*, then it was fine, wasn't it?

That was her thinking—and the nanomachines went along with it. They were delighted at the chance to do "something interesting," an opportunity that presented itself only very rarely for them. It seemed that news of the event had already proliferated via the nanomachine network across the entire world...

"Why do you take up arms against us, Beast King Marl?!"

"Why, you ask? One needs not a reason to fight in the name of justice! Why do *you* sully your hands with such foul deeds?!"

Naturally, the ones speaking the lines were not the Dolls themselves, but their handlers, Pauline and Mile.

"Bwahaha, then I might say the same to you. Does one need a reason for which to do evil? Dare I say: because it's fun?

Counting up all the money you've earned is simply delightful! Haaahahahaha!"

When it came to the role of a villain, Pauline was a natural.

"Both gold coins and the lives of men must be spent wisely!" the princess knight Cherry interjected. "What is the worth— where is the meaning?!—in hoarding your coins and living a life without purpose?! I will show you how my spirit burns!!"

With that, a fierce battle raged once more between the three, and the crowd—children and adults alike—went wild! The adults, seeming to forget that this event was for the sake of the children and that they were merely present as spectators, joined in the cheering, a great clamor spreading throughout the hall.

And Mile, watching as the battle continued to rage atop the stage, thought to herself that it was time to begin the final showdown...

Ka-shink!

Tumble...

"Oh..."

Ogar's sword struck Cherry's breastplate, and it went clattering to the floor. Suddenly, Cherry's naked chest was in full view.

There was nothing else beneath to hide her breasts, which were now dewy with moisture. No shirt, no undergarments— nothing.

And, for some reason, they were sculpted in full detail.

The adults stared in shock, the young boys with intense interest. The girls stomped upon the boys' feet.

"She's braless!! It's over! This match is oveeeeeer!!!"

Now, granted, they were quite different from the garments that Mile knew back on Earth, but this world did still have items that ladies wore over their chests. In her mind, Mile referred to these garments as "bras," and in her panic, the word had slipped out.

Despite her peculiar choice to give the female Doll such a well-sculpted bosom, Mile had not included any garments for her chest. She simply had not thought that far ahead.

Even though she was a Doll, having Cherry continue to fight half-naked would absolutely be sending the wrong message to the children. Therefore, Mile decided to call the match to an immediate stop rather than waiting until the final blow was struck.

Plus, it would be unforgivable to continue such a scandalous spectacle in the middle of a church, at an event that had the church and an orphanage as its sponsors.

"But whyyyyyyyy?!" Mavis cried out, devastated that her grand finale had been so abruptly cut short. Her protests were ignored. Mile, in a great hurry, used her superior authority to issue a command to withdraw to the nanomachines who had been entrusted with making the Dolls move, and the figures all shuffled away into storage—after the nanomachines controlling them had cleared out, of course.

One of these days, Mile would have to sit down and have a heart-to-heart with the nanomachines who had participated today, in order to apologize and recognize their services.

In fact, at the moment, Mile was sitting on the ground having a conversation inside her head with the nanomachines. With her eyes closed, it looked from the outside like, rather than

participating in a conference, she had dozed off. Other than the
nanomachines who lived in the strands of Mile's hair, most nanomachines rarely had a chance to contact her directly, and so a
lively exchange was in progress.

After that, the gathering came to a lackluster end.

This did not mean it had been a failure. In fact, it would not
be out of the question to label it a huge success.

Following the wardrobe malfunction, the adults who had
come to observe took to the stage, putting on their scariest faces
and ordering everyone to keep their lips sealed about what they
had witnessed today—and so the "DolWres" incident became a
secret, known only to those who had been present in that room.

The children were dying to talk about the astonishing spectacle, but as it turned out, the only ones they could talk to about
it with were the other urchins and orphans.

The shared secret granted them a sense of camaraderie and
connection.

By a means that she never expected, Mile's aim was accomplished.

Furthermore, the sponsors who had been in attendance, now
realizing that the orphans had a group of considerable wealth and
skill to assist them, increased their contributions to the institute
in the hopes of strengthening their connection to Mile and her
cohort.

Grants from the Crown then increased severalfold as well, the royal family stating that it would be remiss of them to let support from private citizens outstrip their own. Of course, in truth, they too secretly hoped to appeal to the Crimson Vow, but the girls themselves were entirely oblivious to this.

Later, a messenger from the "invited guests" appeared, asking a slew of questions in regard to the Dolls. In response, he received a slew of answers: The dolls had been discovered within the ruins of a faraway country, and they had no idea how they were constructed; no, they only moved if the operator was within ten meters of them; no, they would only respond to the commands of the first person to command them; no, it was impossible to reassign operators; yes, but when, previously, they lent one to a magical researcher who wished to study them, the next day that researcher's atelier was blasted apart by an explosion, et cetera, et cetera—until, disappointed, the messenger gave up and returned home, dragging his feet all the way.

One day, Mile and the others were walking down the back roads of the city when they again encountered the urchins from before.

"My, you all look well! How is work going for you?" Mile asked.

The children grinned and replied, "It's goin' great. Those guys at the orphanage have gotten all these grants and donations now, so they're livin' comfy. Plus, we've completely moved outta the odd job business around here, so that seems like it's pretty good for them, too. Well, it probably sucks havin' to fend off all the guys that want them to do dodgy or illegal things, but we definitely don't take on that sorta stuff anymore..."

"Whuh...?"

Well, this was new. Having been unaware of such a shift in the world order, the Crimson Vow were unable to mask their shock.

"W-wait, how did this...?"

Seeing the shock upon Mile's face, the boy who was speaking mirrored her expression with one of equal surprise, asking, "What are you talkin' about? It's all thanks to that get-together you put on. Apparently, just afterwards, the orphanage started gettin' a bunch more money comin' in. All the adults who were watchin' started givin' 'em lots.

"As fer us, we got a chance to build our own reputations and abilities as hunters on our own two feet, not relyin' on anyone else. We don't need those odd jobs around town when we can go huntin' and gatherin' out in the fields and take down little monsters and such... Well, to be truthful, it ain't entirely all on our own. It's all thanks to our Big Bro and our Lady of Grace."

The girls had no idea who the boy meant by "Big Bro" or "Lady of Grace," but it was clear to them that there were those in this world who had lent their strength to these urchins. How splendid. How splendid indeed...

Later, when the urchins returned to the abandoned shack that served as their lair, they gave their report to Big Bro.

"We saw the Lady of Grace earlier."

"I see."

"She's lookin' as cheerful as always. Honestly, I can't imagine her not lookin' that way."

"I see."

"What's this, 'I see, I see'? Are you really okay with not ever seein' her? Even when she came to check in on us, you just hid away and didn't even call out or anythin' before she left! If you keep slackin,' some other guy's gonna snatch her away!"

"I see... That would be bothersome, wouldn't it?"

"So hurry up and go talk to her..."

At their urging, the youth known as "Big Bro" grimaced.

"It's not time. I'm still not worthy of her. I need to become a better man fi—"

"How long are you gonna keep draggin' your feet on this?!"

"For as long as I have to. That's the path to 'sophistication,' as I think they'd put it where she's from."

"Sophistication?"

"Yeah, sophistication."

"I don't get it..."

At this, the youth only laughed.

Later, unbeknownst to Mile, a new title had been given to the spectacle put on at the Solidarity Conference:

"BraWres."

Mile herself had in fact labeled the event "DolWres" for short, but apparently, the word she had shouted at the close of the scene, "braless," had left a far stronger impression.

Thankfully for Mile, only a very small portion of the population was even aware of the name, and so after a while, it slipped away into the dark corners of history. There it died, the hapless originator of the term never the wiser...

CHAPTER 39 |

A Town I Once Knew

"L ET'S STOP IN THIS TOWN TONIGHT," said Reina. "If any good, quick jobs show up, then we can earn a little money while we're here, too."

It had been nearly ten days since the Crimson Vow departed from the capital. It was almost evening when they arrived at a small town and Reina made her proposal. The other three nodded in agreement.

They had decided as a group that while they were traveling, they would not use up any of the money they had earned while living in the capital. Using money that had been earned ahead of time would make for too luxurious of a journey and would directly contrast the practical nature of their venture. All the money they had earned so far was stored away. The money for their journey was its own coffer. In fact, they hoped to use this opportunity to add even more to their savings.

"Well then, before we find an inn, let's stop by the guildhall and see what's going on around here."

"Okay!"

They could not possibly reserve a room without knowing whether there were any appealing—or at least interesting—jobs around. Depending on the terms of a job, they might be setting back out immediately, and even a client providing lodging for them was not an impossibility. Although the chances of such a thing were incredibly low...

Creak...

As always, the moment they opened the door of the guildhall, all of the hunters who were already present turned as one to look.

No matter what hall or in what new place they stopped, it was always the same. But of course, this was a habit of hunters, so one could expect nothing less.

And, as always, the onlookers were split into two groups— those who saw that they were only a bunch of little girls and immediately looked away, interest lost, and those who harbored too much of the *wrong* sort of interest and continued to ogle them.

Or not.

"Hey, is that...?"

"The 'Copper Cutter'?"

"That's the girl who snips away other hunters' self-confidence and pride! So she's come back home..."

As the commotion in the guild arose, so did the four girls' panic.

"Aah! Miss Mile!"

A voice called out to them from behind the reception counter, drawing even more of the room's focus to the four girls.

That was when the memories came flooding back, and Mile suddenly shouted, "Oh! Miss Lowry!"

"It's *Laura!*"

The receptionist corrected her, and Mile muttered to herself, "I did think the streets of this town looked awfully familiar..."

Soon after, the guild master, who had been told the news, came running down from the second floor, clutching Mile's hands with his and swinging her around, tears in his eyes.

"You... you finally came back to us! Please, just wait here for a little while—we'll have a feast!"

With that, he ordered Laura to go and make some reservations at an eatery, then flew back to his office to finish up his remaining work.

"What was that all about?" Reina asked, glaring.

"Ahaha..."

Mile laughed dryly before explaining.

"So you're saying," Reina replied, once Mile was through, "that that guild master is the one who endorsed your enrollment for the Hunters' Prep School?"

"Ah, yes. He is."

"Then that means he's your benefactor, isn't he?! And it's thanks to him that we all met! But...for a guild master, who would have to take full responsibility if anything went wrong, to give his endorsement to a little girl who he'd only just met, he would either have to be a fool, an idiot, or some old creep with an ulterior motive. So, which one is he? He didn't really seem like an outright fool, so..."

"Er, uhm. I-It's because he's a good person!"

"Come again?"

"I said, he's a good person!"

Ah, so he's a softhearted idiot, then... the other three correctly concluded.

The girls checked the board but found only worthless jobs posted there and decided to give up looking for work in this town. They would head out first thing in the morning. Just then, Laura, who had finished making their reservations, returned, and shortly after that, the guild master once again descended from the second floor, too.

"Well then, shall we?"

The girls were not about to turn down free food. They followed happily behind the two guild employees.

They arrived at an inn of a reasonable size for such a small town. On the first floor were a dining hall and kitchen. The third floor had living quarters for the innkeepers and their family along with storage space, while on the second floor were rooms for the inn's guests. Since they were already there, the girls decided to reserve a room at the inn before they dined. That way, it wouldn't matter if they stuffed themselves so much they couldn't walk.

"I'm so glad you've come back to us. Welcome home! Laura and I saw you at the graduation exam. What a splendid fight that was..." said the guild master.

Mile was shocked.

"Huh? You came to watch?"

"Yes, of course! Why, I wouldn't pass up the chance to watch the one I recommended making her formal debut! Plus, thanks to you graduating with such high marks, my reputation's grown as well. I was the recipient of this year's New Talent Discovery Award, and my rank as a guild master has gone up! And it's all thanks to you, Miss Mile!"

The guild master was truly overjoyed.

"Of course, we enjoyed watching the rest of you all as well. Miss Pauline, where can I start? You specialize in healing magic, but then there was that small but powerful firebomb! And the healing magic itself—why, that would rival any court magician—no, perhaps even surpass them! A healing spell that can mend a broken bone in an instant? Wow! And Miss Mavis, when you used your Godspeed Blade, your sword moved so fast I could barely even see it! And Miss Reina! You specialize in attack magic, but your iron-clad defense was so intimidating that you sealed the victory without firing a single spell!"

Apparently, the guild master had watched each of their fights with rapt attention. As he gushed over them, the girls couldn't help but feel a tad embarrassed, but it was not really a bad feeling. They all thought that they had put on a splendid performance as well and could accept his words not as pure flattery but as honest praise.

"And of course, there was Miss Mile's fight! That was truly amazing!"

And with that, the guild master began to reminisce:

It was a head-on fight against Gren, the great sword wielder, leader of the B-rank party the Roaring Mithrils, and an A-rank hunter himself—a high-speed bout against an A-rank swordsman on equal turf, daring to go sword-to-sword without using any spells. Then, there was the powerful volley, the tactical footwork, and the magical blade she had shown off!

It was as good as a fight between two A-ranks. If only a minimum period of time as a registered hunter and the requisite contribution points weren't required for promotion, he would insist that she take the A-rank test immediately.

It was because he had witnessed her skill with his own eyes that he had given his endorsement.

What began as a failing on the part of his subordinate had now, on the contrary, become a point of promotion for himself. The feeling that he had somehow cheated his way into this victory was not insignificant, but it was not as though he had done anything embarrassing or wrong. He had endorsed her enrollment in the prep school to cover for his subordinate's mistake, fully prepared to take responsibility on the off chance that anything should go awry. It was as though the Goddess herself had smiled down upon his faithfulness...

Remembering all this, the guild master was deeply moved.

And so the festivities began, with Laura telling the lively tale of Mile's "Great Sword Slicing" and "Copper Coin Cutting" incidents, which she had not witnessed firsthand but had heard a great deal about regardless.

The whole group—save for Mile, who was still underage—all had a bit of wine. (Though, truthfully, there was no minimum drinking age in this country. Mile had placed restraints on herself, owing to memories from her past life...)

In exchange, Mile and Reina ate like pigs—so much so that whoever was paying would normally have been in agony, holding their head in their hands. Yet, as far as the guild master—whose pay had risen in tandem with his rank thanks to Mile—was concerned, such matters were trivial.

Seeing how thrilled the guild master was that the Crimson Vow had been doing so well, the girls decided to tell him the truth about the Elder Dragon-Beastmen Investigation Incident—or at least as much of the truth as would not cause any problems. Since a fair amount of time had passed, they thought he had probably already heard some twisted version of the story in the form of rumors anyway.

The guild master, overjoyed at receiving such valuable information, drank the stories right up. For a guild master, who usually only heard news of what was causing trouble, a success story like this was the sweetest wine.

This girl was like a supernova, a shining beacon of hope for the guild: a girl who would without a doubt rise to an A-rank—no, S-rank would be well within her grasp—who he himself had discovered and had lifted up to the world (or at least, who had come to be lifted).

The renowned party of beautiful young newcomers—all four of whom had graduated at the very top of their class and become household names within a day of their graduation—had graced this town with their presence. The girl who he had given up on ever seeing again had returned and brought her new allies back with her.

This was the dawn of a sparkling future for the guild in this sleepy little town. Perhaps they would now be able to contend with their own difficult jobs, which they had been forced to forward to branches in other towns or the capital in the past.

Their branch. *His* branch.

The branch that he himself led, from the guild master's chair...

This was the greatest day of his life.

These were the fancies that drifted through the guild master's mind.

The next day...

The guild master ended up having a bit more to drink than he intended, but even so, he would never dare be late to work. Granted, he did not arrive before the morning job rush as he usually would, but such early arrivals were merely for the sake of warding off scuffles. At the very least, he got going well before the second morning bell (around 9 AM), with plenty of time to spare.

The receptionist, Laura, always arrived well before the guild master. While she was in between clients, he popped over to where she sat behind the reception counter, showing no sign of being hungover from the previous night's festivities, and struck up a conversation.

"I wonder if the Crimson Vow are off on some job today, then?"

"Ah, yes," Laura replied. "They stopped by early this morning, thanked us for last night, and then said their farewells. They talked a bit with the hunters who were present at the time before heading out..."

The guild master bobbed his head in approval.

"Oh, it must be nice to be so young. Showing up first thing in the morning and heading off to work without even taking a break. So, which job did they take?"

"Well, none of them."

"What?"

The guild master cocked his head, perplexed.

"Well, they said that they would be heading straight on to the next town, and since there didn't seem to be any suitable escort duty requests currently available, they didn't take anything at all... They did say that they might hunt some of the monsters from the daily requests or attempt to harvest some for parts along the way..."

"What?"

The guild master could not make sense of what he was hearing.

"No...but...I thought that those girls had come back to this town to live here and that they were going to work here as hunters, and..."

"Hm? What are you saying, sir...? They're a group of hopeful rookies looking to make their mark on the world. You can't expect them to move to a backwater town like this with barely any jobs to go around. They merely stopped by to see us on their travels—isn't that obvious?"

"Wh... Wh-whaaaaaaaaat?!?!"

The guild master crumpled to the floor, all the color draining from his face.

His happiness had been nothing more than a fleeting dream...

"I hope there are some fun jobs in the next town!" Mile remarked cheerfully as the four walked down the highway.

"Not *fun*, Miley! *Profitable!*" Pauline corrected.

"No, what we really need are jobs that will give us the most promotion points so that we can hurry up and rise up to B-rank and then A-rank..." argued Mavis.

"So then," said Reina, "all we need to do is find jobs that are fun, with good pay, and that'll get us a lot of promotion points—right? Now then, on to the next town! And if we come across any daily-task monsters or harvest-worthy animals, we'll hunt those, too! We four may be lacking in power, lacking in sense, and lacking in experience—but most importantly, we're lacking in money!"

The other three grimaced.

However, this *was* a journey of self-improvement and a

journey to earn money. And so, as always, the three replied in unison:

"Yeah!!!"

Considering that they were on a journey without destination, Mile had left the decision-making up to Reina, with her experience of a life on the road. Now she thought back to the town they had just left: *My, isn't it nice to happen upon old memories like that?* Yet she failed to realize the most important thing:

That town was the one that she had first arrived in when she fled her home country. From there, she had gone directly to the capital, which was located right in the middle of the Kingdom of Tils. Now, they had departed from said capital and arrived at that town...

Mile did not stop to think where they would end up if they continued traveling straight ahead.

And so, the Crimson Vow proceeded. Down along the highway, with their beloved capital directly at their backs and their hearts full of wonder at what might lie waiting for them further down the road.

"What did you say?!"

In the royal office of the Kingdom of Tils, a scene was unfolding. Within the walls were the king, the prime minister, the sword master Count Christopher—a living legend who had risen from the ranks of a humble hunter all the way to nobility—and the guild master of the capital branch of the Hunters' Guild.

"Did I not tell you to ensure they remained with us?!" the king yelled in rage, hearing the guild master's report.

Count Christopher tried his best to pacify him.

"Now now, Your Majesty, as the Master said, it is not as though those girls intend to relocate to another country entirely. They're on a journey of self-improvement, where they hope to find interesting new trials—jobs that are challenging, *worth* doing. It's only a natural thing for young hunters to want to do."

"Now that you mention it, you've said that you did the same—didn't you, Christopher? Traveling around the land when you were a hunter. And even since you became a count, there've been rumors of you sneaking off to other countries without the permission of the palace..."

"Ah, hahaha...."

The count tried to laugh the accusation off, scratching his head. Then he continued, offering up a bit more in the guild master's defense.

"W-well, a hunter does what a hunter does... Anyway, when there are gaps in their journey, or once they've had their fill, I'm sure they'll come back here and settle down. I was the same, wasn't I? After all, the girl named Pauline has family here still, as well as a business that her family runs. And Lady Mavis is a member of one of our country's noble families. Plus, for Mavis, should push come to shove..."

"Should push come to shove?" the king asked.

The count gave a wicked grin.

"We make her a knight—the thing that she's been dreaming of. Once appointed to knighthood, she'd be in for life. Then we pair her up with some promising young lad from another martial line, and she'll have no desire to travel off to any other land, remaining here to spread her skill and talent throughout this country."

"Hm..."

The count's proposal seemed to finally calm the king down.

"However, there's still Mile. What do we do about her? She hails from another country, doesn't she? Is there not a possibility that she'll simply return to the land where she was born?"

"Not from what we've gathered from speaking to her classmates. The rumor is that she was the daughter of a formerly noble family, chased from her home country for some reason or other. The fact that she has such soft and delicate hands, which do not show the marks of life's difficulties, and that she often says and does things that demonstrate an ignorance of the wider world are testament to the truth of that theory. If all this is true, then our plan is obvious."

The king urged the count to continue with his eyes, incensed that he would stop just when things were getting good. In response, Christopher raised the thumb of his left hand and jabbed it toward himself.

"We make her just like me. She's a little girl who's lost her country, her home, and her status as a noble. Your Highness has borne witness to her ability and decides to make her a noble again. Don't you think that your faithful subjects would find this quite the inspiration?"

"I see!!!"

The cry came at once from all three of the others in the room, who were deeply impressed by the count's proposal.

Obviously, there was no reason to raise her to the rank of counthood like Christopher. They could make her a baroness, or give her the lifelong peerage of a knight, or even simply a baronetess—which was barely a noble but significant nonetheless.

"Guild Master, have you any objections to this?" asked the king. "If we pursue this, it may set a precedent..."

The guild master looked a little troubled, and his reply was noncommittal: "Well, ah, if we're speaking of precedents, technically such a thing has already happened a number of times before..."

"What?!"

"Er, well, just as Count Christopher said previously, a hunter does what a hunter does... For most people who become hunters the normal way, it's quite standard to travel to different countries in your youth. Even amongst the graduates of the Hunters' Prep School, a number of individuals have already set off on journeys without waiting the full five years. We did not forbid this because to do so would have drawn the ire of hunters as a group...

"Of course, we don't permit them to formally relocate out of the country. We make sure they are aware that this must only be a temporary expedition and that their travels outside of our borders do not count toward their five years of service to the country. We impress strongly upon them that after a certain amount of time has passed, they must return home.

"Those girls are incredibly young and abnormally skilled. We considered that they might find themselves courted by strangers from other lands and tried our best to get them to stay, but it seemed that they were already aware of the precedent. Plus, they threatened to become quite a nuisance to the guild, so in the end we could not deny them..."

"........."

The king and prime minister appeared grim. Count Christopher, of course, was already aware of this.

"Considering the timing, one might wonder whether those girls' sudden actions have something to do with *that* incident..."

"Indeed, I was considering that..." said the king.

The prime minister and the count nodded in reply.

"In that case, this might be a good thing. We don't have to pay for any formal jobs, and should anything out of the ordinary happen... Why, they are merely a single group of hunters acting independently for whom neither the country nor the guild can be expected to take responsibility. At the same time, should those girls achieve great success on foreign soil, then they are still citizens of this country and on the register of this country's guild—which means that their achievements can be claimed as all thanks to us."

This time, the count was the one to knit his brows at the king's shrewd analysis.

"Well, they are still a group of wide-eyed young rookies. Perhaps we should have a bit more consideration for them..."

And so, it was finally decided that the Crimson Vow would be allowed to do as they pleased.

However, they were absolutely forbidden to re-register, or take up permanent residence, in another country.

They were forbidden to become entangled with strange, foreign men.

They were forbidden to get involved with men from their own country as well, should those men be unsuitable or troublemakers.

And if they were to achieve any great recognition, they would be considered for the peerage.

Thus was the official ruling.

And so, in a closed room, entirely unbeknownst to the Crimson Vow, the hurdles for any potential future romance on their parts had just been raised extremely high.

Of course, whether or not the girls themselves would obey these rulings was another matter entirely...

CHAPTER 40 |

Carriage Ride

"**P**LEASED TO MAKE YOUR ACQUAINTANCE. We're the Crimson Vow, the C-rank party who accepted your escort request."

"Hello there! Pleased to meet you as well!"

Mavis, the official party leader, greeted the merchant who was their newest client. He met them with a cordial reply, blessedly showing no signs of shock that he was being greeted by a group of young girls.

On this particular day, they had taken on a job escorting a small-scale caravan, consisting of three merchants and five wagons, from a town near the national border to a town in the neighboring kingdom. Including the Crimson Vow, the three merchants, and the two extra drivers, their party totaled nine members. Naturally, three of the wagons would be driven by the merchants themselves.

This was a fairly standard setup for merchants leaving from the countryside, in contrast to the larger caravans that departed from the capital and other big cities.

The whole thing started when Reina said to the others, "Even if it's just for the sake of appearances, I wonder if it would be better, when we first leave the kingdom, to say it's because we 'took on a job that took us across the border.'"

Everyone readily assented, and since guard duty would bring them a bit of pay for little work, they decided to spend the next few days killing time and making money on daily extermination and harvesting requests until a suitable escort job appeared.

So that they would not miss out on a job that perfectly fit their criteria, only three members of the party went out to work at a time during those few days, each taking a turn waiting back at the guildhall, just in case. It was Reina's turn at the guild when the ideal job appeared. The moment it was posted to the job board, she snatched the posting with lightning speed, the likes of which might only be seen from a group of ladies when a department store marks a rack of designer clothes down to 90% off.

As soon as she finished the job-acceptance paperwork, she headed straight to the merchants' shops to confirm that they would be leaving the next morning, and pin down any other such details, before heading back to the inn to await her companions. Since her work was finished, there was no reason for her to stay put at the guildhall all day and nothing wrong with her lazing around the inn for a while.

And now, the caravan was departing.

Naturally, rumors about the Crimson Vow had yet to make it *this* far. Even if there was a bit of buzz about the party around the capital, they were still but a C-rank party. The only parties who would be talked about all the way to some little town in the middle of nowhere would be S-rank or A-rank parties at the very least. Stories of B-rank parties might make it out to the neighboring towns and villages now and then, but only every so often.

Therefore, the girls chose to forget that they had a bit of renown around the capital. If a group of C-rank hunters were to introduce themselves with, "Folks know us around the capital as..." it would be laughable at best.

For now, they were going back to their roots, living humble lives as a band of no-name rookie C-rank hunters. So they had unanimously decided.

They were divided in two, with Mile and Pauline at the head wagon and Mavis and Reina at the rear. Through careful consideration, the group had decided that this arrangement yielded the optimal balance of front and back line, as well as a favorable distribution of offensive ability.

In addition, it was only natural to put Mile, with her location magic, at the head of the train. While Mile strongly disliked using magical shortcuts like that for the party's benefit, her companions were already well aware of the existence of her location magic. Plus, they were on a guard duty job, where people's lives were on the line, so she couldn't afford to be such a stickler about it.

As they drove, Mile spoke only with Pauline and the driver. As always, she sat atop the canvas roof of the wagon, with Pauline sitting beside the driver on the bench. Given that they were at the head of the train, the driver of this wagon was not one of the merchants but a trained professional. Therefore, he would never do anything so insolent as to look up the skirt of a girl who was sitting behind him.

As far as this kingdom was concerned, Mile had a working knowledge only of the capital and the town where she had first registered as a hunter. Outside of those two places, she had been to a number of other towns and villages, but only as part of her job, and never for very long. Therefore, she had no particular interest in either their route or their destination. Even if she were to inquire as to the name of the highway they were on, she wouldn't know it, and if she were to be told the names of any of the towns, she would soon forget them. A guard's duty was nothing more than to fend off and defeat any attacking bandits or monsters. It was not their place to go poking their noses into the affairs of the merchants who had hired them. All that mattered was that they stuck together. Beyond that, there was no need to sweat the details.

Plus, this time, Reina had been the one to handle all of the paperwork and negotiations. She was a merchant's daughter, after all, so she was no rookie when it came to travel or business. Therefore, Mile felt no reason to worry. Besides, it was more exciting to visit a new town for the first time without any prior knowledge of the place, wasn't it?

Incidentally, Mile was the only one who was in the dark as far as their destination—Reina had filled in Mavis, who was sitting with her during their journey, and Pauline, when Mile had been off hunting for supper the previous night.

Mile's memory was good, but it was not good enough to recall a route that she had only seen one time, over a year ago, when she was traveling the other way in quite a great hurry. And after all, the scenery, viewed from the opposite direction, was a completely different beast.

They were very close to the border now.

And so the procession marched on. Mile was riding high, blissfully unaware of what awaited her.

"Gee, thank you, girls..."

The merchants and drivers grinned as they stuffed their faces with grilled meats. As always, the Crimson Vow were cooking up a meal of the meat they had hunted during the trip—their treat.

"Wow! Storage magic, huh? I've seen mages use it before, but none of them could ever hold as much as you can. Man, must be nice..."

For a merchant, such a talent was quite enviable. That said, being able to store and remove a tent, still fully erected, had to at least be slightly unusual. Just what *were* the upper limits of this girl's storage capacity?

"I mean, to be frank with you ladies, I was a little worried, seeing that you were just a group of young girls. But honestly, this is..."

Another of the merchants spoke, gazing across the roaring bonfire, the mountain of logs stacked beside it, the healthy-looking workhorses, and the mounds of jackalope meat.

Mavis had gathered the firewood. Knowing that green wood would not burn easily, she chose fallen trees, chopping them up in an instant with her sword.

Reina had wordlessly raised a bonfire in the blink of an eye.

Pauline had restored the horses' energy with her healing magic.

And Mile had produced the tent and the meat from nowhere.

Naturally, the merchants had hired escorts many times before. They were well aware of the abilities of the average C-rank hunter. Thus, they didn't even need to see the Crismon Vow on the battlefield to grasp that they were leagues beyond that level.

They had already crossed the border hours ago, well before the sun set.

The border was not the sort of thing that was marked off by walls or barbed-wire fences. There were neither soldiers nor lookouts patrolling it. There was neither the budget nor the numbers to deploy guards all along the length of an extended perimeter that ran largely through uninhabited, undeveloped lands—and such a thing would have been meaningless anyway.

Most major cities were strongholds, with their own walls running around them. However, there was no need to waste such fortifications on towns that were not of strategic importance. The defense of such places fell to the fighting strength of the local soldiers, mercenaries, and hunters.

Truthfully, even on modern day Earth, most national borders were just as open. Of course, there were still plenty that were strictly guarded.

And obviously, the purpose of those more closely observed borders was twofold: both for the sake of turning away anyone who might dare enter and to prevent the flight of any citizens from within...

The following afternoon, they passed through a crossroads. They had proceeded a short way past the junction when Mile suddenly sensed a suspicious presence up ahead. She halted the caravan and gathered everyone around.

"There's a strange formation assembled up ahead of us. There are two horses stopped on the road, with eight people beside them. There appear to be six others surrounding the group."

"Hm? That sounds like..." Reina began.

Mile nodded.

"Yes, exactly..."

"Some bandits and a wagon they're attacking, most likely!"

"If there's one wagon and eight people, I don't think they're carrying goods. It's probably a passenger carriage..."

Mavis and Pauline were of the same mind.

"It doesn't look as though there are any other ambushers lying in wait... Mind if we go look?" Mile asked the merchants.

While under employ as a guard, it was against code for a

hunter to leave a client waiting alone without their permission. After all, they were being paid by these merchants—not the riders of the carriage that was apparently under attack.

Furthermore, there were six attackers ahead, and they were only four young girls, two of whom did not even appear to be of age.

Should the tables turn on the girls, there was the possibility that the attackers would discover the existence of their band of travelers as well and that the merchants themselves could end up hurt. There was no way that wagons as laden with goods as theirs could possibly flee from a group of bandits.

Only a fool would risk waiting around for who knew how long, braving any danger that was to come—and these merchants were not to be taken for fools.

Their reply was immediate: "Go right ahead, please!"

Hearing this, Pauline appeared somewhat shaken, while the other three shared toothy grins. For Pauline, who was raised as a merchant, this was a wholly unexpected reply, but then suddenly, she grinned as well, as though quite pleased with their response.

"The reward for taking bandits is three gold a head. If we can bring them in alive to be sold off as slaves, that gets us a cut of at least seven gold. That's ten coins altogether. And, there's six of them, so... Gwehehe. Gwehehehehe..."

Her smile was a sinister one.

The merchants grimaced, perhaps worried as to whether all of the Crimson Vow would make it back safely—or perhaps merely due to Pauline's terrifying laugh. Still, the merchants had enough faith in their abilities to allow them to do battle, and Pauline sounded utterly certain that they would be bringing each and every one of those bandits back alive.

"Give it up already! Get outta there!"

The man who appeared to be the head of the bandit troop surrounding the carriage shouted his threat for the umpteenth time.

Because of the way the carriage was surrounded, even if they were to try and urge the horses on to make their escape, they would be cut down before they could even begin picking up speed. Either the reigns, the driver's arms, or his head would be quickly severed.

Customarily, in order to avoid having an extermination force sent after them, most bandits assaulting a passenger carriage would avoid harming the driver, the horses, or the carriage itself, at least as much as possible. However, if the victims tried to run or resist, then all bets were off. Therefore, most drivers would not attempt to oppose the brigands, neither resisting nor making any move to escape.

No one could criticize them for this. Just as anyone would, the drivers valued their own lives over the lives of others.

As long as the passengers kept quiet and obeyed, it was unlikely that they would be killed, anyway. It was only their belongings that would be stolen—though trying to run or having their carriage overturned might see them lose their lives, too.

There is *a chance that the thieves might try to kidnap the women*, the driver thought to himself. Obviously, this would be an unfortunate turn of events. Though they wouldn't be *killed*, they might still be taken to live with the bandits or sold off elsewhere. Still, even that fate was better than death.

Talking himself out of his own feelings of guilt, the driver stayed put in his seat, not saying a word.

However, the passengers were not going to stand for this.

It was only natural that they would not sit idly by while their money, their luggage, and their other valuables were taken, especially when they also knew that having their loved ones stolen away would truly be the end of the world for the families of the women and girls on board.

For their part, the bandits did not dare approach the carriage casually, remaining outside and merely ordering the passengers to disembark instead. After all, there was a possibility that a guard, soldier, or hunter might be riding among the passengers—not to mention any man willing to put his life on the line to protect his wife.

Yet in truth, there was scarcely anyone among the seven passengers inside who could hope to truly stand up to the bandits. There was a single young hunter. There was one middle-aged merchant who carried a short sword for self-defense. There was a girl of around ten years old. The rest of the group consisted of a young married couple with zero combat ability to speak of and a little girl of five or six who appeared to be their daughter, as well as one slight old man wielding a cane.

"Sorry, guys. There's no way that I can take on six bandits on my own. We shouldn't try to resist them," said the young hunter.

No one could blame him. He had not been hired on as a guard, and there was no way he would be coerced into leaping to his death in a battle he had no chance of winning.

The most pressing matter for the passengers was concern over whether or not the bandits might try to take the youngest girl away.

As for her mother and the ten-year-old girl? They would *definitely* be stolen—there was no question about that.

Just then, however, the ten-year-old said something quite unexpected.

"With my magic, I should be able to take out at least one of them, maybe two. That way, the others will be occupied with carrying their injured allies, and they might just give up on dragging you all along with them. The likelihood of it working isn't incredibly high, but it's better than doing nothing."

"Wha...?"

The married couple stared at the girl, eyes wide with shock.

"B-but if you do that, then you'll be..."

"Considering what would happen to me if they took me away, I would rather die now," she said with a shrug.

She spoke coolly, but her hands were trembling. She was still a little girl, after all.

"If that's where we're goin', then take me along with ya."

Everyone stared in surprise as the elder cut in.

"What? I've already lived a full life. I don't have much longer in this world, but if I can squeeze in one heroic act before I leave it, that'll get me in good in the next! Bahaha!"

"Then I'll join, too," added the middle-aged merchant with the short sword.

"A-and of course we'll fight, too!" said the young married couple, though no one truly expected much of either of them.

"What the hell are you all talking about?! If you keep this up, then I'm gonna have to fight, too!" the young hunter shouted, sounding peeved, even as a grin spread across his face.

"Now then," he continued, "it's just like the little miss said. We don't have to kill all of them. As long as we can wound two or three of them bad enough that they won't be able to take the ladies away, then we'll have won. Even if they kill us after that, nothing can take that victory away from us.

"Once the battle's decided, it's unlikely that they'll try and go after the survivors on this side. If word started getting out that these guys were bandits who massacred everyone they attacked, that'd be a big problem for them. We're the ones who chose to fight, so I'm sure they'd like to keep their reputation for not pointlessly killing those who surrender.

"Of course, if we manage to take them all down, and there's some of us still standing, with enough juice left..."

The young hunter gave a wicked sneer.

"Then we snatch up any bandits who are still alive and drag 'em back to the capital as a trophy! And we can all split the reward!"

And so, the tactical planning began.

"Enough already! Get outta there! If you all don't come down from that carriage…"

As the passengers continued to ignore his threats, the leader of the bandits grew angrier and angrier, until finally, he signaled to his subordinates with his chin.

At this, one of the underlings hoisted himself up onto the back of the carriage, pulling up the canvas in an attempt to crawl in and drag the passengers out by force. Just then…

"Gyah!!"

He tumbled to the ground.

"Gyaaaahh!! My eyes! My eyeeeees!!"

He struck the ground hard enough that his screams were not surprising, but then the man began to roll around on the ground, his hands pressed to both eyes.

"What?! What the hell did you all do?!"

There was no real point in the leader of the bandits asking this question. The answer was plain to see.

The man had been stabbed in both eyes. That was all there was to it.

He had thrust his head beneath the canopy, with both of his hands occupied. Even an infant could prevail if such a perfect target was offered up to them utterly undefended.

With this, the bandits' fighting forces had already been reduced by one, without even knowing how much combat potential still lay within the passengers' ranks. Furthermore, when it came time to retreat, they would be at least two men down, with one of their unin-jured members having to help the now-blinded man along to safety.

"Damn it!"

The chief raged, but now, short of climbing the stairs into the cabin, which were already barricaded, there was no easy way into the carriage. They could not pull themselves up with their arms to try to squeeze in, because if they did, they would inevitably be attacked from within by the passengers' blades.

They could torch the carriage, but doing so would mean the loss of both the valuables and the women, making this whole ven-ture a net loss. That said, there was no way they could just pack up and go home now, either.

"Cut the canvas! If anyone inside gets hurt then it's their own damn fault!" the chief ordered, his underlings brandishing their swords and spears as they closed in on their target.

Just then...

"Don't take another step!"

Suddenly, four women in hunters' garb appeared from around the bend behind them.

The bandits froze immediately in shock, but when they took a closer look, all they saw before them were two children between twelve and thirteen and a pair of young ladies around sixteen or seventeen.

A truly veteran C-rank hunter would be able to take on two bandits apiece, but with such youthful opponents, there was no way that the five bandits could possibly lose. Plus, the four girls together would fetch quite the pretty penny.

Clearly these were four idiots who thought far too much of their own strength. The chief sneered, yelling, "Forget the wagon for now! We're takin' these ones in alive! Try not to hurt 'em too much, though—the price'll go down!"

"Is that their angle, then?" asked Mile.

"Guess we better try to take them in without killing them either. Doesn't matter if we hurt 'em though. We can always fix them up with healing magic later, so we don't have to worry about it diminishing their price as labor slaves," Reina replied, with a snort.

"We don't need all four of us to take down these guys though. Who's gonna do it?" Mile asked.

Reina thought.

"Hm, the one who's the best at getting it done without hurting them would be... Pauline, you're up."

Pauline nodded.

Mile took a running stance, steeling herself in the event that the bandits should try to take the passengers hostage. Well, even if they did do such a thing, they could deal with it.

Without uttering a sound, Pauline began incanting a spell in her head.

The bandits, assuming there was no way that such a little lady could cast an attack spell silently, figured they would be fine if they simply attacked her the moment she began speaking. Plus, even if she could attack with magic, it was unlikely to be anything more than some sad little fireball, without much power or speed. Since they were far enough away, they could easily fend off something like that.

The two little ones were nothing to speak of. The majority of the bandits' attention was focused on Mavis. But, then...

"...Guh?"

"Ngah!!"

"Geheeeeee!!!"

The five bandits suddenly clutched their skulls and fainted in agony.

A violent, indescribable pain, like a slow burn, spread throughout their eyes, noses, mouths, and throats. And it wasn't just in these sensitive parts but also in the exposed skin on their faces, necks, arms, and legs.

It continued to spread beneath their clothing, all the way to a certain place on their backsides, with a horrible, slow burning...

"Agh, agh, aghhhhhh!!!"

"Gyaheeeeee! Sh-she's a devil! A deviiiiiiiil!"

The five men writhed on the ground. The sixth, who still had his hands clutched over his eyes, was outside of the effective range of her spell, but as he was already incapacitated, she left him be.

"Magic in the air, dissipate and send your powers away!"

Pauline dissolved the spicy components from the air, but what had already entered the men's bodies and stuck to their skin remained.

"Passengers," Mile shouted, "we are the hunting party the Crimson Vow! We have defeated these bandits, so please, be at ease!"

Surprised, perhaps, to hear the voice of a young girl, one of the passengers timidly peeked out from behind the canvas.

"Wh-what?! Goodness, it's true! Everyone, look! Those little girl hunters just wiped out all the bandits!"

The man, who, judging from his appearance, was a merchant, shouted to the others. The top of the carriage opened up wide, and all the other passengers poked their heads out as well.

"Whoa! Whoooa!!"

"W-we're saved! We're saved, aren't we, darling?"

One after another they cried out in joy and relief.

Pauline, meanwhile, muttered to herself, "Somehow, I don't think we're going to be able to run up too high a charge for coming to their aid..."

Mile and Mavis, who possessed the most brute strength, were left to the task of binding the bandits, who were still writhing and thrashing in pain. Naturally, they used supplies that were stored in Mile's storage space.

For once, they used completely normal rope for this task. Anything more, AKA. "technology that was far beyond that of this world," would be overkill in this situation.

Pauline went back to fetch their employers, while Reina was put in charge of negotiating with the carriage party.

It hadn't been their intention to profit off of a situation like this, but they also did not work for free. Not insisting on payment would set a troublesome precedent for other hunters so, even if they only charged them a pittance, it was at least necessary to establish the fact that they had "received compensation" for their labor.

The young hunter was the first to disembark the carriage, walking all around the vehicle and inspecting it as though to ensure that its condition was still sound. Then, one by one, the other passengers stepped out. There was the middle-aged man who looked to be a merchant; a refined elderly gentleman with trim white hair and whiskers; a young married couple holding a small girl's hands; and another girl of around ten years old, who appeared to be traveling solo.

"Wha...?"

As she saw the last passenger, Reina raised her voice in surprise. Hearing this, Mile paused what she was doing and looked toward the carriage. She let out a cry of shock as well.

"Whaaaaaat?!"

The girl, who was returning from her home in the provinces after a long vacation, was not wearing her own clothing, but rather, the uniform of her academy. It was not, incidentally, that she could not afford other clothing. Back in her home town, the fact that she had been able to enroll in an academy in the capital lent her quite a bit of status, so her parents had insisted, again and again, that she wear her school uniform as she traveled.

Reina immediately recognized that uniform. And so did Mile.

Very timidly, Mile asked, "U-uhm. Wh-wh-wh-what was the name of this kingdom again...?"

"Huh? U-um, this is the Kingdom of Brandel... Oh, I see! You've just come over from Tils! You're already well past the border!"

"G..."

"Gh?"

"Gyaaaaaaaaaah!!!"

"...And so, I enrolled in Eckland Academy!"

The young girl, Phelis, who claimed to be a first year at Eckland Academy, happily regaled them with her tale.

After the incident with the bandits, the marching order of the caravan had been rearranged slightly. At the head was the carriage with the passengers, as well as the captured bandits inside. Pauline had laid her healing touch on the man whose eyes had been gouged, restoring his sight so that it was good as new—though it was unclear whether this was out of kindness or merely consideration for the price he would fetch when he was turned over to be sold as a laborer.

Behind the carriage was the merchants' former first wagon, where all of the Crimson Vow rode. On the off-chance that anything should happen to the carriage, they would be able to respond immediately.

Since this new arrangement had left the carriage jam-packed, and because the bandits were likely to be a bad influence on growing young ladies, the couple and their daughter decided to take to the rear wagon, while Phelis, the little student, rode along with the Crimson Vow.

So that there would be enough space in the cart, Mile

packed some of the merchants' goods away in her storage space. Observing this, the merchants all stared at her, speechless, causing Mile to feel more than a twinge of guilt.

Reina had negotiated their reward with the passengers, but as far as "negotiations" went, it had been a lax one. The amount that she proposed to them was (to Pauline's great displeasure) a low one, so the passengers offered no complaints. On the contrary, they happily assented. Additionally, they wished to combine their processions until they reached their intended destination. Provided that the passengers did not mind traveling in tandem with the carts, which moved far slower than their carriage, the merchants agreed to the arrangement, and so, the contract was settled.

Just a short while ago, the passengers had been on the verge of losing their possessions and their lives. If they could have a squad of unbeatable guards traveling at their side, any fee was more than justified from their perspective.

Since this would be treated as an emergency job request, contracted on-site, it would be processed after the fact. However, pending an inquiry, it would in fact be treated as an official guild assignment. So the Crimson Vow would have to pay a processing fee, but it would also net them promotion points—though because the amount Reina had asked for was low, the guild's cut would be low as well, which might engender some bitterness...

Because these passengers did not appear especially affluent, and because they were already traveling in the same direction, the amount they had requested was a low one. Though everyone knew it was common practice to take advantage of such emergency situations to extort the hapless clients for all they were worth, the Crimson Vow's workload was not increasing by much—and, outside of Pauline, the girls were not the kind to take advantage of someone in a moment of weakness.

And so, the Crimson Vow sat listening to young Phelis's stories. However...

Mile could not hold back any longer. Finally, she asked the question that had been weighing on her mind since she had seen Phelis in her uniform.

"Um, so, are there any cats living around your school?"

Phelis looked a bit startled, but then answered with a big smile, "There is! Is that a common thing, then? We have one at Eckland, the honorable Lord Cricket Eater!"

"Cr-Cricket Eater???"

"Lord?"

The four all spoke up at once: Reina, Mavis, and Pauline surprised at the outlandish name and Mile at the stately title and address.

"Yes, the messenger of the Goddess, the honorable Lord Cricket Eater. He is the beloved companion of the Wonder Trio, the divine sisterhood who received the Goddess's blessings, and he lives in their care. Now and then, he blesses the rooms of we first and second years with his presence as well, doing away with the bugs and mice on our behalf."

"........."

Sensing how still Mile had suddenly grown, Reina looked her way, but Mile was already catatonic.

When it came time to make camp for the night, Phelis rejoined the other passengers.

"...Mile. This is the place, isn't it?" asked Reina, some time after dinner.

"...It is," Mile replied.

"You do realize that we're heading toward the capital, don't you? Between the merchants and the carriage, we're contracted twice over."

".........."

Mile was lost for words.

You knew this the moment you looked at those passengers and saw the uniform, didn't you, Reina? Mavis wanted to ask, but even she knew that this was not the time or the place.

"So, what do you want to do?"

"...ends..."

"Hm? What was that?"

"I w-want to see my frieeeends!!" Mile wailed. "I left without even getting a chance to say goodbyyyye!!!"

Reina patted Mile on the head as tears streamed down her face.

"It's okay, Mile. It's okay to cry sometimes—and to think of yourself and what you want. You're still only thirteen years old, after all. We may have been your classmates at school, but we're all much older than you, so you can think of us as your big sisters."

"W-weeeeeeeeh....!!"

Watching Mile wail and cling to Reina, Pauline smiled gently, while Mavis fidgeted, her hands trembling.

By the looks of it, she wanted to be in Reina's place.

However, Reina appeared to be utterly unaware of this, or at the very least, feigned ignorance, paying Mavis no mind. Mavis's shoulders slumped in disappointment.

The Home of Yesteryear

I T WAS SEVERAL DAYS LATER.

The merchants and the carriage arrived safely in the capital, and the Crimson Vow received their job-completion stamps from both parties, along with the payment that came directly from the passengers.

Because the merchants had already made their deposit with the guild, as was the norm, the payment for that contract came from the guild's coffers. However, the passengers had contracted the girls directly, so they were expected to pay them out of their own purses. Should the job be something done outside of the guild, the Crimson Vow could pocket all the money, but if they wished to have it processed as a guild job, the girls would have to pay the guild their cut.

Granted, there was scarcely a hunter around who would go and purposely involve the guild in a job that was already completed just to pay the guild their processing fee—but the Crimson Vow were not just any hunters. They wanted those promotion points, they wanted to be B-ranks, and they wanted any tasty morsel of a job that would improve their reputation to appear in the official guild records. Accepting an emergency contract would reflect well on them—and besides, it was not as though they were wanting for money.

They parted ways with the two groups in front of the Merchants' Guild and then headed for the Hunters' Guild.

Before they passed through the city gates, Mile had stowed herself away inside the wagon, and the moment they left the caravan behind, she darted away into a back alley while the others waited. When she returned shortly after, her hair was golden, her eyes were brown, and her face was one that they did not recognize.

With her hair and eyes, it had merely been a matter of altering the pigment, and she had camouflaged her face by bending the light waves around it. She had not made drastic changes to any of her features, but together, the effect was enough to make her look as though she were a different person entirely.

The other three stayed as they were. They had no acquaintances in this country that they knew of, and even if they should happen to be recognized, it was not as though it would cause problems for them to encounter someone they knew. As far as everyone but Mile—who would be in grave danger if her true identity as "Adele" were revealed—was concerned, this city was nothing more than another stop on their travels.

And so, once Mile's transformation was complete, the four of them headed off to the guild without a care.

In her hand, Mavis gripped the end of a rope, with six men fastened to it. These were of course the bandits, who they had dragged down from the carriage.

Of course, the men's wrists were tied together, but their arms were bound tightly to their bodies as well—snug as a bug in a rug, one might say—so there was no possible way they could try to run or fight at full power. In addition, noose-like coils were knotted around their necks.

Indeed, the way they had been bound, so that they could not possibly escape, was almost excessive.

Exactly who was responsible for this was unclear.

Here she was, for the first time in so long, in the capital of Brandel Kingdom.

Mile had lived in this city for nearly a year and two months, but she had never once set foot in the Hunters' Guild.

As she nervously passed through the door of the guildhall, the bell jangled, and all the hunters present turned their way. Then, the moment they saw that it was only some party of rookies, their attention dissipated, and the hunters returned to what they had been doing before. In every guild in every town they had ever set foot in, this was the customary reception.

"Pardon me. We would like to have a completed escort job and an on-site emergency contract processed," Mile requested at the reception window.

"Oh, certainly! Step right this way!"

The clerk moved out from behind the counter to lead Mile to a conference table. The paperwork required for emergency contracts was a bit more complicated than that for a normal job.

After Mile came Reina, Pauline, and Mavis—and behind Mavis, six bandits on a rope, who shuffled their feet through the open door.

"Wh...?!"

All the hunters sitting around at their tables, and all the guild staff behind the counters, suddenly sprang straight up.

"Oh yes, by the way, we would like to turn in some bandits as well." Mile hurriedly amended her request.

Apparently, she had already forgotten.

The proceedings at the guild were concluded without incident.

The processing for the emergency on-site contract and the inquiry around it went smoothly, and the reward money for turning in the bandits, along with their cut for the bandits' future sale as criminal slaves, was as expected. What was unexpected was the envelope that the driver of the coach handed them, inside of which was a small bonus reward from the coach drivers' union.

Even if the money they received was not much, recognition like this improved the guild's reputation as well, so they were more than happy to receive the honor—and the promotion points that went along with it. And so the Crimson Vow left the guildhall with smiles plastered across their faces.

"Mm..."

After the Crimson Vow exited the hall, the clerk who had processed their paperwork looked contemplative.

"What's wrong, Sharon?" asked her coworker, worried.

The clerk, who still looked rather uncertain, replied, "Hmm, it's just, those girls who were here a moment ago... I get the feeling that I've seen them somewhere before. I mean, if you had come across a party of cute young kids who could capture six bandits all on their own, without injuring the bandits and without taking any injury themselves, you'd think that you'd remember them, wouldn't you? Argh! I just can't think of it! I've got nothing but brain fog!"

It was only natural that the clerk could not place the Crimson Vow. She might have remembered if she had been dealing with someone who looked exactly as she recalled, but only a vague resemblance could not be expected to ring any bells. It would be one thing, too, if they were faces she had seen countless times, but in this case she had only caught glimpses of their likeness, now and again, in the figures sitting upon her boss's desk...

Plus, the one who had that unmistakable silver hair had altered her appearance.

"Mmm, nngh..."

"Enough already! Just forget about it, and get back to your work!" her coworker scolded.

And so, the clerk known as Sharon gave up on remembering.

Thus, a potential branch of all the possible paths of history crumbled into dust.

That evening, Mile and the others decided against taking a room at an inn. In order to best minimize the risk of Mile being discovered, they planned to leave the capital that night, as soon as all their affairs for the day were in order.

"All right, so, following your lead, we'll head over there some-time after they're done with dinner for the evening. Have you finished up your letter?" Reina asked.

"Ah, y-yes, here it is..."

Mile withdrew a letter from her storage space and handed it to Reina.

"Good. We should try and eat early ourselves. Don't look so wor-ried, Mile. We'll be in and out of there before you know it!" Reina assured her with a broad smile, the letter pressed safely to her chest.

Late that evening, once classes were over, and both extracur-ricular activities and dinner for the boarding students had con-cluded for the night...

Three girls passed through the front gates of Eckland Academy.

Perhaps they were students returning from an after-school outing. There was a girl with red hair, wearing an academy uni-form. She was followed by another girl who was particularly well-endowed in one area, wearing a gym uniform, perhaps having gone out for some exercise. They were likely third years, though the gatekeeper found his eyes unfortunately drawn to the parts of the second girl's body that did not appear to belong to a twelve or thirteen-year-old at all.

The last to come traipsing through the gate, looking rather embarrassed, was a girl with golden hair and the appearance of a swordswoman—likely the older sister to one of the other girls.

There were no problems here. It was far from the sort of scene that required an investigation of any sort as they did not appear suspicious in the least.

So the gatekeeper thought to himself, as he continued to keep his watch.

Knock knock!

"Hello? Who is it?" Marcela asked, hearing a knock on the door of her dorm room.

A voice from the other side of the door replied, "A thief..."

"Why the heck would you say that?!" another voice scolded.

"Sorry, it's just that Mile always answers like that in these kinds of situations..." the first voice replied.

"Since when?! Anyway, what are you gonna do if she starts thinking we're acting suspicious?!"

They were already acting plenty suspicious.

Marcela rubbed her temples with her middle fingers.

It had been quite a while since she had felt this particular variety of exasperation. She felt almost nostalgic somehow.

"...So, who's there?"

"A thief..."

"Enough with that already!"

Intrusions like this were common around the time a new group of freshmen entered the academy.

They wanted to talk to her.

They wanted to be her friend.

Please, be my mentor!

Grant me the Goddess's protection as well!

You'll take me into the Wonder Trio, won't you? Or rather, I suppose that would make us the Wonder Quartet! Ho ho ho!

However, Marcela had turned them all down. She had not expected anyone to come crawling back now after all this time.

Just as she was pondering how to handle the situation, she heard a tiny voice. They had been making such a huge fuss before—why speak softly now?

As she pondered this question, she had the distinct impression that her ears were playing tricks on her.

"Bakery. Wringing from the air. Crooktail's bone. Stepmother and stepsister. Somewhere in the countryside..."

Slam!

"Gyaah!"

Reina had pressed her face to the door, whispering, when suddenly that door was flung open at full force.

Reina toppled back, blood streaming from her nose.

"...My apologies."

It was several minutes later.

Thanks to Pauline's healing powers, the blood pouring from Reina's nose had stopped, the pain vanishing with it.

"Th-that's fine. I know it wasn't on purpose..."

After hurriedly dragging the three girls into her room, Marcela ran off to fetch Monika and Aureana. They each brought their own chairs and crowded into Marcela's dorm room.

Reina, Mavis, and Pauline sat on the bed, while Marcela, Monika, and Aureana each perched on their chairs, facing them.

When it came to an interrogation, it was usually the one who had the higher vantage point who had the upper hand. This principle was what led Marcela to choose this particular seating arrangement. Nevertheless, Marcela could not have lived with herself if she did not offer a proper apology for what she had done.

However, now that that was over and done with, she had no mercy left to spare.

"Let us cut to the chase. The color of the ribbon on your uniform is the one worn by third years. However, I have never seen anyone like you in our year. And you there, in the gym clothes. Those are also of the color worn by third years, but again, I have never seen you before. In other words, you all are trespassers, impersonating students.

"Over half of the students at this school are young ladies of noble birth. As a result, I have no doubt that being caught on these grounds illicitly would be deemed a capital offense..."

The blood drained quickly from their faces.

"W-wait! T-take this!"

What Reina pulled from her breast pocket was a letter, placed inside something that looked like a split bamboo rod.

As she handed this item over, she shouted, "O-onehguy-day-gozighmass!"

"C-come again? I have no idea what you just said."

"Er, well, that's just something else that Mile says in situations like these..."

Truly, Reina was in no position to be judging others.

"What in the world is this?" Marcela asked, though she had already correctly judged that the item was a letter.

She withdrew the document from its container and flipped to the back.

...where the sender's name was not written.

However, Marcela had already realized the truth.

The words that had been whispered from outside of the door. This mysterious trio who she somehow felt that she had seen before.

Somewhere or other, she knew she recalled seeing these three girls, though not in the flesh.

The wheels of her Adele Simulator spun at full tilt...

"Lower intelligence, separate from common sense, and

increase carelessness times five..."

The Crimson Vow were rather taken aback by this strange incantation, but Monika and Aureana looked on, calm and knowing.

And then...

"There!"

Suddenly, Marcela thrust her right hand out into the empty space beside Mavis.

At the same moment, Monika and Aureana dodged, startled.

And then, the seemingly empty space in front of them shuddered, and the silhouette of a human—with Marcela gripping it by the collar—materialized before their eyes.

"Gaaaah!"

"Eeeeek!"

The human figure shouted, and Monika and Aureana shrieked.

"I thought you might be there!" Marcela crowed triumphantly.

"H-how did you...?"

Mile, who had now materialized fully, was speechless. Monika and Aureana looked on in curiosity, eyes round.

Mile had already undone the light-wave-bending magic that she had used to fuel her transformation and had returned to her original face and her silver hair. Terribly shaken, she stared at Marcela in disbelief.

Her sound, her smell—every trace of her should have been perfectly concealed.

There was no way that Marcela could have known she was there. It was impossible!

As Mile wracked her brain, Marcela replied, coolly. "...How

did I know? That's simple: It is because you are you, and I am me. Did you truly believe that yours truly would be unable to detect you?"

Yet even as she spoke, her eyebrows slowly began to knit together. Moisture welled in the corners of her eyes.

Then, she threw her arms around Mile, squeezing her tightly.

"Uuh... U...uwah..."

"Adele!"

"Oh, Adele!"

As Monika and Aureana threw their arms around her from both sides, Mile began to wail, too.

The others watched, tears streaming down Mavis's face as well, while Reina puffed her cheeks out unhappily.

Even as she clung to Mile, her tears overflowing, Marcela cast a sidelong glance at Reina, understanding her expression instantly.

...Looks like I've got a rival!

Mile continued to weep, completely unaware that any of this was happening.

They were on the brink of something truly terrifying—and the only one who realized it was Pauline...

"So, what happened with everything here after I ran away...?"

Once everyone finally calmed down, the time came to fill each other in.

Mile isolated the room with a sound barrier, and Marcela, as the representative of the three, began her tale.

"Since you left, we have made a number of connections and obtained some information of undeniable veracity. First off—and this is something it rather pains me to say, Miss Adele—your father is no longer alive. He was charged and found guilty of the murders of your mother and grandfather and of trying to seize control of the Ascham family legacy after chasing away the sole legitimate heir—which would be you. All of this constitutes a capital offense. When you're charged with an offense like that on three counts, there is no escaping your sentence, no matter what defense you offer up. Then again, it was not as though there was anyone willing to speak on his behalf—not a soul would defend him.

"You *were* aware, Miss Adele, that you are the sole legitimate successor of the Ascham line—the only one who still carries the family blood? And that your father, who had only married into the family without any legitimate claim, was nothing more than a steward until you were able to assume official control of the estate?"

Mile nodded.

She had never been told any of this directly, but based on her own recollections—as well as everything she had observed after her reawakening as Misato and the details she was able to infer through the lens of Misato's superior knowledge—she had determined that there was a high probability that this was the case.

However, no matter how horridly this man had behaved in life, he was still Mile's father. And so, Marcela relayed this news with a grave expression, in consideration of Mile—or rather, Adele's feelings—but Mile did not appear bothered at all.

The only memories she had of him were from before her reawakening and the subsequent integration of Misato's experiences with Adele's. In truth, those memories were few, and none of them were good.

He was a stranger for whom she felt nothing.

No, he was a *monster*, who had murdered her kindly mother and grandfather and mistreated young Adele.

As far as Mile was concerned, this was all that man was to her.

The only father she had was the one she called Father in another life, when her name was Misato.

"I see. What of the others? What's become of the house of Ascham now?"

While Marcela was rather stunned at how entirely unshaken Mile appeared, she continued her exposition.

"Your stepmother was charged with the same offenses. Anyone else who was complicit to or abetted their crimes, as well as anyone who perjured, accepted bribery, or who tried to flee prosecution, was charged accordingly."

"And my stepsister, Prissy?"

"Ah, well, it was judged that a child as young as her could bear no true sin and that she only behaved in the manner she did under her parents' influence. However, she did lose both of her parents to their felonies, and there's little guesswork involved in knowing the fate of a young girl who has lost her status as a noble. There was talk of sending her to a convent, but your father's family, even if they had no means—or really, any desire—to save their own son, still wanted to protect their granddaughter. They have adopted her as their own daughter.

"His Majesty permitted this, for it seems that our fair kingdom has truly been blessed with a benevolent ruler. I daresay she may be able to strive for some measure of happiness yet, not as a noble by name with any shred of rightful inheritance, but as a common girl, under a noble family's care..."

"I'm glad."

Though Prissy had been cruel to her in many ways, it had after all been nothing more than childish bullying; it was not as though the girl's actions ever had any longstanding impact on Mile's life. Mile's response, and the warm smile that accompanied it were reflexive, at the joy of knowing that her stepsister, who had committed only the crime of being born to rotten stock, had not met some terrible fate and would still be able to strive for a normal existence.

That's just the sort of person Miss Adele is, isn't it? That's why it's so good to be her friend!

Mile's kindness never falters...

So her two sets of friends, new and old, appeared to be thinking.

"So, Miss Adele, control of the Ascham household now falls to you. Though your whereabouts were unknown at the time, his majesty issued an official decree to this effect in the gathering hall at the palace. In other words, you are now the head of the house of Ascham, her Ladyship, the Viscountess Adele von Ascham.

"For the time being, his Majesty has assumed direct control of the Ascham territories, but as the issues with your family and the attempts on your life have been resolved, he intends to return your inheritance to you posthaste upon your return and relinquish the office of controller of the estate.

"Currently, the house of Ascham is one known to have been shaken by scandal, but the moment that you reclaim control, the Crown will dispatch managerial experts and reputable stewards, house staff, and the like to assist in the redevelopment of your territories. Once that redevelopment is successful, thanks to your involvement with Her Highness, the third princess Morena, you will rise to the rank of Countess, after which you will be engaged to His Highness the Crown Prince or His Highness, the second prince.

"In the case of the former, your status would rise yet again, putting you on the same level of succession as the second prince. Alternatively, in the case of the latter, you would become a Duchess upon—"

"Welp! Now that everything I needed to do in this country is taken care of, I guess we better get going on to the next one!"

"Yeah!!"

"Huh?"

Mile cut in abruptly, interrupting the discussion of her own affairs. With this, and seeing the speed with which the other three girls voiced their approval and stood to leave, Marcela immediately lost her cool.

"Wh-what? Now wait just a moment! Where do you think you're going?! Miss Monika, block the door! Miss Aureana, the window! We won't let you get away agaaaain!"

"Hff hff hff hff hff hff hff..."

The seven girls, scattered about the room, writhed in exhaustion, their clothes rumpled.

Indeed, the battle—more a catfight than an all-out brawl—had finally fizzled to a stop.

"Wh-what's with these girls?! How could we lose to a group of mere students?! Ones younger than us at that!!" Reina screamed, pinned to the ground.

Indeed the battle had ended in utter defeat for the Crimson Vow.

Seeing as they were in a girl's dorm room at an academy, fighting against enemies who were not hunters but merely civilian students—students who, moreover, were not even bad people—they had to avoid causing any unnecessary harm to the girls. Therefore, the Crimson Vow had to try to merely suppress their enemies and escape using only brute force and restrictive magic, ruling out fire magic and other more deadly techniques. Yet while their opponents were not strong, the Crimson Vow could not manage to compete with the girls' speedy restrictive and water magic, and were easily overwhelmed.

"B-but how...?"

Despite her self-imposed limitations, Mile was utterly stunned that she could be so easily overwhelmed by the opposing group's spells.

Marcela replied, smugly, "You were gone for over a year, Miss Adele. Did you really think that we spent all of that time fooling around?"

"Wuhh... St-still, improving *that* much is crazyyy!" Mile wailed.

"Now then," said Marcela. "Shall we continue our conversation?"

"So, if I just sell the estate and pocket all the proceeds..."

"Are you out of your mind?!" Marcela shouted.

Mile's proposal was swiftly denied.

"Your family's land is a gift from his Majesty, the king himself. In return for protecting, governing, and developing that land, you are eligible to receive the privileges of a noble! It's not something you can just sell off like an old cow!"

Mavis nodded emphatically as well.

"So in that case, I'd have to relinquish everything to the king... Or else turn it over to a relative..."

"Well, yes, that is the usual course of action. When a noble household is unsettled by scandal, their lands are confiscated or their manor demolished, with the noble themself confined to house arrest, his children disinherited, and ownership of the estate reassigned to some distant relative or the like. However, that is only what applies under normal circumstances. That is not going to be the way things work out for you, Miss Adele."

"Huh?"

Marcela continued to crush Mile's plan into tiny pieces.

"Do you really believe that his Majesty would allow you to escape so easily? The son of your grandfather's elder sister, or some such relative, has already tried to force his claim to the Ascham family estate, but his Majesty quickly denied him. This fellow was incredibly obstinate about it—no matter how many times he was told that there was already a legitimate heir, he insisted that anyone who had absconded from the country to whereabouts unknown should be disowned from the family. There was some anxiety that he might try to harm you or otherwise interfere with you in some way in the future, and I believe the whole thing turned out rather unfortunately for him...

"Anyway, the situation seems to imply that his Majesty is intent on having you, Miss Adele, serve as the head of the house of Ascham..."

"........."

Mile was amazed. She was amaz-eggs and bacon.

"Wh-what do we do...?"

Mile and the Crimson Vow fretted.

Meow!

Just then, a black cat slipped through a window into the room.

"Oh! Crooktail!"

Mile grinned as her old friend Crooktail, known to others as "Cricket Eater," slinked around her back.

"He's just trying to leave his scent on you, isn't he?" Mavis asked.

"No, his back is itching, isn't it?" Pauline wondered.

"No, I'm pretty sure he's asserting his dominance, isn't that right?" said Reina. "Like, 'Yes, this person is my servant.'"

"Sh-shut up!" Mile roared, with unusual vehemence.

It was only following a desperate plea from the Crimson Vow that the Wonder Trio finally agreed to allow them to leave.

"Well, I suppose it is far too soon for you to be tied down by any engagements or marriages. We are all still only twelve years old, after all. Enjoy your freedom for a little while longer."

It should be noted that, despite Marcela's assumptions, Mile had a birthday early in the year and was already thirteen.

"M-Miss Marcela..."

Tears glistened in Mile's eyes.

"You can spare us a little more time, though, can't you?" Marcela asked. "I'd like to talk about what's happened since then."

"O-of course!"

For some time after that, Mile and her old friends had a lively exchange about all that had occurred since Mile—or rather, Adele—left the academy. Reina and the others listened quietly. They would have plenty of time to talk with Mile from there on out, so they had no interest in interfering with the scant time that the younger girls had together—a time that meant the world to Marcela and the rest of the Wonder Trio.

✧ ◈ ✧

"So, should we get going soon?"

Reina finally cut in, seeing that the four girls appeared liable to keep talking until the sun rose if they let them.

The later it got, the more inconvenient it would be for them to leave. Students passing through the gates in the late evening were one thing, but students coming and going in the middle of the night or early in the morning were certain to give the guards pause, and they hardly wanted to be detained and questioned.

Regrettably, even good things must come to an end. Marcela and the others were all too aware of this.

"I suppose you must. However, this is not our final farewell, Miss Adele. I'm sure we will be seeing each other again very soon."

"Y-yes, absolutely!"

What the four girls would regret most would be a final parting.

"Oh, that's right!" Marcela said, as though suddenly remembering something. "The three of us have a bodyguard. They don't follow us around during school hours, but they accompany us whenever we leave the premises, and tail and investigate anyone who is not a student or their associate entering the school grounds."

"Wh...?"

The Crimsons Vow's faces twitched.

"Oh, but I believe you all should be fine. Miss Adele could not have been spotted, and besides—the pair of you were wearing academy uniforms, while you appear to be their older sister. I bet they thought nothing of it. It's still early enough that you should be able to pass yourselves off as an older sister returning home and her younger sisters coming to see her off.

"Please do take care, though, next time you come to visit. I get the impression that any letters or packages addressed to us are being inspected before they make it into our hands. The last time I asked my father to send me a package, when it arrived I found that there were gaps in the wrapping paper and the packaging showed signs of tampering. Inside, the papers were all in disarray, as though someone had hastily opened and shuffled through them."

"........."

Everyone was stunned at Marcela's prudence.

I-Is this girl really the same age as Mile? Reina wondered. *Though, come to think of it, while Mile's an airhead most of the time, she can be really clever in a pinch. The lesser nobles of Brandel are a force to be reckoned with!*

I would have never noticed or even thought of something like that, thought Mavis. *To think that I could be outwitted by a twelve-year-old girl... How pitiful.*

The two could not hide their shock at Marcela's insight in spite of her age. Only Pauline looked on with a smile, as if to say, *Hm, well done...*

However, there was something that none of them realized.

Though Marcela always took the reins as the leader of the Wonder Trio, the smartest of their group was not, in fact, Marcela, but the quiet and inconspicuous Aureana.

The reason that she sat so quietly—not speaking, only observing—was so that she could commit all that she noticed to memory and analyze it later. It was Marcela who led the pack, but when it came to the important decisions, Aureana was the one to guide her on the correct path. Usually, Marcela assumed that she had come to a conclusion on her own.

Aureana had entered the academy not on a noble's coattails or via the standard admission but as a penniless commoner who had overcome the mile-high hurdle of the academy's scholarship exam. *She* was the true ace up the sleeve of the Wonder Trio.

And so, the Crimson Vow left the academy behind.

With a casual and confident stride, they strolled through the front gates. Mile had once again used her light-bending magic to enter stealth mode so that she could not be detected by the naked eye.

As they passed, Mavis nodded politely to the gatekeeper, who smiled and waved his right hand in reply.

"This seems like a good spot to get changed. Over there, on the left," said Mile as she passed into an alleyway, still rendered invisible by her cloaking.

The other three followed behind her, no one particularly surprised by the instruction. They had already changed like this before entering the academy, after all.

Plus, they were exiting the capital late at night.

While this was not especially strange for a merchant or a

hunter, it would be an absolute no-no for a young female student wearing the uniform of Eckland Academy. In such ensembles, they would most certainly be stopped and questioned.

Plus, while wearing a normal uniform was suspicious enough, seeing a little girl with a prominent chest wearing gym clothes that were strained by her size would most certainly warrant an investigation or an arrest.

"Please don't ever make me wear this agaaaain!" Pauline wailed, her skin burning from the stares of all they had passed by going both to and from the academy.

Truthfully, even within the school, all of the guards' eyes had been focused on her...

As always, Mavis had gotten off scot-free because the uniforms were nowhere *near* her size. She averted her eyes.

"All right, let's just get you out of that before it... Oh."

Mile suddenly trailed off.

"Ah..." the other three responded.

A group of five thugs had suddenly appeared, all of them wielding cheap swords.

They were surrounded.

"Oho! We got us some Eckland students, don't we?! You girls know it's awful late to be hangin' out in alleyways like this. Y'all come out to play? And whoa! What's with you there, missy? You're really lookin' for some, ain'tcha?!"

"See?! This is why I didn't want to wear this!" Pauline shouted at an empty place beside her—not out of fear, but rage.

"Yes, yes, here you go."

Mile, still hidden, took the group's staves and swords out of storage and handed them to Pauline, who in turn handed Reina and Mavis their respective weapons.

Truthfully, a mage's staff had nothing to do with magic. It was a simple bludgeoning weapon used for self-defense, not a magical wand. However, Mile got the impression that the staff was something that Pauline truly did need in this particular moment.

The thugs, meanwhile, gawked in surprise, having just watched the weapons poof out of thin air.

"St-storage magic? I bet we could sell these girls fer a ton!"

While it might stand to reason that someone who could use a power as rare and difficult as storage magic might also be strong in other areas, the ability to use it did not always correspond to combat magic abilities. In fact, there were many cases of individuals who were exceptionally skilled in utility magic and utterly hopeless when it came to attack spells.

And so the thugs, judging by Pauline's age and her meek and mild appearance, reckoned that combat magic likely was not her forte.

Why were they so careless? Put simply, it was because they were thugs.

In addition to the first girl, they faced only a child and a swordswoman. With five of them and three of the girls, the thugs figured that apprehending them would be a cinch. They circled in, swords in hand.

Naturally, they had no intention of killing their prey. If they killed them, the girls wouldn't be worth a single copper—and plus, they wouldn't get to have any fun with them.

One of the thugs facing Pauline came toward her, brandishing his sword. The sword was merely there for the sake of disarming Pauline if she attempted to use her staff. A staff swung around by a woman was little threat to begin with, this thug believed. Plus, at such close range, there would be no time for her to cast a spell.

"Jet Spray!"

Bwoosh!

"Gaaah!"

The man screamed and pressed his hands to his face as two small, powerful jets of water, wrought by Pauline's silent incantation, struck him directly in the eyes.

"My eyes! My eyes!!"

He had yet to drop his sword, but striking a man who was standing still, his hands over his eyes, was a mere trifle—like taking candy from a baby.

Pauline struck him with her staff before knocking his sword away.

And then, her assault continued.

Bam bam bam bam bam bam bam bam bam bam bam bam!

Yes, it was a technique that Reina had perfected. A hurricane of blows dealt by a staff. The most frequent target was Mile.

Though the water jets had been powerful, they were not forceful enough to gouge the man's eyes out or cause him to go blind. It was but a simple jab.

It was after this that Pauline's real attack began. She began to strike the man in earnest, venting all of her anger and frustration.

Bam bam bam bam bam bam bam bam bam bam bam bam!

"O-oww! St-st-stop iiiiiiiiiiiiit!!"

The other four men, stunned at their companion's unbelievable defeat at the hands of a support-magic user, rushed in to rescue their ally and take down this unexpected foe. However...

"Icicle Javelin!"

Four icy spears suddenly flew toward two of the men, striking each of them in the gut.

"Wha...?! You can do spell-free casting, too?!" shouted one of the men who had not been hit by Reina's attack, frozen in shock next to his companion.

Reina's two targets writhed on the ground, unable to speak. Naturally, she had been holding back, and the tips of the spears were blunted, so they had not pierced the men's flesh. However, they had still been struck by two very intense gut punches.

When it came to performing magic, neither Pauline nor Reina spoke their full incantations aloud, enacting the spell with only a shouted keyword.

Compared to totally silent casting, 'spell-free casting,' or speaking an incantation in your head and then uttering the spell's name, was at the next highest degree of difficulty. There were very few mages who could use an attack spell in this way.

"I guess that means I'm up last, huh?" Mavis called out to the remaining two, swinging her sword at incredible speed, as though she was warming up for the real thing.

The two men turned on their heels at once and tried to make

a break for it.

Suddenly, the air before them shimmered, and a human form appeared.

"You're not getting away that easily."

"Gyaaaaaaah!!!"

"Think that's enough?" asked Pauline.

"Yeah. Any more than that would be a waste..." answered Reina, after relieving the men of all their possessions and binding them hand and foot.

Mile confiscated all of their swords, knives, and other weapons, packing them away in her inventory on the logic that they might come in handy later.

"These guys aren't hunters, so this isn't any of the guild's business," Reina contemplated. "They don't seem like proper bandits either, just a bunch of lowlife thugs, so we won't get any special reward for capturing them, and I don't think they'll sell 'em off to the mines, either... In other words, turning them in alive won't net us any coin, and since it's unlikely they'll receive a very severe punishment, there's really no good reason to bother.

"So I think this is good enough. I'm sure it'll hurt for these guys to lose even garbage swords like these, and I'm sure that if they go wandering around unarmed, all the people who they've bullied in the past will find some way or another to deal with them... Or, I suppose I should say, I'm sure *some* passerby will find them rolling around on the ground, all tied up like this..."

The other three nodded.

"Now then, let's do this," said Mile. "Shroud of Darkness!"

After Mile withdrew Reina and Pauline's regular clothes from storage and handed them over, she summoned a barrier of darkness several meters in radius around them, and the two quickly changed. Mile and Mavis, who were, of course, already in their own clothing, had no reason to change. The shed uniforms were then placed back into storage.

The four passed through the city gates without further incident.

Seeing hunters making a hurried exit in the middle of the night was not an especially rare sight.

As of yet, they had not detected any sign that Mile's—or rather, Adele's—presence had been discovered. However, it was better to be safe than sorry. With magic to light their way, the Crimson Vow quickly moved as far as they could away from the capital.

"So, they're gone, then."

"Yes. They've left us."

After the Crimson Vow made their exit, Marcela and the others sat in a daze for some time. Finally, they began to come back to themselves.

"Well, the most important thing is that they're safe and that they're enjoying themselves," said Marcela, but her expression was clouded.

"Um, your face is..." Monika started, but no one asked her to elaborate. They all knew what she meant.

"Journeying for the rest of your days at Adele's side, huh?"

"........."

It was rare for Aureana to misread the room so acutely. Monika and Marcela were deeply silent.

"Um, Miss Marcela, Miss Monika, I've been doing some thinking..." she continued. "In just a few months, we'll be graduating. Miss Marcela, you'll be returning to your home to begin bridal training, and Miss Monika, you'll be helping out with your family business while doing the same. As for me, I'll be working a civil service job somewhere in order to pay back my scholarship loan.

"If Adele happens to return home after we've all parted ways, we may never see her again. If Adele starts asking around to find us, she'd be in grave danger of being discovered by an associate of the Crown, some obstinate noble, or affiliate of the church..."

"Oh." The other two were lost for words at this revelation.

"And so, I was thinking... Now that the two of you have far more value to society than just being a noble's or a merchant's daughter, it shouldn't be a problem if you take a bit longer than usual to marry, should it? Say, even if five or ten years go by—even if you're eighteen or twenty-three—before it happens, you shouldn't have any issue still netting some worthwhile proposals, should you?"

Just where was Aureana going with this?

The moment the two of them realized what she was getting at, their eyes began to sparkle.

Though Marcela had sat in a daze since Adele's departure, the wheels in her head suddenly began to turn at full speed.

"After we graduate, suppose we got ourselves into the employ of Her Highness, Princess Morena? Have her prepare an official post for us—something like 'The Viscountess Ascham Search Party,' directly under her command. With that, we would be working in service of the Crown, which would help toward the repayment of my scholarship and gaining valuable work experience that no noble could ever be ashamed of. Even a merchant parent would never complain about a job that gets you connections to the Crown and the royal family. Plus, you'd receive a large stipend and wages..."

"I'm iiin!"

"Y-you're a genius!!!"

"Aha..."

"Eheh..."

"Ahahahahahahahaha!!!"

We will find her.

We have the 'Super Adele Simulator' on our side, after all.

And when we find her, we can send information back to Her Highness, now and then. "The search for Viscountess Adele von Ascham continues," etc.

And all the while we'll journey with a normal young hunter named Mile at our side.

It may only be for a brief period in these few decades we call a life.

But those few moments are sure to be fun and exciting—the treasure of a lifetime. Memories that sparkle like diamonds.

Somehow, I just know it...

Didn't I Say
to Make My Abilities
Average in the
Next Life?!

The Crimson Vow vs. The Wonder Trio
The Battle for Mile

SOMETIME LATER in a certain kingdom, the Crimson Vow were walking through town when suddenly a voice called to them from behind.

"My, it has been a while!"

On this particular day, Mile was off on her own taking care of some individual business, so Reina, Mavis, and Pauline were working as a trio. The moment they turned to see their interlocutor, disgust spread over Reina's face, clear as day. "Bweh! You all again…?"

"You should never greet a young maiden with so crude a response as 'Bweh!' That's not language that a proper lady should even be using in the first place," said the newcomer.

"Well, aren't you proper?! I don't have any use for that fancy noble-ish talk of yours."

"I am not 'noble-*ish*'! I am a true and proper noble!"

"But Mavis and Mile don't talk that way," Reina replied.

"Wha...? P-please don't ever compare me to those two! If you're going to do that, why I'll have to start comparing the peddler's daughter to 'Jane the Hustler'!"

"...My apologies." Reina's apology was sincere.

"Um," said Mavis, rather uneasily, "Just who is this 'Jane the Hustler' who you're comparing me with?"

"Forgive us!"

The two bowed their heads in apology to Mavis. Apparently, this "Jane the Hustler" was quite the seedy character.

"So, what do you all want this time?" asked Reina.

The girl placed her hand to her heart and replied, "We have come to take back what is rightfully ours: Miss Adele. She belongs at our side!"

The girl's two companions gave an emphatic nod.

"We are the three splendid sisters blessed by the Goddess..."

"The Wonder Trio!!!"

Kaboooom!

With no regard for the fact that they were in the middle of town, the Wonder Trio—Marcela, Monika, and Aureana—struck a pose as an explosion sounded and tricolored smoke streamed behind them.

It was very much reminiscent of the Crimson Vow's performance at the graduation trial of a certain Hunters' Prep School.

"Nnh..."

Reina clutched her skull.

"Damn it, we can't lose to them! We are three allies, bound at the—"

"Quit it!" Reina shouted, chopping Mavis in the forehead to cut her off. "Anyway, let's take this somewhere else! Come with me!"

Seeing how a crowd was beginning to gather at the commotion they had caused, the six girls quickly changed locations.

"Now then, what is it you wanted?" asked Reina.

"I already told you!" Marcela yelled. "Miss Adele belongs with us..."

"Ah, yes, yes, once upon a time there was a poor young girl who believed such foolish things..." said Reina, aping the manner of Mile's Japanese folktales.

"Please do not mock me! Just what do you ladies know of Miss Adele? Do you truly believe that she is happy remaining with you? Are you certain that you are not merely a pack of leeches, relying on Miss Adele for every little thing?"

"Wha?! Wh-what did you...? You're always going on about 'Adele *this*, Adele *that*'... No girl by that name exists anymore! The girl you're referring to is Mile, a C-rank hunter, our classmate and roommate at the Hunters' Prep School! If you're looking for someone named Adele, then maybe you need to take your search elsewhere.

"She is the one who *chose* to leave her old name and home behind to live as 'Mile, the rookie hunter,' so if you're so willing to ignore that girl's wishes and continue reducing her to who she was back then, then maybe *you* are the ones who are doing her a disservice!"

"Wh-wh-wh-wh..."

"Whatcha got to say?!"

"What are you saying?!"

"Grrrrrrrrrrrrrngh..."

With each barb, the girls struck harder and harder at each other's most sensitive spots until they both were seeing red. Monika and Aureana, as well as Mavis and Pauline, looked back and forth between the pair nervously when suddenly the two shouted the decisive words at one another:

"Bring it!"

"Let's settle this!"

"First of all, we must decide the method of combat. That way there won't be any whining and complaining from you lot afterward saying, 'Oh, that match was a setup, so it doesn't count,' or 'You only won because you chose something you're good at.'"

"That sounds like something *you* would say!"

"Nnh..."

"Mmnh..."

"Grrrrrrrrrgh..."

Since at this rate the two seemed likely to end up stuck in an eternal feedback loop, the other four took it upon themselves to lead the discussion, mutually agreeing on a mode of combat.

Well, to put it more precisely, they agreed on a method of *deciding* a mode of combat.

Each side wrote four different contests on a piece of paper, and then each was required to choose two entries from the other side's list. Those four chosen entries became the chosen modes.

The results of this were the following: a cooking battle, a shopping battle, a comedy battle, and a battle of smiles.

For each contest, both sides would select one representative from their team to compete. The team itself was free to decide which member would represent them.

As it would be necessary to have Mile herself serve as the judge for these contests, they parted ways, resolving to reconvene the following day with Mile in tow.

"Tomorrow, we're gonna show you all what's what, once and for all."

"As shall we! Go on now. Enjoy your final evening with Miss Adele."

"Grrrrrrrrrngh..."

And so, the next day arrived.

"Wh-what the heck is this...?"

Mile, who had been detained by Reina early that morning and forbidden to eat breakfast, was not in the best of spirits. Her stomach growled. However, she knew that her friends would not force her to do something so heinous as skip breakfast without good reason, so, while she was annoyed, she allowed Reina to escort her down the stairs after breakfast had concluded. When she reached the dining hall and saw that there was only one occupied table in the room, she gasped.

"Miss Marcela, Miss Monika, Miss Aureana! It's been ages! So that's what this is all about? Gosh, you guys...!"

Mile blushed and giggled. Utterly ignoring her, Reina announced, "Now then, let's begin!"

And so the flames of battle were kindled.

"Round One: A Battle of Culinary Skill!"

"Huh? Wha? Huhhhh?"

Mile was baffled.

"Our side will be represented by Aureana."

"And we'll have Pauline. Let's do this!"

Mile still had no idea what they were doing, and so glancing at their befuddled friend out of the corners of their eyes, Aureana and Pauline headed straight for the kitchen. At some point, the owners of the inn, apparently having been notified ahead of time, had taken seats at a table in the back of the room. One got the impression that they would be participating in the tasting. That way they could steal some recip—ahem, further their interests in the culinary arts.

It was at this point that Mile finally grasped what was going on.

Ah, okay. They're each going to try and make a special dish for me to enjoy, and then I'll have to select a winner. I remember there being a TV show like this a long time ago, back when cooking shows were popular...

Thirty minutes later, two dishes appeared before Mile.

In the interest of fairness, both dishes were prepared using only ingredients that were already available in the inn, with any specialized or expensive additions prohibited. Furthermore, they could each prepare only one dish. Just what dishes might they be able to make out of such limited ingredients...?

Mile grabbed one of the plates and pulled it toward her.

Chomp.

"Oh..."

Chompchompchompchompchomp!

"It's so good..." she uttered, almost without thinking.

Pauline grinned.

She had prepared karaage using the magic-infused cooking style that Mile had perfected.

Using only standard ingredients, she concocted a perfect karaage seasoning, and with a pan, oil, and a little skill, along with her own culinary knowledge, she succeeded in perfectly recreating the cooking Mile normally did with magic. The fact that she had accomplished what was normally wrought by complex magics with only manual techniques meant that she had, in truth, surpassed Mile. The dish was nothing short of a miracle.

Of course, she had used chicken instead of rock lizard meat, but this meant that she had actually recreated the original dish Mile knew from her previous life without even knowing it.

As for Mile, she had never thought the day would come when she would be able to eat karaage cooked by someone other than herself. There is no joy more universal in this world than having your own dish recreated by someone else's hand. The fact that it was so perfectly seasoned only elevated her joy to another level.

Seeing how thoroughly satisfied Mile appeared, Pauline knew that her victory was all but assured.

Then, Mile started on the second dish.

"Hm?"

Chompchompchompchompchompchompchompchomp!

"Th-this dish..."

Mile was stunned.

Aureana explained: "It's an old family recipe of mine, passed down from my grandmother, to my mother, to me—our special technique for making a stew out of whatever ingredients are available. I thought that it might be something you would enjoy..."

Hearing this, Pauline smirked inwardly.

Mile, who was by birth a viscount's daughter, most surely had a discerning palate. By nature, she was the sort who would happily gobble down anything put in front of her without complaint, but if she *had* to compare the two dishes in terms of flavor, the one she would give the highest marks to would surely be...

"This is delicious! I've never eaten this before, but somehow it fills me with nostalgia... Both of these dishes were absolutely amazing, and I would love to eat both of them again, but if I *had* to choose then I would pick this one!"

"Wha...?"

Pauline crumpled to the floor in shock.

Indeed, Mile was incredibly fond of the taste of home cooking, and she liked the style of improvised cooking that was passed down from grandparent to grandchild. This was the sort of cooking that she always yearned for. In her previous life, she was on bad terms with her grandparents, and her mother was not especially good in the kitchen. In this world, she had only ever eaten the food prepared by chefs in her noble home, as well as the prepared meals at dorms and inns and such. Indeed, she had yet to ever encounter such a meal.

"Sorry, Pauline. Your fried chicken was delicious, but I assume the point of this contest wasn't just which dish tastes better but which one I like better—right? So, I choose this one."

Yes, while Mile might normally mince her words and soften blows with bejeweled turns of phrase, when it came to matters of food and war, she was a viper.

"Well then, that would be the match! Let's move on to the next one, shall we?"

The Wonder Trio left the inn in high spirits, with the Crimson Vow—sans Mile—dragging their feet behind. Only the innkeeper and his family remained in the room, quietly tasting all the food that was left behind.

"Round Two: The Shopping Challenge!" Reina announced after the group had relocated to the capital's shopping district. "The goal of this round is to find the item that Mile would most enjoy, for the cheapest price. You will each receive three silver pieces, with which each representative will purchase a present for Mile. Our side chooses Pauline!"

Pauline was up to bat again. Owing to her previous defeat, she was smoldering with a fighting spirit and raring to go. If there was nothing else that she knew, it was the art of commerce, and she was so confident she could burst.

"And we will choose Miss Monika!"

If it was a matter of commerce, this competition would be

too difficult a challenge for Aureana, the commoner, or Marcela, the noble. Monika was the natural—the only—choice.

"You have thirty minutes, starting now. Begin!"

At the signal, Pauline and Monika rushed off into the shopping district, each with their three silver pieces clutched tightly in hand.

Thirty minutes went by.

"...A pendant?"

Indeed, Pauline had purchased an adorable pendant.

"You don't really have any decorative accessories to wear besides the ribbons you use to tie back your hair—right, Mile? Of course, wearing a ring would make gripping a sword more difficult, and gemstones are reflective, so there's a higher probability of being spotted by a monster or human enemy. Materials that might make a sound if they strike something are dangerous, but I thought it would be nice for you to at least have something to wear while you're in town. You're still a girl, after all!"

"Th-thank you, Pauline!"

Mile gladly accepted the gift.

"Eheheh..."

Seeing how she smiled, the Wonder Trio unthinkingly grinned as well.

"...What's this?" Mile asked, receiving the next gift.

"I'd suggest you peek inside to find out—carefully, so that no one else can see."

"O-okay..."

Mile thought this instruction a bit suspicious, but she did as Monika said.

"Huh...?"

It was underwear.

Inside the package was a pair of underwear.

"Underpants?"

The moment Pauline heard Mile's muttered question, she was certain of one thing:

She had won.

"We caught a glimpse of you yesterday, Mile, Just how long are you going to keep wearing that same old underwear?"

"What? But I wash them regularly, and I have plenty of spares..."

"You dummy," said Monika. "No matter how many pairs you have to cycle through, eventually they're going to stain or start to wear out. Sooner or later, they'll just fall apart. Why haven't you replaced them? It's not as if money is an issue for you anymore."

Mile hung her head.

"That's... it's because..."

Suddenly her voice began to warble, tears welling in her eyes.

"Th-that's because they're the ones Miss Marcela gave me... Th-the first gift I ever got from a friend..."

"You wha—?!" Marcela shouted, turning red. "That's the nonsense reason that you're still wearing them?!"

"It's not..."

"Hm?"

"...a nonsense reason. It's not a nonsense reason! It's really the first—the very first...one I ever got..."

As Mile wept, Monika patted her on the back, consoling her.

"So then, won't you wear these, too? They're a present from all three of us."

Mile gave an emphatic nod through her sniffles.

And once more, Pauline crumbled, her hands and knees planted on the ground.

Anyone watching could see that the Wonder Trio had prevailed again.

"Round Three: Comedy Battle!" Reina announced, displeasure clear on her face.

They were now in the Crimson Vow's room at the inn.

"Whoever makes Mile laugh the quickest wins! First up, the Wonder Trio!"

Aureana was the first to step forward.

"Adele, you remember Cricket Eater, right? Well, he found himself a wife and had some kids. And then his missus ran out on him, leaving him to bust his butt raising the kids she left behind!"

Pfft!

As this battle was a time trial, Aureana forewent any joke with a punchline that would take a lot of time to build up to, opting instead for a one-liner. Without skipping a beat, Mile fell for it, snorting with laughter.

Pauline was already holding her face in her hands.

"Next up, Pauline!"

The Wonder Trio looked puzzled at the announcement.

"Why do you choose Pauline every time?! Are you truly that lacking in variety? Maybe *that's* why you're so fixated on Miss Adele..." Marcela said, sounding exasperated.

Reina shouted back, embarrassed, "Th-the best battle strategy is to offer up the combatant who's most suited for the fight, isn't it?!"

"Well, it's not like I really care, anyway. And I suppose your tactic is not in violation of the rules."

Marcela looked at her smugly, as if her response were perfectly crafted for the sake of ridiculing the others. Reina gritted her teeth. However, now was not the time to make a fuss. The fact that neither she nor Mavis would be of any use in this scenario was simply obvious, even if Reina herself was loath to admit it.

And now, Pauline, already shaken by the record set by the Wonder Trio, stepped up to the plate.

"Gya-aha-gahaha! St-stop it, Pauline, stooop!"

Yes, Pauline had leaped straight over to Mile and begun tickling her sides.

"The winner is Pauline! One point for the Crimson Vow!"

"Objection!!!" the Wonder Trio roared, in what was, for them, rare form.

Reina sneered and said, "Oh? I don't recall a rule that said that the method couldn't be a physical one. The only stipulation was, 'whoever makes her laugh the fastest wins,' wasn't it? Isn't the one who can think of the best approach—or in other words, the smartest method—the one most suitable to be Mile's companion? Does this not count as a mark of superior ability? Or do you intend to contest the victory after the fact, based on a rule that never existed, just because you lost?"

"Gah... V-very well, then! Now, it's time for the next match!"

Overhearing this exchange, Mile tilted her head quizzically.

"Round Four: A Battle of Joy! This is the final contest! Whoever can make Mile the happiest shall be the victor! First up, the Wonder Trio!"

The Crimson Vow had gone first in both of the first rounds, so the Wonder Trio stood to begin the remaining two.

This time, Marcela took the stage.

"Miss Adele, we three shall be by your side, now and always. Even when you retire from being a hunter, even if you get married, even if you have children—we shall always remain friends. Our families will grow together, and we shall always, always, live a happy life together..."

"M-Miss Marcelaaaaa!"

Mile threw her arms around Marcela, overwhelmed with emotion.

"O-objection!" shouted Reina.

"...What is it now?" Marcela asked coolly.

"Obviously, I'm objecting to you leveraging the outcome of the battle for the possession of Mile in order to win a victory before that victory's even decided! I don't care if you tell her you'll

be by her side, but what's this 'we three' nonsense?! Are you planning to chase us away and keep Mile all for yourself?"

"Oh really? Are you saying that there is a precedent for that
objection? As long as we do not break the established rules, then
we are free to do whatever we want, aren't we? Who was it now
who was speaking of obtaining victory via the 'smartest method'?"

"Uh... Guhh... Y-you little—"

"What was that?"

"You vile little—"

"What are you all talking about?"

"Huh?"

As Reina and Marcela glared at one another, Mile's voice
came from behind them.

"I keep hearing you talk about 'possession' and who's 'suitable'
to be my companion... Just what is all this about?"

She was angry. Mile, who appeared to have grasped the true
meaning of these events, was well and truly mad.

When Mile was fuming and pouting, her cheeks all puffed
out, she was nothing to worry about. That just meant that she
was a little peeved. However, when she had no expression at all...
That was when you knew that a calamity was about to strike. You
could tell from her face, but more so, from her harsh and cold
demeanor. When she got to that point, you had better apologize
quickly—or else there would be hell to pay.

And then, there were the times when Mile moved beyond her
expressionless state and showed her anger again.

That was dangerous. That was incredibly dangerous.

To date, the only time anyone had ever witnessed this was during the battle with the elder dragons when she thought her friends were going to die.

This is bad!!!! everyone thought as one.

"I did think that it was awfully strange... This morning, I was having a lot of fun. I thought that all of you were staging this competition in order to entertain me, and I was enjoying it. But then, the atmosphere got tenser and tenser, and you all started saying weird things. In which case... I see now. I understand what's going on here."

"A-aaaah, um, well..."

Reina and Marcela both stammered nervously. The other four took a few steps back.

"I am no one's prize!!!"

"W-we're sorryyyyy!!!" the whole group shouted.

Mile was terrifying when truly angry. She was always so good-natured. And yet...

"Just *what* were you intending to have me do? To make me choose between my friends?! Miss Marcela!"

"Y-yes?!"

"Miss Marcela, if you had to choose between Miss Monika and Miss Aureana who to remain friends with, and were forced to cast the other by the wayside, which of them would you choose?"

"Wh-wha?! How could you possibly expect me to choose?! How could I toss one of them away, just like that?!"

Then Mile turned to Reina and said, "Reina, who would you choose? Between Mavis and Pauline?"

"Wha...? You can't expect me to make that choice!"

So said Reina. However, Pauline thought back to the night where she was nearly abandoned alone at the inn and muttered to herself, "I would definitely be the one left behind."

"My point exactly." Mile continued. "And *that* is the sort of choice you all were trying to force me to make. You decided this all on your own without even asking my opinion."

"Ah..." The six fell completely silent.

"But seven people is way too many for a C-rank party... A split of the earnings would be too low," said Pauline.

"Yes, and with 1.5 on the front line and 5.5 on the backline, the balance would be atrocious," added Marcela.

Naturally, Mile was the one split into 0.5. She counted half for each side.

What the two girls were saying was true enough, but then Monika lobbed in her own bomb.

"Surely having too many mages is a problem, but aren't our roles important as well? As far as origins go, we have two daughters of merchants and one daughter of a traveling peddler, along with three nobles. We'd have two chiefs of staff, and a third, Adele, in special circumstances. We'd have two people who like to handle finances and negotiation and two who like to take charge. Along with one who surprisingly takes the reigns in emergencies..."

"Who's this unexpected emergency leader you're talking about?"

Mile's question went ignored.

"This is hopeless. It absolutely wouldn't work."

"It *is* hopeless."

"I think it is..."

Everyone was suddenly pessimistic.

However, Mile, as per usual, was unable to read the room.

"Don't worry, guys! In my country there's a saying: 'With enough captains, a ship can climb a mountain!' With enough people putting their heads together, the impossible becomes possible!"

"Mile, are you sure you know what that means? Do you really think that's the correct interpretation?" asked Mavis, eyebrow raised.

For Mavis, who came from a family of knights—in other words, a military family— it was far too easy to imagine the fate of a small platoon that had too many captains.

"In any case, Miss Adele," said Marcela, "I believe that traveling with us, the Wonder Trio, is the best choice for you."

"Don't just hop right back into it and start saying whatever you want! Plus your party's name is the Wonder *Trio*, isn't it?! It's not a 'quartet'—it's a 'trio'! You can't have your numbers going up! Mile is ours!!!" Reina vehemently objected.

"I don't know what we'd do without Mile! She's our precious piggy ba—*dearest friend*, after all!"

"Just a minute! What were you about to say, Pauline? Piggy ba...? Just what were you trying to saaay?!?! Also, did any of you hear a word of what *I* just said?! We've looped back around to the beginning..."

"Maintaining the status quo would mean that Mile has to remain where she is."

"Are you saying that you would try to drag Mile away by force? Did you not hear anything that she just said?"

"Don't suddenly remember what she said when it's convenient for you!"

"No, but we should be the ones to look after Miley..."

"What do you mean, 'look after'?! I'm not a child!"

"But aren't you?" the group asked in chorus.

"Graaaaaaaaaaaaaah!!!"

And so, things dragged on as they always did.

In the end, another pointless day drew to a close with absolutely no progress whatsoever...

CHAPTER 42 |

Spice

AFTER SOME TIME, the Crimson Vow reached a certain town. They still had not escaped the reaches of Brandel's borders, but as there were no signs of Mile having been discovered, there was no reason for them to rush. Plus, even if someone did find her out, they could easily shake off any pursuers.

"Why don't we spend the next few days in this town? We've been walking for several days straight now, but we do still need to try and make a bit of money. If we came all the way to another country just to plow straight through it, then it kind of defeats the purpose of going on tour. I want to at least be able to say that we did a few jobs while we were here in Brandel. If anything comes up for Mile, then we'll just pack up and book it for the border immediately."

Reina was right, the other three realized. It had in fact been some time since they had last taken a job.

"Spices?" Mile suddenly asked.

The other three followed her gaze.

*Spice Gathering. Payment determined by amount and variety
of spices acquired. Please speak to client for further details.*

"Are you saying we should take this one? Just how does one
come by spices? This is the first time that you've visited this town,
too—isn't it, Mile? You don't have any acquaintances or associ-
ates in the area, and we have no way of knowing what kind of
spices grow around here... But then again, I guess you'd know
about that sort of thing. You're so good at cooking, after all."
Reina sounded skeptical, but Mile just grinned.

"It'll be fine," said Mile. "I've already got a bit of an inventory
anyway. Plus you'd normally expect people to go to a specialty
shop or the town market or make a request for something like
spices from the merchants' guild. So if they're sending their request to the Hunters' Guild it means that..."

"Something else is going on?" asked Mavis.

Mile nodded.

Reina shrugged. "It doesn't look like there are any other interesting jobs, anyway. I'd like to think that by now goblin hunting is a little beneath us. It's probably good experience for us to
take weird jobs like these now and then. Is that all right with
you all?"

Naturally, Mavis, Pauline, and Mile, nodded.

"Very well then! This will be our first job in this town!" Reina announced, moving to tear the posting from the job board, but Pauline hurriedly stopped her.

"Hang on, you can't just rip it off! This doesn't look like it's just a one-time job. Plus, the job isn't truly accepted until we've spoken to the client and agreed on the terms. The final processing isn't going to happen right here and now!"

"Oh, whoops!"

And so the Crimson Vow proceeded to the clerk to gather further details about the job before leaving the guild behind them.

"So this is the place," said Reina, standing before a restaurant and looking up at the sign looming over them. It was a rather unnecessarily grandiose sign.

"In we go!"

She proceeded through the door, upon which hung a sign that said "Temporarily Closed." The other three followed her.

Indeed, the client who had requested this particular job was the owner of this particular eatery—an incredibly run-of-the-mill, or perhaps a little more high-class than normal—establishment known as "Calamity."

A shop called Calamity that's looking for spices... What a peppery turn of events! Lights, calamity, action! Er, wait—isn't "calamity" an English word that means like, "plague" or "disaster?" I've got a bad feeling about this... Mile thought to herself. However, no one in this world spoke English, so it probably didn't actually mean anything. It would have to be a coincidence.

"Pardon us, we saw your posting at the Hunters' Guild, so..."

When it came to most official exchanges, Mavis was the one to take charge. She was the oldest and seemed the most earnest, after all... And, of course, she was the true party leader.

Yes, the leader of the Crimson Vow was Mavis. Even she seemed to forget that now and then.

"Oh, came to take the job then, did you?"

Hearing Mavis's voice, a man who appeared to be in his forties emerged from the kitchen.

"We can't produce our own spices around here, and it's gonna be a long while until the next shipment, so we've been in a bit of a pickle! But uh, do you have any leads on spices? They aren't something that you can easily come by in this area, and of course normally we'd go to a shop or the merchants' guild, but they don't have any more to sell. I've already spent most of my dough, so I wouldn't be handing this off to the hunters' guild—which really is rather expensive—if I were looking for something easy to find," the man explained, appearing half-optimistic and half-concerned.

As he went on to explain, this shop used an extravagant amount of high-quality spices in its recipes. (Well, compared to Mile's experiences from her previous life, they were actually quite stingy with them, but...) Though their ingredients were expensive, they were considered a high-class establishment, so they still managed to turn quite a profit.

Though the shop was well managed, very recently, a calamity

had occurred: the merchants who were meant to deliver spices to the shop from a far-off town were assailed by bandits and all their stock plundered.

Bandit attacks were incredibly rare on the route that they took, but, like it or not, that is what had happened.

Thankfully, as the shop had not received any goods, they did not have to pay for them, and they immediately placed another order. However, the spices originated from far away, and apparently, the suppliers had been hit with an unexpected influx of orders, meaning that they were going to be out of stock for some time yet.

For a high-class restaurant known for its well-seasoned dishes, not having spices was entirely out of the question. They had even decided to accept a slight decrease in quality in order to try to scrape up the necessary spices from nearby sources. However...

"The ones who normally enjoy dishes with high-quality seasonings are usually nobles or particularly prosperous merchants. The general populace typically doesn't even visit any restaurants. They just use pungent herbs and vegetables with a lot of salt. Once you start introducing real spices, you have to raise your prices, or else your profits go down and you can't stay in business. Our customers know good food when they taste it, and they come to prefer it over the cheap stuff.

"Generally this is not a problem for us, since using high-quality spices is our shop's selling point. We're the kind of place that the common man can only visit a few times a year, so the high prices are no issue. In fact, I'd say being pricey gives us more cachet. Of course, spices are a rather rare commodity to begin with. Now that we've already scraped up as much as we possibly can, there isn't much left to find. We've already gotten everything we can from our neighbors, both on the capital side and on the border side..."

Apparently, this job was not going to be an easy one.

Somehow, I don't think we'll have most of the problems that normal hunters would encounter, thought three of the Crimson Vow.

Indeed, *three* of them thought this.

And it was the *normal hunters* who were doing the thinking.

"Well, you can let us worry about how it'll get done. As for the terms of the job..."

Taking the reigns of the conversation from Mavis, Pauline hashed out the details with the shop owner. The result of their discussion was that, given the fact that they had no idea of the type, quality, or amount of spices they would be able to secure, the job would not be billed at a flat rate as with most task requests but treated as a regular mercantile transaction.

No matter how much the shop owner wanted the spices, if the restock fee ended up being too high, the shop would be in trouble. So it was agreed that he would pay no more than 1.5 times the standard market rate. Any more than that and it would start to dip into their profits.

On top of this, they mutually agreed that even if they failed, the Crimson Vow would not be required to pay a penalty fee, and it would not be recorded as a job failed but as a "job completed with zero results." This was a complicated task, and even if the Crimson Vow *were* to fail, it would cause no further hardship for the shop. After all, at that point, the job could still be made available to other hunters.

With this arrangement, there was almost no risk for the Crimson Vow. Even in the worst-case scenario, all they would end up suffering would be a waste of their time. Such was the beauty of Pauline's negotiating skills.

"With that, I believe our discussion is complete. We will present this contract to the guild along with our job acceptance report."

With Mavis offering up the last word, the four moved to stand.

"Just a minute."

Apparently, however, the shop owner was not finished.

"While you're here, I want you to try our food. We only have a small quantity of the spices that we've previously acquired from afar, so I'll make a little something with those and scrounge up another dish that can be made without spices. I'd like you to try both. If it gives you a bit more strength, things'll turn out better for all of us!"

It was unclear whether he truly believed that, whether he merely wanted to show off his cooking skills, or whether he thought that this might be the only chance for these hunters, a typically impoverished group, to taste such high-class cooking for themselves...

No matter what his thought process might be, there was certainly no reason for them to refuse.

Plus, Reina had already plopped back down into her seat, the drool practically running from her mouth.

"Pardon the intrusion," Mavis had no choice but to reply. "It seems as though we will be taking you up on that offer..."

After a short while, the owner brought out two dishes that were visually indistinguishable from one another and placed them before the girls.

"Here are two versions of a spicy beef stir-fry with garlic scapes, chives, mushrooms, and wild vegetables. One is made with our usual spices, and one is made without. The unspiced one has been supplemented with more pungent vegetables, local herbs, and salt for flavor."

They all tried both of the dishes to compare, and...

"They're completely different!" said Mavis.

"They really are," added Mile, apologetically. "No offense meant to your skills, sir, but no matter how much work you've put into salvaging the unspiced one, the flavor pales in comparison."

The shop owner grinned and replied, "No offense taken. In fact, I'll take that as a compliment, a testament to just how good our seasoning is. I think this will help you understand just how crucial it is for us to get those spices. As long as I've gotten that much across, then having you try out these dishes was worthwhile."

Now that the man mentioned it, what he said was true. The four certainly did feel more inspired now to acquire the spices on Calamity's behalf.

"Please. We aren't just some fancy eatery for nobles to frequent but a part of the community—a local, high-quality shop where the common man can experience a bit of luxury now and then. We may not be cheap, but what we share with the people is a dream, an aspiration, something that they can acquire if they just reach a little farther.

"To tell you the truth, what I love the most is to see the happy looks of satisfaction on the faces of our customers who can enjoy this luxury only a few times a year. That's why I want to reopen this shop as soon as I can. And for that, I absolutely need those spices."

The four girls nodded and stood. Not the smallest scrap of food was left on their plates.

"What—are y'all heading out already?" asked the shop owner. "I've still got more dishes for you to try!"

And so, they sat themselves right back down again.

The Crimson Vow left Calamity behind and headed straight to the guild, where they made their report to the clerks and handed over the contract with the terms that had been established during their discussion. Then they set off into the nearby forest.

"So Pauline, why did you decide to include that provision for job failure in the contract? You know I already have a ton of spices packed away in my inventory. Even if we only gave him those, there's no way that the job could be labeled a failure..."

"It's for insurance purposes!"

"Wha...?"

What Mile should have been surprised by was the fact that the people of this world had already hit upon the concept of "insurance." Of course, the insurance of this world didn't work exactly the same way as that of modern-day Earth—but what left Mile truly flabbergasted was Pauline's inscrutable actions and the fact that she would bother with such a thing on a job that they had no chance of failing at all.

"All right then, are you gonna spill the beans or what?"

"Huh?"

The moment they arrived in the forest, Reina clapped Mile on the shoulders. Mile was perplexed.

"You weren't really planning on just handing over all the spices you use for your own cooking to the guy and calling it a day, were you?!" Reina continued pointedly. "So, what's the plan? You gonna use your location magic to figure out where the wild peppers grow? Or are we gonna track down those bandits and retrieve the stolen spices?"

Mavis and Pauline listened in with bated breath, wondering which option Mile was going to choose.

"We aren't doing either of those things! First off, we aren't going to be finding any fields full of peppers around here. As for the bandits, how are we supposed to capture them when we don't even know which bandits they were attacked by or where?!"

It was a reasonable response.

CHAPTER 42
SPICE

"Aw, come on..."

The other three were completely dejected.

They had become thoroughly spoiled by Mile's abilities.

"Obviously, we're going to be making the spices!"

"Whaaaaaaaat?!?!"

And yet, she still managed to surprise them.

"All right now. Pauline, you make an Ultra Hot Waterball in this pan here. Slowly now, make sure it doesn't spill. Careful..."

Pauline faced the pan that Mile had produced from storage and cautiously began her spell.

"Waterball... Ultra Hot..."

Ker-plunk.

A bright red liquid sloshed into the pan, filling it up to the brim. A noxious aroma drifted up from the vessel.

"Now, I just need to figure out how to break this down..."

Mile thought hard.

Judging by the smell, the Ultra Hot magic definitely employed some sort of capsaicin. This liquid, brought into being by magic, was a physical substance. If she could just remove the capsaicin components from the liquid, they could probably be used as spices.

She had no idea if this physical substance had been brought about by molecular conversion or whether it had been transmitted there from somewhere else, but all that really mattered to her at the moment was that it existed *now*, so she tried not to think too hard about it.

The root of the spicy taste that came with spiced food was typically either something like the capsaicin found in chili peppers—habanero and the like—or else the allyl compounds that were found in wasabi, mustard, garlic, and so forth. However, those allyl compounds were highly volatile, so their use in cooking environments was fairly limited.

Furthermore, when it came to spices, there were also substances such as nutmeg, ginger, cassia, cumin, coriander, pepper, cinnamon, sage, thyme, bay leaves, et cetera. However, what the shop owner was after were most likely those spices of the capsaicin variety. With that in mind, the other possibilities became irrelevant.

This was the reason that Mile had asked Pauline to employ her Ultra Hot magic. However...

"If we simmer it for a while, there's a chance that all the spice might go out of it, even if the spice elements—unlike allyl compounds—are chemically stable. Plus, heating it up until all the liquid evaporates might take a long while..."

The boiling and evaporating methods would probably prove rather inefficient in producing a large amount of spices—and plus, even with a number of pans, they would only be able to collect a small amount. Realizing this, Mile racked her brain for alternatives.

And then suddenly, she was struck with an epiphany.

"That's it! According to a modern physics book I read ages ago, there might just be a way! The 'LovePlus Demon'! No, wait— that was a different sort of methodology. That one was, 'If a being of sufficient intellect to know every facet of a dating sim's code existed, then they could predict the outcomes of every route of the game,' or something like that. That's not right at all!

"Right—I remember now! The principle I was thinking of was something like: 'A vessel of lukewarm coffee is divided into two portions with a shutter. If you employed an omnipotent demon to open the shutter only when the faster moving molecules moved from right to left, and when the slower moving molecules moved from left to right, then you could divide the liquid into hot and cold without introducing additional energy into the system, thereby decreasing the entropy.' So if we used something like that...

"Oh, yes, yes—that was it! The 'Maxwell House's Demon' principle... Anyway, in reality, there's been a reduction in information here, and as a result, an increase in entropy, but that's got nothing to do with me! And besides, I don't have to rely on any demons because I have my nanobuddies..."

Mutter.

Mutter... mutter...

Suddenly, a chattering seemed to fill the air around her.

Mile, however, did not notice this and began to attempt a spell.

"Nanomachines inside the pan form a thin membrane in the middle and use that shutter to separate the two sides into moisture and capsaicin..."

Gyaaaaaaaah!

She heard a noise.

"Okay, forget that. Just separate out the capsaicin particles however you want, nanos. Oh yeah, and since we don't actually need the moisture, you can just get rid of that."

Shwoop!

The next moment, all the moisture had vanished from the saucepan, leaving only a small amount of red powder remaining on the bottom of the dish. (Incidentally, capsaicin actually crystalizes into a white powder, but the nanomachines, of their own judgment, concluded that that would not seem especially "spicy," and, ever prudent, decided to add in the red coloring themselves.)

I wonder what was so awful about the partition method... Mile pondered, tilting her head.

"What in the world were you just muttering to yourself about?" asked Reina. "Is this the magic-made spice you were talking about?"

She stuck her fingers into the pan and took up a pinch of the powder, giving it a curious lick.

"Gaaaaaaaaaaaaaaaaaaaaah!!!"

It was pure, crystallized capsaicin. On the Scoville scale, it would have a value of 16,000,000 units. For comparison, this was roughly 3,200 to 6,400 times the heat of your standard Tabasco sauce, which has a rating of around 2,500 to 5,000 Scoville units. It was not a level of heat that your average human could bear.

Mile had rushed to stop her, but she was a moment too late.

"...! ......!! ....!!!"

Reina fell to the ground writhing, unable to speak.

Pauline, who had been about to stick her finger in to taste it as well, froze, white as a sheet.

"R-Reina, open your mouth, hurry! Stick your tongue out as far as you can!"

Through gobs of tears, Reina steeled herself and followed Mile's directions, thrusting her tongue out.

"Ice Water!"

Mile struck Reina's tongue with a beam of magical water.

Because capsaicin locks onto the portions of the tongue that sense heat as well as the pain receptors, numbing the tongue with cold water would dull the sensation, while the powerful stream blasted the molecules away. And then...

"Heat!"

Capsaicin does not easily dissolve in water, but it does in oil, so she withdrew some cooking oil from her inventory and heated it, using that to wash Reina's tongue. Finally...

"While that cleans off your tongue, take this and drink it very slowly!"

With that, she pulled out the final ingredient, some heated milk that was still warm from the inventory, and handed it to Reina.

Despite Mile's quick thinking, Reina was still in pain, but she had gotten past the worst of it, so she endured quietly, not bothering to complain to Mile.

Seeing this, Mile recalled the tale of a certain boy detective.

Lick...
"Hm, this is potassium cyanide!"
Collapse.

"I-Is this pure chili powder?!"

Pauline gaped at the capsaicin powder that had suddenly appeared, her eyes like that of a nuclear physicist.

"Yes," said Mile. "Well, this is technically only the component of a chili pepper that makes it spicy, isolated here on its own."

Hearing this, Pauline appeared to be in a trance.

"This pure spice came from *my* magic... For as long as I have magical power, I can make this high-priced ingredient over and over again! This is the work of a god. It's like I can shoot gold coins from my fingertips! With this, I'll be filthy rich, like no one ever was! Unparalleled riches!!!"

Though it was not the same as pepper, which was often worth literally its weight in gold, chili was a very high-priced ingredient by weight, as far as foodstuffs went. Plus, this was the spice in pure, crystalized form. Of course Pauline would be riding high.

Oh, this is bad... Mile fretted, watching her friend.

At this rate, Pauline was going to start suggesting that they go into high-volume production of this chili—or rather, capsaicin powder—so that they could make a fortune... Well, actually, she was already saying it.

At this rate she's gonna go over to the Dark Side. I can't let that happen...

Quickly, Mile poked a hole in the rising soufflé that was Pauline's dreams.

"We can't do that, Pauline! If we made a fortune off of this

CHAPTER 42
SPICE

powder, it would spell disaster for the spice industry! It's not just producers or transporters who would suffer—think of the ramifications for international trade. Besides, given that we would have no record of having purchased it, having transported it, having stored it anywhere, or even having paid taxes on it, the authorities would catch on to us in a heartbeat. And all the nobles and officials and merchants and criminals would come crawling out of the woodwork, asking us for information and exclusivity and tax money..."

"Erk."

Pauline was, of course, a merchant's daughter. She understood exactly what Mile was getting at. If they didn't tell people that they had acquired the product by magic, they might be abducted, tortured, or even arrested for import fraud and tax evasion. On the other hand, if they *did* spill the beans, they might be murdered to keep the secret from getting out—or else the secret *would* get out, and the price would plummet. It would be a fatal blow for producers and brokers of chilis, and it would cripple their own profits as well.

And of course, the biggest problem would be that Pauline's special Ultra Hot magic would begin to spread.

Thus far, the Crimson Vow, as its originators, were the only ones who knew about this magic. Only a few dozen people so far had witnessed it (or rather, been on the receiving end of it), and for the most part, those people could not use magic. Even for the ones who were capable mages, it would be incredibly difficult to determine the source of the spell's effect from seeing it just one time.

Besides, any mage who would sully their hands with criminal acts was not much of a mage to speak of at all. If they had any significant amount of power, they would be more than able to make money by legitimate means. Furthermore, any such person who had made an enemy of the Crimson Vow had since been imprisoned and sold off for labor.

So, as things were, there was little worry of any knowledge of this particular magic being spread to other people. However, if it did get out, and mages with criminal intent began using Ultra Hot-type magic...

The balance of power between mages and melee fighters would crumble entirely and those criminal mages would become unstoppable!

As all this ran through Pauline's mind in a single instant, the blood drained from her face.

"I-In that case, won't even this little bit we made right now cause a problem?" offered Mavis.

"Erk!"

Mile faltered.

"Uhm, well, it's... you know!"

"Know what?" Mavis and Reina asked, suspiciously.

"This is this, and that is that!"

"........."

And so the mass-production of the synthetic spices began.

Pauline used her Ultra Hot magic, while Mile used her isolation magic, and then the jars were stored away in her inventory.

Obviously, they could not march back into town *too* quickly—that would be suspicious. Therefore, they made the collective decision to stay a while longer and produce a large amount of the product for future use. As long as it was stored in Mile's inventory, it would not deteriorate, and it could also be used as a weapon. While Mile and Pauline were busy putting the powder into the various containers that were already inside Mile's storage space, Reina and Mavis set to work packing it into vessels of bamboo and grass that could be tossed like grenades and other such weaponry.

These were weapons that could sap all the fight from an opponent without injuring them. It truly was a humane means of combat.

However, as Reina sat quietly packing the hand grenades, a strange, wicked grin hung on her face.

There could only be one reason for this.

She couldn't accept being the only one to suffer. Misery loves company, after all.

In the midst of her work, Mile caught this smile out of the corner of her eye and began to think, desperately, of how to devise some countermeasure should one of those grenades suddenly be lobbed her way...

That evening, the Crimson Vow returned to town and took a room at an inn. Initially, they had planned to camp out for three days to feign the amount of time it would take to go hunting or gathering for goods; however, the longer they stayed away, the longer Calamity would remain closed.

Plus, they were already doing something that was outside the norm. It made little difference if it took three days or one to do it.

By now, such things were of little consequence to them.

It was possible that they had breathed in too many of the spice particles and gone funny in the head. They had inhaled too much curry and gone mad, just like Hanada Kousaku, the Curry General of *Houchounin Ajihei*, and his Black Curry.

Still, for the sake of making it look like it had at least taken them a *little* more time—and because they were now eager to call it quits for the night rather than heading straight for Calamity, they journeyed to the inn to take a load off.

They could do it tomorrow. That's a saying they have in Spain, isn't it? *"Hasta mañana,"* which in this case meant, "The deadline doesn't haftah mattah-nya!"

...Who let that catperson in here?!

"So, anyway. We got them."

"...What do you mean, 'so, anyway'? Well, I suppose... Let's just see 'em!"

Given how quickly the girls had returned to him, the owner of Calamity held out little hope for their results, resigning himself to receiving only the smallest bounty, offered up merely for the sake of form and in the hope of earning a job completion mark.

For one, the Crimson Vow did not appear to even be carrying anything, which meant that their offerings could not have been anything more than what they could stuff in their pockets. However...

Boom!

From out of nowhere, a massive bucket suddenly appeared atop the table. Inside the bucket was a strange red power.

"Wha...? No, d-don't tell me..."

Instinctively, the owner reached out to touch the powder, but Mile swiftly seized him by the wrist.

"Tch!"

Reina, robbed of a new ally in suffering, glared at Mile, fangs bared.

"R-Reina, you're really scaring me..."

After finally persuading the owner not to sample (?) the powder directly, they procured a small pot full of soup and mixed a tiny amount into it. And then, when he sampled *that*...

"Pwah!"

He collapsed.

"W-water..."

"Here you go!"

Thinking that just such a thing might occur, Mile had already prepared a glass of cold water and stored it away in her inventory. Unlike in Reina's case, the owner would not have the pure product lingering on his tongue, so the water should be enough.

Mile had to try desperately to restrain herself from instead withdrawing some earthworms that were still stored away in her inventory from the time they had all gone fishing, just for the sake of a joke. It probably would be less than prudent to offer a client a glass of cold "*worm*-ter."

After a short while, the shop owner was back on his feet. Naturally, he had a few questions.

"Where in the world did you get your hands on this? No, wait, more importantly—what *is* this stuff?"

"Oh, well, this is a pure, concentrated version of the components of chilis that make them spicy. Unfortunately, the supplier swore us to absolute secrecy..."

"........."

The owner stared into the bucket with frighteningly serious eyes.

"So, how much of it would you like to buy?"

Leave it to Pauline to cut straight to the chase.

The market price for pepper was five silver per gram. It had roughly the same value as gold. Chilis were nowhere near that pricey, usually netting 1 silver per gram. This was still fairly expensive, but one gram of powdered spice worked out to a very large amount—so much so that you wouldn't even use a tenth of it in one dish. Incidentally, if you used a full gram in a single dish, even that was only 1 silver's worth, which in Japanese money equaled about 1,000 yen. And at any rate, the owner was only buying the spice at a 1.5x markup from the market rate. He could break even by just raising the prices of his dishes slightly, so it wasn't a big deal.

There was probably about five kilograms there before him... At market rate, that would come to around 50 gold or five million yen in modern-day Japanese currency. At a markup of 1.5x, that would be 75 gold. Plus, it was already around 5,000 times hotter than standard chili powder—only a fraction of the normal amount of this special powder would still be more than enough.

Even so, the Crimson Vow obviously could not price it 5,000 times higher than the normal rate, and they were very curious as to how the shop owner would value it. While they all stared each other down, the owner casually stuck a finger into the soup from before and tasted it again, deep in thought.

Finally, he reached his conclusion.

"I'll give ya ten gold for the lot."

"What?"

The owner was an honest, hard-working individual who loved to cook. Therefore, Mavis, Reina, and Mile were shocked at hearing such a low price presented. Only Pauline showed no signs of surprise.

"Might I ask the basis of that appraisal?" she asked pointedly. "Bearing the standard price for chilis in mind."

The owner flinched slightly, but then recalled that he was only facing a little girl, and his resolve swiftly returned.

"It's too finely processed. There's no hint of the original

peppers. That's why the price has gone down. This is merely spice—it has none of the complex flavors of a chili pepper. In fact, the price I gave you is already an undeservedly high one for less-than-third-rate, inferior goods such as these. But, since you did go out and do the job properly, I thought I'd cut'cha a break! Ahaha!"

The owner gave a forced laugh, but Pauline only peered at him, her eyes like ice.

"And what of the fact that, because it's so spicy, you'd barely need to use any of it?"

"Oh? I'm pretty sure that was just a mismeasurement on my part. It's just a little bit on the spicy side."

"How much do you suppose it cost us to acquire this quantity?"

"There's no way a group of greenhorns like you would have the money to stock up for very much. I bet you stole it from somewhere or got it on the cheap, right? Look, just hand it over already, and don't make trouble. You are gonna tell me where you got this from, aren'tcha?"

"Mile, put it away!"

"On it!"

"Huh?"

At Reina's command, Mile put the bucket full of spice back into storage at once.

The owner gaped, wide-eyed, at the suddenly empty space.

"That's a 'complete, with no results,' then."

The Crimson Vow moved to leave, but the owner rushed to stop them.

"Wha...?! W-wait! *I'm* the one who hired you all, so..."

"We failed to reach a mutually satisfactory agreement on the price, so the negotiation is a failure, isn't it? The job was complete as contracted, with no penalties on either side. That was indeed the original contract. It says so on the guild record, in fact—in writing," Pauline reminded him.

"Guh..."

The owner, backed into a corner, began to panic.

"W-well, what I meant was, I only have ten gold on hand right now! I definitely didn't think that I was going to buy that much off of you fer just ten gold! Obviously we can't keep much gold in the shop at one time. We'd get robbed blind if we did. I have to go withdraw the rest from the merchants' guild, so it's gonna take me a bit! Please, come back here this evening. I'll have it ready for you then!"

How suspicious.

The Crimson Vow all shared the same thought, but they nodded to acknowledge his words and left the shop behind them.

"So, what do you think?" asked Mile.

Pauline shrugged.

"It's not looking great. First off, he tried to avoid giving us a price. Then he tried to drive the price down, probably because he was underestimating us. And after that, he attempted to sniff out our source."

"And here I thought he was a true artist, someone concerned

with flavor above all else..." Mile said, disappointed. "If he hadn't tried to belittle us or squeeze our source out of us, I might've been inclined to even charge him less than market price. It cost us nothing to make it, and it is true that it's incredibly spicy without much smell or flavor, which makes it very difficult to cook with, after all."

"Well," said Reina, "I guess it just goes to show that all it takes is a pile of money to bring out someone's true colors."

She cast a sidelong glance at Pauline, who did not seem to notice.

Sighing, Pauline said, "I get the feeling that even if we wait until evening, it isn't going to change anything."

"Well, in that case, why don't we go hunt something while we're waiting around, so it's not a total waste of our time?"

"Yeah!!!"

Mavis's proposal was well received.

That evening, the Crimson Vow returned again to the gourmet eatery, Calamity. There, they sat across a table from the shop's owner, each side facing the other.

"Now then, shall we continue this afternoon's negotiations? We have yet to hear your new proposal regarding a price arrangement. How much are you willing to pay?"

Pauline's voice was cold. Clearly, she no longer regarded the man as a suitable trade partner.

"First," he replied, "I wanna see the goods again. I can't risk forking over a bunch of money just for you to take it and then say, 'Oh, we actually already sold it all somewhere else.'"

Pauline nodded, and once more, Mile withdrew the bucket full of powdered spice from her inventory and placed it atop the table. Seeing this, the owner grinned.

"Now then, how about you tell me where this stuff came from? Give me that, and I'll raise my price to eleven gold for the lot."

"Ahhhh..."

The four girls let out a prolonged sigh. This was, in fact, a waste of their time.

As the four moved to stand and leave once again, the owner clapped his hands twice. The side door opened, and five fellows, who appeared to be hunters in their thirties or forties, appeared. Two of the men stood blocking the doors, while the other three surrounded the owner, as if to guard him.

"Well," said the man, "I thought we could handle this peacefully, but I guess you all wanna do it the hard way. You three—capture them!"

"Ahhhh..."

Once again, the Crimson Vow let out a great sigh.

"Well, uh, I'm not exactly sure why you want us to capture them," said one of the men. "It doesn't look like you're in danger or anything. You just had a failed negotiation, didn't you? Taking them prisoner for that alone would make us criminals..."

Apparently, these were not some thugs on the owner's payroll but just a group of normal hunters.

"They're clearly wagon-raiding bandits! That bucket there contains the spices that were stolen from us. They waltzed in here out of nowhere trying to sell my own goods back to me, and when I offered eleven gold pieces to get them back, all they wanted to do was keep drivin' up the price! So I'm gonna bring them down and hand them over to the authorities! Now hurry up and capture them!"

Even with these excuses, it could cause quite a lot of trouble to falsely imprison someone. Especially given that they were dealing with a group of young girls, it was entirely possible that the hunters would be given a red mark or even have their licenses revoked. They were not about to do something so imprudent.

"Mister, we were hired as your guards. We have no reason to capture a group of young ladies who have made no move to cause you any harm—whether or not they're bandits. Though I suppose, if they *were* bandits, there would be a reward out for them, and, as good hunters ourselves, I can't see why we *shouldn't* want to cooperate with you... Have you any proof?"

The owner pointed straight at the bucket on the table.

"That! That right there is the product that our shop ordered from far away, which was stolen by bandits on its way here!"

The hunter turned to the Crimson Vow and asked, "Is that true?"

Fwp fwp fwp!

The girls shook their heads in unison.

"To begin with, that bucket contains a specialty spice that we obtained all on our own. It's not something that you can get anywhere else. Why don't you ask the owner there where it is that he ordered it from?" Mile started. "It would probably take a long time to confirm his claims with the source, but I'm sure that if you asked around at the neighboring shops and with the merchants' guild, they could tell you whether such a source exists, whether they have ever sold such a product, and whether this product is one that is typically used by this store."

The hunters' gazes all turned toward the owner.

"M-my sources are a proprietary secret! That's not something you go flapping your gums about! Why don't *you* all tell *us* where you got that from and prove *your* innocence?!"

"Oh?" said Mile, a look of feigned shock on her face. "But didn't you just say that a source was something you shouldn't go flapping your gums about?"

The hunters snickered.

"Wha..."

"Plus," she continued, "regarding those stolen spices, didn't you tell us just yesterday morning that they had been stolen before you even had a chance to receive the goods—so you hadn't lost any money on them? In which case, the stolen goods were never your property but that of the spice merchants, weren't they? Are you really trying to say that you have a legitimate claim to their goods?"

The hunters looked on in surprise as the owner stammered wordlessly.

"Furthermore, did you *really* order this great an amount? Are you saying that the amount you ordered is exactly the same as the amount in this bucket?"

"Y-yes! I ordered five kilograms—it's a perfect match!"

As the owner made this claim, a grin spread across Mile's face.

"In that case... Allow me to clear up your misgivings!"

One after another, Mile drew out a variety of containers in many shapes and sizes, lining them all up on the table. Altogether, they contained an enormous amount of spices.

"Huuhhhhhhhh?!?!"

There was a cry of shock, not only from the owner, but from the five hunters as well.

"St-storage magic!!!"

The whole group was, of course, shocked at just how many vessels had appeared, although given that the owner was already aware of Mile's storage magic abilities, he did not share the hunters' surprise on this count.

"I would say that this is proof that these spices are not something that we merely stole from some caravan, wouldn't you?" said Mile, facing not the owner but the five hunters.

The hunters nodded emphatically.

"Um, so. Judging by what I overheard earlier, I'm guessing that you all are hunters who were hired for what you thought was going to be a normal, legitimate guard job?" Mile asked.

The man who seemed to be the leader scratched his head and replied, "That's right. It was a job that just got posted this morning and wasn't discussed very much ahead of time. He told us that he was dealing with a group of hunters and that he wanted to have us ready as a show of force just in case the negotiations got a little hairy. We were supposed to show up and look intimidating when he gave us the signal. He said it was just a group of little girl rookies, so it would be no big thing—and that we'd get a feast of good food and booze this evening for doing just a little bit of work. So of course we grabbed that slip the moment we saw it..."

"In that case, I would say that the circumstances here are clear, are they not? This man wove a false tale in order to try and steal these spices away from us and secure our supply route for himself—and aimed to make you all do something criminal in the process. Our possession of these spices clearly contradicts the owner's testimony earlier. Plus, if he truly thought we were bandits, wouldn't the usual course be to contact the authorities rather than contracting hunters at his own expense? This man has hired you under false pretenses, given false testimony, and tried to force us to reveal our secrets. Would you all be so kind as to serve as witnesses to this with the guild and the city guard?"

"Y-yeah, absolutely. If we didn't, we would get a job failure marked on our record or even be labeled accomplices to a crime, which would be bad for us, obviously. Yet we also have a request: please attest to the fact that our party never made any mistakes or did anything illegal—we were only deceived!"

Mile readily agreed. The hunters looked relieved.

"Now, as for our culprit..."

The man suddenly appeared queasy.

"You knew that these spices were not stolen goods, but you tried frame us as criminals just to get your hands on them. Furthermore, you didn't even have any rights to the stolen goods in the first place. You deceived the guards you hired from the guild and tried to make them accomplices to your crimes. Before we turn you over to the authorities, by way of the guild, is there anything you would like to say for yourself?"

As Mile offered the man a last word, he began to argue desperately. "I-I meant you no ill! This isn't that serious—"

"Oh, 'no ill?' The thought never crossed your mind that you might be doing something wrong? You're saying that for you, this is a completely normal procedure? That it didn't make your conscience sting even a little bit?"

The Crimson Vow and the hired hunters all glared down at him as though the man were little more than a pile of dirt.

"Huh? Uh, no, that's not what I meant! I just..."

"If you could try and trick someone into a criminal act with *no* ill will, then I just shudder to think what atrocities you might commit when an evil mood *does* strike you..."

And then Mile landed the finishing blow.

"Also, are you going to tell me that you intended to fight against the hunters who you *yourself* hired through the guild?" She turned to the other hunters. "What does the guild do in matters like this?"

"It's seldom seen, but such acts of malice toward the guild are committed now and then. Not only will he no longer be able to place requests with the guild, but he'll be taken in and turned over to the authorities. If things had gone south and we'd ended up fighting you girls, there might have been some casualties. He won't get off lightly, I can tell you that."

As he listened in on this exchange, the owner went white as

a sheet. Seeing how terribly he was trembling, Mile thought to herself, *Well, I guess we've frightened him enough.*

"So then, what made you decide to do this?" she asked.

The owner desperately replied, "I j-just really wanted those spices! I thought that if I could get my hands on a spice like that for cheap—not just temporarily but for the foreseeable future—then I could start selling dishes that were chock full of spice for lower prices... I know it's no excuse, but I figured that if I had a cheap, nearby source of seasonings with that much heat, then even if it was lacking in flavor or aroma, I could mix it up with normal chilis and use a few other tricks to make do! If I could get it as cheaply as possible, then all my the less-fortunate customers, for whom this food was out of budget so far, would be able to enjoy this spicy food whenever they liked, without a care...

"You all are traveling hunters, aren't you? If you all lived around here then there's no way I wouldn't have noticed a group of such memorable young women as yourselves. In other words, you're going to be leaving town soon, aren't you? And so, your source!" He collapsed, hands on the floor, his head hung in shame. "I just wanted so badly to know how you got your hands on that spice..."

The girls were a bit troubled.

From the get-go, they had thought the owner was rather arrogant. However, given that his position as their client gave him a bit of an elevated standing, and that they were, of course, only a group of young girls, they had not thought too much of it. It was not at all rare to meet some stubborn older gentleman who was passionate about his craft.

Besides, when it came to his cooking and his customers, he seemed incredibly sincere.

If only they had not been the ones to take on this job.

If only they had brought him a normal kind of spice in a normal amount.

If only things had gone that way, then perhaps the man could have proceeded through a normal transaction and continued to run his business as a normal restaurateur.

Their own misdeeds had driven this man to the path of crime and sent his life into disarray.

As they realized this, a crippling unease set upon them.

"So then, what did you intend to do if seeing your hired guards did not persuade us and things came to blows?" asked Mile.

The owner stared blankly and replied, "What? I mean, you all are no match for them! I just figured that you girls would quietly surrender in order to protect yourselves or that you would easily be captured, and then you might tell us where you got the spices in order to prove that you weren't thieves. Then I could discover the source that way..."

"And then you intended to turn us over to the authorities so that we could be jailed—even executed—for a crime that we didn't commit?"

The man raised his voice in shock.

"O-of course not! I would never do such a thing! All I really wanted was the source, so after I got you to tell me that much, I was going to give you your gold, apologize for the misunderstanding, and let you go!"

The explanation was sound, but Mile wouldn't let him off the hook so easily.

"What if we didn't tell you?"

"...What?"

"What I'm saying is, what had you planned to do if we decided that we valued our loyalty over our lives and refused to tell you our source? Were you still going to turn us over as bandits? Or did you plan to torture the information out of us?"

The owner's face went blank and took a few moments to return to his original expression.

"...I didn't think about that."

"Huh?"

There was a chorus of confusion throughout the room.

"I didn't think that far ahead..."

Somehow or other, it seemed he was telling the truth.

"Well, at any rate, there was never any possibility of that happening in the first place."

"Huh??"

The owner's and the hunters' voices overlapped.

"I mean, if it had truly come to blows, we would have just knocked all the other hunters out and turned all six of you in to the authorities, letting them know we had been attacked by robbers."

The hunters sneered at Mile, with expressions that seemed to say, "Hey now, enough with the jokes, kid."

That was when Mile snapped.

At first, she had merely been trying to gauge the shop owner's intent, or rather, how far ahead he had planned. Once she had done so, her intention was to wave the whole thing off, like, "Oh well, there wasn't a chance of that happening anyway, so it's whatever, honestly." But clearly, these men were not taking them seriously.

Any hunters who would stand for letting themselves be so belittled would never make it in this line of work.

"Reina! Pauline!"

"Firebomb!"

"Ice Needle!"

At Mile's signal, the two swiftly cast their spell-free spells, and a small ball of flame, along with a modest barrage of ice needles, appeared above their heads. They had been holding these spells in their heads from the moment the other hunters appeared, ready to cast them at a moment's notice. This was a natural precaution for mages.

"What?! Spell-free casting?!"

The guard hunters' eyes went wide.

Then, Mile drew a copper coin from her inventory (pretending to pull it from her bosom), turned to Mavis, and flicked her fingers.

"Mavis!"

"On it!"

Her sword slashed in the blink of an eye, and Mavis's left hand flew from the grip of her sword through the air.

As you may have guessed, it was the special trick that Mile herself had popularized: the Copper Coin Cutter.

When the girls went drinking with the guild master back in the town where Mile had first registered as a hunter, Mavis had heard Laura describe this special technique, which Mile had used to impress the hunters in the guild there. Later, Mavis begged Mile to teach it to her, and so the trick was passed on to her.

However, for as much as it was called a "trick," that did not mean that it was the sort of thing that just anyone could pick up if given the right instruction. It was a technique that Mavis could only use because she was wielding a sword that had been forged by Mile.

"Wh...?"

Impossibly, the hunters' eyes opened even wider. In Mavis's open palm, there was the copper coin cut cleanly in two. They turned to look back at Pauline and Reina, the firebomb and ice needles still floating above their heads.

"P-please forgive us!!!"

The hunters went pale, imagining just how things might turn out if a real battle erupted. Now, they knew the Crimson Vow's true strength.

"M-man, I really didn't expect this. You all are so young... You have such a skilled swordswoman; these two mages, who are as good as B-ranks; and as for *you*, you're little, but... You're the brains of the operation, aren't you?" asked the fellow who appeared to be the hunters' leader.

Mile shook her head. "No. Compared to Pauline's black-hearte—ahem, *resourcefulness*—I am but an infant. I am a swordswoman-slash-mage."

From beside her, Reina added, "And really, Mile's the strongest of all of us—whether with magic *or* swords."

"Wha..." The five hunters shrunk away.

They're terrifying. These girls are terrifying!

The Crimson Vow's reputation had yet to spread across national borders.

Of course, they had made a name for themselves at the graduation exam, and with a few other incidents, but in the end, they were still just a group of rookie C-rank hunters. It would be strange if people in other countries *did* know their name. It was one thing in the capital of their own country, where plenty of people had attended the exhibition and seen their prowess for themselves, but even in the Kingdom of Tils, hardly anyone outside of the capital itself had even heard of them.

There was a small chance that some people knew about Veil, the boy who had vanquished the leader of the Roaring Mithrils. That was all according to Mile's plan...

And now, it was time to deal with the owner.

It would be one thing if this were a routine job, but Reina, Pauline, and of course, Mavis, were useless when it came to such an unusual situation. Thus, they let Mile take the reigns. Every aspect of this operation had been left up to her judgment.

Mile thought for a bit, then faced the shop owner and spoke.

"That'll be twelve gold pieces."

"Huh?"

Everyone, save for the Crimson Vow, stared at Mile in confusion.

"What did you just say?" asked the lead hunter.

"I said, twelve gold pieces."

".........."

Silence spread throughout the room.

"But why?!" the leader screeched angrily.

And so, Mile explained.

"I don't think that the owner here is a bad person, deep down... He merely had the incredible chance to get his hands on the spice of his dreams, which stirred up a bit of evil in him..."

"No ordinarily honest person would ever stoop that low!" The leader of the hunters protested. "If he's the kind of guy who would do this, I guarantee you that he would definitely do the same thing all over again in similar circumstances! To make matters worse, he'll have learned from this experience. Next time, he won't bother hiring a legitimate guard, but instead some actual thugs, and I doubt that whoever he sets his sights on will be nearly as strong as you. They'll probably be tortured by those thugs or their buddies and end up strung up as criminals on false charges. You do understand that, don't you?!"

He was, in fact, correct.

However, Mile rejected his argument.

"It's fine. I'm sure the owner is already reflecting on his actions, and he won't try anything like this again in the future. Besides, the specialty spice we offered him was something that we'd already brought along with us in storage. It's not made anywhere around here, and there's no possible way for the owner to get in touch with the producers. Plus..."

"Plus?"

"If he ever does something like this again, we'll come back and deal with him. And when we do, we'll be sure to stuff a *ton* of this spice down his throat. The same amount as what's in that bucket right now, perhaps..."

Hearing this, the owner began to tremble.

An experience like that would spell death for him, both emotionally and physically.

When the guard hunters saw this, they snickered.

"Anyway," Mile continued, "if he swears he'll never do it again, then I suppose we can let him off this once. Even if we turned him over to the authorities, it's not like he's a bandit or anything, so we wouldn't get any reward for it. Moreover, we wouldn't be able to sell our spices, so we wouldn't make a profit. Besides, you'd be losing the best restaurant in town—it's really a lose-lose situation. Therefore, I think we can just let him off, though not without a bit of a penalty."

"A penalty?"

"Yes. Say, for example, he has to pay each of you one extra gold coin on top of your promised wages, for wasting your time. Five gold in total..."

"All right!!!" came a chorus.

"I-If he really is reflecting on his actions, th-then I guess it would be all right to let him go just this once! We mustn't forget that compassion is an important part of being human!"

The moment they heard Mile's proposal, the leader and his allies' attitudes changed immediately. Mile looked to the owner and saw him nodding his head fervently. Apparently, the matter was settled.

She stored away all of the spices, save for the bucket they had brought out initially, ignoring the owner's small sigh. Understandably, the man did not have the strength of heart to suggest that they sell him any additional spices. It was clear from the fact that Mile had only brought out the one bucket initially that she had never intended to sell him any more than that. Now recognizing that she had clearly obtained the product from some far-off land and would not want to be relieved of her stock all at once, the owner understood it was only natural she would reject any further requests.

In fact, neither the claim that the spice was "not made any-where around here" or that she had "brought it along in storage" was technically a lie. They had made the product themselves, so it wasn't something anyone else in the area would be able to provide, and they had in fact carried it from the forest in storage. So really, Mile had told the whole truth. If anyone should misinterpret her words, why, that was no fault of hers, was it?

The owner retreated to the shop's hidden vault and came back with a leather sack, handing twelve gold coins to the Crimson Vow and one each to the other hunters as he signed each of their job completion forms. The guard hunters' pay had already been deposited ahead of time at the guild, so they would retrieve it once they gave their report there.

✧ ◈ ✧

CHAPTER 42
SPICE

"So, now what?"

"Hm, what to do...?"

After leaving the restaurant behind and giving their report at the guildhall, the Crimson Vow huddled up near the job posting board. They had originally planned to spend several days in this town, but now that the spice matter was settled, there did not appear to be any other interesting jobs available.

As usual, if other hunters were to hear them hemming and hawing over what jobs to choose based on interest alone, they would be furious, but as it stood the Crimson Vow were not hurting for money. Plus, while the aim of this journey was ostensibly to find out what the elder dragons were after, at the moment, that much was merely incidental. Their main goal for now was to better themselves, earn more promotion points, and to have fun traveling with their friends.

This did not mean that they might not still take on boring, low-level hunting and extermination jobs now and then, depending on the circumstances, but, if at all possible, they would prefer to do unusual and interesting jobs—ones that would temper their skills and grant them new experiences.

For young maidens, time was a precious thing. They could not afford to waste it on tasks that were not worth their while.

Indeed, Mile had said something along these lines.

This time, it wasn't, "I just want to be a normal girl!" but instead, "We don't have any time to waste!"

"Should we head on to the next town?"

"Yeah, that's probably a good idea."

"Guess you're right."

"I just want to get out of this country already so we can relax."

With their opinions all in alignment, they decided to head for the border at once. They were already very close, so it would take them no time at all to reach the next kingdom.

"In that case, let's head back to the inn, let them know we're leaving, and head on out."

"Yeah!!!"

Several days later...

Calamity, the restaurant that had been temporarily shut down due to a shortage of spices, was now back in business—which was booming. Though the quality of the menu's flavors had decreased somewhat, they had a brand new menu full of dishes that were packed with spice and their prices slashed to be well within reach of the common man. However, the posting indicated this was a limited-time offer. They happened to have obtained some spices for cheap, and once their supply was all used up, it would be back to the normal dishes and prices.

When all the other restaurants heard the news of how Calamity had obtained such cheap spices by placing a request at the Hunters' Guild, they would rush to do the same. However, there were no other hunters around who could fulfill such a request. The owners all shrugged, thinking to themselves, *No matter. There's no way the amount of spices that a single party could have brought in will last Calamity very long. Once they run out, they'll have to close again until their regular shipment comes in.* Yet somehow, the "limited time" offer showed no signs of ending—even well after the reordered spices had finally arrived from their faraway source.

Through much experimentation, the owner of Calamity had come to the conclusion that using the spice powder in its pure form made dishes far too spicy—nay, dangerous even. It did not dissolve well in water, but it did mix well with oil, alcohol, and vinegar, so he began making solutions of those, which made the substance easier to use. This was also far more efficient, going a long way to stretch the amount of spice he had available.

Recall, this was a powder of pure capsaicin. Even very watered down, the heat would still pack quite a punch. Thus, he was able to continue effectively using his supply for a very long time.

Finally, when his supply began to run low, the owner of the gourmet restaurant Calamity stored away the last pinch of his special spice in a little glass vial, tucking it into his hidden vault. He stared at that vial for a short while and then returned to his work.

What might the owner have been thinking as he gazed at that tiny glass container? Only the man himself would ever know.

Didn't I Say
to Make My Abilities
Average in the
Next Life?!

CHAPTER 43 |

The Inn

"**I** KNOW IT'S STILL PRETTY EARLY IN THE DAY, but the next town after this is kind of far. Why don't we stop here for the night?"

It had been three days since they left Calamity and the town in which it was situated. The first night, they stopped at an inn in a tiny village, and the second two nights, they camped out, hunting animals, exterminating low-level monsters, and gathering medicinal herbs and specialty foodstuffs along the way. There was still a fair bit of time until evening, but rather than spending a third night in the rough, they decided to overnight in the town where they had just arrived.

The Crimson Vow had long since crossed the border from Mile's home country, and now they stood within a small provincial town in the neighboring country. Without the fear of being pursued by someone from her native land, Mile finally appeared at ease.

"This place is pretty small, so we'll be lucky if there are even two or three inns in town. We'll pick the best-looking one and stay there," said Reina, and the group nodded.

The various pros and cons of an inn had a large effect on what their physical condition would be like when they departed the next morning. The food needed to be good, the beds needed to be soft, and they had to be able to get a peaceful night's sleep. When travelers who often camped out went out of their way to spend the money for an inn, it had better at least fulfill those basic provisions—or there would be complaints. When paying for such a luxury, there was no sense in staying somewhere subpar just for the sake of scrimping.

On the other hand, just because an inn was costly did not automatically mean that it was good. And each inn had its own selling points, like amazing food or having its own baths... It was always a matter of cost versus value, as well as one's individual preferences.

In short, the only thing to be done was to investigate all the options and decide for themselves.

Because this town was so small, it had only an outpost of the Hunters' Guild, rather than a proper branch. Normal hunters would come to such a place to sell off the prey they had hunted and herbs and such they had gathered, as well as turning in their extermination trophies for points and rewards. However, the Crimson Vow had no need to sell their stock in some backwater place like this where they would almost certainly receive a lower price than elsewhere. As long as the goods were inside Mile's storage space (read: inventory), they would never spoil, so it was better to simply hold out until they were at a larger branch where they could get a better rate.

Still, it did behoove them to at least show their faces at the office. There was a chance that there might be some interesting jobs available, and they might be able to glean some information from the other hunters, too.

And so, they popped in to scan the intel board and the job board.

There was nothing. No useful information, no interesting jobs, no lucrative jobs—nothing. All they found were incredibly standard job requests and dailies: goblin hunting, herb gathering, and all manner of boring things like that.

"So I'm thinking we just stay the night here and then head out first thing in the morning?"

The other three nodded fervently at Reina's proposal.

Of course, checking the boards was not the only reason the four had stopped in at the guild outpost. They still needed one more important thing: a recommendation for an inn. Once they were finished checking the boards, they headed straight to the reception desk to ask for more information.

"What the heck was that about?!" shouted Reina.

As the Crimson Vow left the guild outpost behind, they walked through the town square, looks of utter bewilderment upon their faces.

"Mm..." Pauline replied. "I guess our only choice here is to investigate the inns for ourselves."

The information they had received about the town's inns was incredibly peculiar.

Apparently, there were two inns in this town. That was typical. It was precisely what they had expected. However, when they asked which of the two the clerks would recommend, the staff members' opinions were firmly divided.

Mavis asked the first young man she saw, who recommended an inn called the House of the Maiden's Prayer. Even if this was only a guild outpost, there was no reason a lower-ranking guild employee would try to deceive a hunter, so they decided that there was no reason not to take the recommendation. Just then, however, another clerk, a young woman in her early twenties, stopped them.

According to the young woman, the House of the Maiden's Prayer was dreadful, and instead they should stay at the Wild Bear Lodge.

Neither of the two appeared to be lying. It was obvious that each of them thought that their recommendation was the truly superior choice. And so, they assumed that this meant that neither inn was definitely good or bad but that it was merely a matter of trivial differences and personal preferences. Therefore, they decided to go with the recommendation of the first young man, who appeared to be in his late teens, closer in age to them. That was when another girl of around fifteen or sixteen, who had previously been helping another hunter, stepped in to voice her disapproval—quite strongly.

"Do *not* go to the Maiden's Prayer! The Wild Bear Lodge is the only reasonable choice!"

However, *another* man in his early thirties heard this and argued, "No, it's definitely the Maiden's Prayer!" But then another middle-aged hunter jumped in with, "How could you recommend that freakin' piece-of-crap inn?! The Wild Bear's the only way to go!" and then...

The situation, thankfully, did not escalate beyond bickering and grumbling; however, seeing that neither side would be willing to concede their point, the Crimson Vow hurriedly took their leave.

"This seems like it's a little more serious than a matter of people preferring one very similar inn over another just because of personal preferences," said Pauline.

"Yeah," Mavis agreed. "Everyone was like, 'No, that inn is garbage, you have to go to this one!' I never thought I'd ever see two groups so divided."

Reina thought quietly as she listened, arms folded. And then...

"All right, change of plans! We'll stay one night at each of the inns. That way we can figure out why their opinions are so divided and what the true source of this problem is!"

Reina was tittering as she said this—she had veered straight into "Let's have fun!" mode.

"Sounds entertaining," said Pauline. "I'm dying to know why it is that they're so weirdly divided on this issue. It might even be a useful experience to help me learn more about managing my family's shop..."

"Sounds good to me!" Mile chimed in. "I've been wanting to do something fun like this!"

"Then it's decided! First off, let's head to the House of the Maiden's Prayer!"

And with that, Reina, Pauline, and Mile were off. Mavis shrugged and followed them.

Soon, they arrived at the House of the Maiden's Prayer. Apparently, it was practically neighbors with the Wild Bear Lodge, which was only a stone's throw away on the opposite side of the street.

"Why?" asked Mavis, surprised at their proximity.

In reality, it only stood to reason. This was a small town, and they were in the town's center, near to the shopping district and the Hunters' and Merchants' Guild outposts. Both inns were in the center of affairs, facing out onto the main road. If you thought about it, this was the most suitable place for businesses such as theirs, targeted not at the locals, but at travelers who were passing through.

"Do you have a room for four available?" Reina asked as they entered the inn, facing the girl of fifteen or sixteen who was overseeing the reception counter.

"Welcome!" the girl replied with a smile. "Yes, we have some vacancies!"

She had a good manner for customer service.

"What? Two half-gold, without meals?"

Reina was a bit shocked to hear the girl explain the prices.

It was five silver per person per night, without meals included. In Japanese money, that would be nearly 5,000 yen. In other words, it was rather expensive. While it would be entirely reasonable to expect to pay like this at a business hotel in modern-day Japan, unlike Japanese hotels, these inns had no power outlets, fridges, TVs, or phones, so their furnishing and operation costs were completely different. Plus, it was not four single-person rooms they were after, but rather, one four-person room.

Still, if half the people at the guild were adamant about their recommendation, there must have been something here that was good enough to warrant such an extravagant fee. In addition, they had come here for the purpose of satisfying their curiosity, so even if it was a little pricey, they were not about to change their minds.

Naturally, they had to pay up front, so Reina pulled two half-gold pieces from her purse and handed them to the girl at the counter.

"Hot water is four half-silver per basin, and it's one more half-silver to borrow a towel."

"That's a lot!" the four girls uttered without thinking.

However, the girl did not appear to even notice. She must have been used to such reactions from customers.

"Our dinner prices are on the menu on the wall over there. You can order food at any time before the second evening bell at 9 PM."

The Crimson Vow turned to look at the menu posted on the wall, and read...

Vegetable Stew	*1 Silver*
Vegetable Stir-Fry Special	*1 Silver*
Soup and Rolls (2)	*1 Silver + 2 Half-Silver*
Orc Meat Steak	*3 Silver + 5 Half-Silver*
Ale	*5 Half-Silver*

"That's a lot!!!" the four of them shouted again, but the girl at the counter only continued to smile blithely.

"What is with the prices here?" Reina grumbled as they entered their room.

"This recommendation from the guild outpost is the real mystery," said Mile. "We need to figure out what it is that warrants these prices..."

Mavis and Pauline nodded.

"Thankfully, since we have our cleaning magic, we at least don't need to worry about wasting any money on that," said Reina.

"But the same can't be said for the food," Mile added. "If there's some kind of secret to it, we can't just forego dinner and eat what we've got in storage..."

Reina and Pauline pouted.

Though the money that they had earned here and there in the

past several days did not amount to very much, owing to the situations with the rock lizards, the bandits, and the wyvern, as well as their recent tussle with the beastfolk and elder dragons, their actual savings were nothing to scoff at. Enough so that coughing up ten or twenty silver would by no means break the bank.

However, most of the Crimson Vow were accustomed to a rather austere lifestyle. Even Mavis, thanks to hanging around the others for so long, had begun to take on a thriftiness that was unbecoming of a young noblewoman.

This disregarded Mile, who was also a noblewoman's only daughter, but no one really thought of her in that way.

Mavis was a noble's daughter. Pauline was a merchant's daughter. Reina was a peddler's daughter. And Mile was simply Mile. She was the singular complex creature that was Mile, no qualifiers attached. At least as far as the other three were concerned.

Thus was Mile's status amongst the Crimson Vow.

"Anyway, the suspense is killing me. Let's hurry up and go eat!"

It was unclear whether Mile was truly concerned about whether the secret of the inn's popularity lay in their food or whether there were merely sirens going off in her head to warn her that her tank was running on empty—as her fuel consumption tended to be rather inefficient. Either way, no one had any reason to argue with her proposal, so they all headed down to the first-floor dining hall.

"Wha...?"

The room was packed. Every seat in the room was not taken,

but there were a ton of people regardless—so many that it could not be only overnight guests eating here but locals as well.

This was a good sign. Any reputable inn tended to have patrons who came simply to eat. However, when they took a closer look around the room, they noticed something incredibly peculiar.

"There's no one here but young men..." Pauline noted.

"Oh..."

Thanks to her...well-developed body, Pauline was suddenly the center of attention and realized this straight away. Indeed, though there were plenty of customers present, outside of the Crimson Vow, there were no women or children anywhere in the crowd—nor were there any elders. They were all young men of ages varying from fifteen or sixteen to somewhere in their thirties.

Now that they thought about it, all of the hunters at the outpost who had insisted that the Maiden's Prayer was the best choice were young men, no older than their thirties. All of the women and elders had favored the Wild Bear.

"I think I'm beginning to understand why the opinions were so divided..." said Mile.

The other three nodded.

"Well, let's just see how their food is," said Reina. "If we don't, then this whole thing will go nowhere."

She had a point. The four of them took a seat at an open table and placed their orders.

"Vegetable stew, veggie stir-fry, soup with bread, and orc meat steaks, please! Two orders of each!"

No matter how overpriced it may be, Reina was not one to tighten her belt and order less just to save a few coins. Much as she might complain, food was food. That was the Reina way. The same went for Mile.

Of course, the order Reina had placed was not for her alone but for the whole table. She had ordered two of each dish so that they could all try each one and still get a chance to eat their fill.

This didn't mean they might not still put in an order for seconds, later.

The girl who had previously stood at the reception counter took their order and relayed it to the kitchen, a voice of acknowledgement echoing back from inside. It seemed to be the voice of another young woman.

"........."

After a short while, the food was brought and placed upon the table. The Crimson Vow gazed upon it.

"It looks completely average..." said Mile.

"Actually, I feel like the portion size is even smaller than average," quipped Pauline.

Naturally, Pauline's complaint was a bit more pointed.

"It smells average, too, and the ingredients are nothing special... Actually—no, it seems like they might even be using cheap cuts of meat, and the amount of meat that's in here really isn't significant." Mavis prodded at the stew with a spoon.

"Maybe they used a lot of high-quality seasonings? Let's go ahead and try it..."

"Hmm..."

The four looked quite uncertain.

"It doesn't taste awful. It's not even that it's actively bad, but..."

"It doesn't taste good, either," said Pauline, finishing Mavis's sentence.

"Yeah," Mile added. "It's kind of like whenever Mavis has tried to make something."

Hearing this, the appropriate phrase popped into Reina's mind.

"Amateur cooking?"

"That's it!"

The food was not inedible by any means, so the Crimson Vow continued to eat, all the while racking their brains over the mysteries that had yet to be solved: of why the food was so expensive and why so many customers readily came by.

After a short while, those who had finished eating stood from their seats and began to leave and a girl of seven or eight appeared from the kitchen to begin clearing the dishes and wiping down the tables. The customers looked upon her fondly.

The last call for orders had already gone out, so after the final set of cooked dishes emerged from the kitchen, another girl of twelve or thirteen appeared from the kitchen, and began assisting the first with the cleanup, while chatting with the customers. Judging by her voice and the conversations they could overhear, this girl appeared to be the chef.

The fact that the food was amateurish now made sense. It was because it had been made by an amateur.

It was possible that the food here was so well reviewed

because it was amateur cooking made by a cute girl. Indeed, in the same way one could relish the taste of food made for you by your lover or imagine the feeling of a father having a meal cooked for his daughter...

The Crimson Vow considered this deeply, trying their hardest to understand.

The girl of around fifteen or sixteen, who had taken their order, and who appeared to be the eldest of the three they had seen so far, now returned to the counter to settle the tabs of the departing customers. Well, that wasn't so strange a thing for her to do. In fact, it was necessary.

However, the Crimson Vow suddenly wondered: *Why isn't the oldest one doing the cooking?*

This mystery was almost immediately solved by a conversation between a customer and the girl who was in charge of the kitchen.

"This must be hard on you, Miss Lafia. You're so young, but you have to do all the cooking all by yourself..."

"Ahaha, if my older sister did the cooking, this place would fall to ruin."

Suddenly, the Crimson Vow understood. They looked at the girl with pitying eyes.

"So are you all still getting guff from those guys at the Wild Bear?"

Oh? Something else was afoot!

The Crimson Vow strained their ears to listen in.

"Ah, yes, it's still the same state of affairs..." the girl said sadly, her expression downtrodden.

"I see. Keep your chin up! You can't lose to guys like that, especially for the sake of your late parents! We all stand behind you, Miss Lafia!"

At this, men sitting at other tables raised their voices in agreement.

Now, the Crimson Vow *truly* understood. They now grasped the reason why there were so many customers, and the place was so strongly recommended, despite the higher-than-usual prices and the fact that the food was nothing worth writing home about—even a bit regrettably mediocre as far as inn food went.

"I absolutely refuse to use this place as an example for our shop. Absolutely, positively, never!"

Pauline appeared utterly disappointed. Mavis and Reina also seemed rather dissatisfied to find that the mystery was not so mysterious after all.

However, something else still puzzled Mile: "I can understand why it is that people would favor this inn, but, um, why is it still only relatively young men? If this were just a matter of compassion, then you'd think that women and elders would be showing their faces here even more..."

"Hmm..."

Apparently, the mystery had yet to be solved, after all.

A short while later, the girl who had gone to the counter called the one named Lafia over and left her to the bookkeeping. Then, the eldest walked over to where the customers were.

"Thank you as always, everyone. It's only thanks to you that the three of us have been able to make a living since our parents passed away. I must keep working hard until my sisters can marry good men," said the girl, dabbing the corners of her eyes.

The men nodded fiercely. And then, a number of their gazes began to drift toward the girls they were after.

Waaaaauuuugh!

The Crimson Vow were taken aback—at first, by the fact that so many of these gazes were turned toward the youngest girl, the one of seven or eight. Though they wanted desperately to think that this was merely a paternal, protective gaze, cast upon a young child who had lost her parents, what truly struck them was...

Suspicious, unnatural, just a little bit flirty... She's playing them!

Indeed, the eldest girl's expression was perfect, her words were perfect, and though no tears were being shed, she dabbed at her eyes with perfect delicacy. She was dangling bait before the men's eyes—in a way that was clearly premeditated.

"What an actress!" one might say. Or better yet, "How terrifying!"

And yet, no woman or elder would be fooled by this routine. No other woman would be taken in by such a performance, and men past their prime no longer had it in them to be fooled by a little girl's tricks.

Which would be why the only local customers who ate here were young men.

All the overnight guests were those who had been recommended here by the young male employees at the Hunters' and

Merchants' Guilds—or they had chosen the place themselves and been charmed enough to find an inn run by three young girls that even the high prices could not force them to relocate...

Finally, the Crimson Vow well and truly understood.

"Mystery solved..." said Mile, as they returned to their room.

The other three nodded.

"Honestly, it was just some stupid gimmick! All the money we spent on lodging and food were a total waste!"

Pauline did not even attempt to hide her discontent. As a merchant's daughter, she would never dream of running a business in such a manner.

"Is it really so bad if three sisters who've lost their parents— some of them still very young—do something a little under-handed to keep their inn and eatery thriving, in spite of being all on their own?" asked Mavis. "They aren't bothering anyone, and they haven't told any lies, much less done anything to break the law, have they? Everyone who comes here has knowingly consented to the listed prices, and they come and shell out for the food anyway. When you do something as an act of charity, you start to feel good about yourself, so really, both sides benefit from it, don't they?

"Plus, I think it makes a lot of sense to get the local hunters on your side, so no weirdos try to set their sights on you. In fact, it sounded like they have been facing some harassment. I really don't think you can blame them for doing what they do."

Pauline cringed, lost for words.

It was true that there were no real victims here. Though the girl's words were a bit manipulative, she could not simply run off to get married and leave her two sisters behind. In reality, it was more than likely that the three of them would all eventually end up marrying someone from this town.

Pauline, however, continued to grumble. She could not accept such practices.

"Still, there's no reason for them to be charging so much more than usual! With that many customers, the normal prices should be more than enough, shouldn't they? If they just shelled out to hire a chef, they could have normal food, but no, they cook it themselves, dishing out tiny portions, with ingredients you can tell are garbage at first glance. Just what, pray tell, is the meaning of *that*?!"

There was no response they could give. There was nothing to be said but, *That's just how they run the place, isn't it?* Plus, no matter what the reason, it was none of the Crimson Vow's business. If they didn't like it, they could stay somewhere else. That was all there was to it.

"Anyway, that's half of our investigation complete! Tomorrow we'll stay at the other one—the Wild Badger Lodge, right?"

"That's Wild *Bear*, Reina..." Mile softly corrected.

The next morning, after having breakfast, they left the inn behind.

As all of their luggage was put away in Mile's storage (read: inventory), they had no need to transport it anywhere, which freed them up to move around.

They'd held out no hope for the quality of breakfast, but it would have been more of a bother to eat elsewhere, and it would be unfortunate to have people think that they skipped breakfast because they were poor. Plus, even if they had embarked on this expedition just for a lark, eating breakfast was still part of their investigation.

With hardly any—or in fact, zero—expectations for what they would be presented with, they placed an order for four breakfasts, and when they saw the plates that were brought over, they were flabbergasted. Honestly and truly, from the bottom of their hearts.

Each plate had two small pieces of bread, a single hard-boiled egg, one quarter of an apple, and half a cup of milk on the side.

This breakfast far surpassed their wildest dreams—in the worst possible way.

"W-well at least they can't charge us all that much for just this," said Reina, but Pauline silently pointed to the sign posted up on the wall:

Breakfast   6 half-silver per person

"That's a lot!!!"

That evening, after a full day of harvesting birds and jack-alopes, as well as hunting a few larger beasts in the nearby forest, the Crimson Vow returned to town.

Given that they did not intend to remain for very long, and since there were no interesting job requests, they busied themselves with the completely average ingredient-gathering jobs that were available. It would have been boring to sit around doing nothing all day, and this town was too small and too rural for there to be any interesting sightseeing.

On the other hand, doing jobs that were boring but required a significant amount of time would be equally bothersome. At times like these, the best jobs were the standing orders for materials, which required no preliminary discussion and allowed them to complete the job however they chose. If they were so inclined, they could always store their spoils in Mile's inventory and cart them off to sell another day in another town—or eat them themselves, whenever they pleased. That said, they didn't intend to hold on to them until they found a *perfect* price...

They headed straight toward the Wild Bear Lodge, not even bothering to make a stop at the outpost.

"So, this is the place."

As was becoming their custom, Reina stood before the inn, her arms crossed in an imposing stance.

"What do you mean, 'This is the place?!'" Mile cut in. "It's right across from the House of the Maiden's Prayer, where we just stayed last night!"

Mavis quickly clapped a hand over Mile's mouth. "Shh! What if people inside hear you?! How do you think those three sisters will feel if they heard that we decided to stay at a different inn for the night?"

"Ah..."

No matter how much of a rip-off—er, generous price to benefit the young sisters—they had experienced the night before, there was still no sense in hurting others' feelings without reason. Mile took a moment to reflect on her words.

"All right, let's go in."

And so, Reina opened the door to the second inn, the Wild Bear Lodge, and the four of them stepped inside...

"A bear?"

"A *bear*?"

"An ursine?"

"B-E-A-R!"

Indeed, they were greeted by a bear.

It had a beard that consumed its face, as well as arms and a chest thick with hair. Its legs were most likely the same. No matter who you asked about this creature, their first thought would have to be...

"A bear."

"Shut your mouths!"

No matter how bearlike this person was, they were very decidedly a *person*. Even Mile, usually quick on the draw, did not brandish her sword against him.

"You have to admit, that's how this seems, isn't it?! The name of this place is so straightforward..."

"It's been named that since my parents' time!"

The man, who seemed to be the owner, shouted at Mile's assertion, but honestly, he did not appear to be all that angry. This was a place of business, and he was accustomed to hearing this from first-time guests. In fact, it had become part of the expected patter whenever someone entered the establishment.

"Might you have a room for four available?" asked Reina.

Instantly, the man's expression morphed back into that of an innkeeper, and he replied, "Sure do. The room'll be one half-gold and two silver. Hot water's one half-silver for a basin, and you get one towel for free. Extras are four copper each."

"What normal prices..." the group sighed in relief.

"Lemme guess, you girls stopped over across the street?" the owner said with a grimace.

The girls nodded.

Truthfully, there was much that they wished to ask the man, but they still had yet to officially take a room and pay him his due, and they were each currently burdened with some small item (a canteen or some other light object), as people would think it strange if they kept showing up totally empty-handed. Besides, they were already interrupting an innkeeper, who was probably right in the middle of the evening's preparations. Forcing him to linger any longer would be rude.

And so, they paid for their room and then began to head upstairs, but they were stopped by the owner, who asked if they needed hot water or towels.

Most likely, he knew that hot water was essential to a young girl's grooming routine. If he'd really thought about it, though, he would have realized that there was no reason a group with two mages would ever need to *pay* for such a thing.

"This place seems decent, even if he is a bear."

"The prices are normal, too, even if he is a bear."

"Nothing else seemed out of the ordinary, even if he is a bear."

"Well, I mean, we can't make that judgment for sure until we've tried their cooking... Even if he is a bear."

And so, the four waited until dinnertime.

"Such normal prices."

The dinner menu had plenty of options, all at standard prices. As always, the party ordered eight diners' worth of meals.

"There's a normal amount. The variety of ingredients is normal. The quantity and quality of the meat is as expected, too," judged Mavis, prodding the soup with a spoon.

"Hm, the main flavor I detect is salt, followed by what's probably locally grown herbs," said Reina, sniffing with her face close to the plate of meat and vegetable stir-fry.

"This steak is cooked perfectly rare, just as we ordered it. It's not overcooked or seared only on the outside with the inside raw. A passing grade!" said Mile, nodding, as she examined a cut of the meat. She was quite fond of rare steak.

"If you factor in that the ingredients are about thirty percent of the cost, as well as firewood and the wear on the cooking tools, the cost of labor, and taxes, these prices are incredibly fair," said Pauline, assessing things from an economic standpoint.

But then...

"Shut up already! Hurry up and eat it before it gets cold!!!" the Bear raged at them.

Hearing this, the other patrons laughed.

The food had been prepared by the Bear... or rather, the owner, along with the woman who appeared to be his wife—though the fact that such a woman even existed seemed incredible. Each had prepared a separate set of dishes, and each carried out the ones that he or she had cooked. Considering the cost of labor, it was probably more profitable for them to do things that way, even if hiring a waitress would mean a slight increase in general efficiency. During times when business was slower, having additional employees was an unnecessary expense.

At this moment, the owner had just emerged from the kitchen, carrying out another customer's order.

"And now, the final measure: the taste..."

The four each carried a bite of food to their mouths.

"I..."

"It..."

"It's..."

"Amazing!!!"

It was absolutely delicious. The food had been made with normal ingredients and normal seasonings, but it was clear that it had been prepared by the hands of an experienced chef.

Even if that chef *were* a bear.

In any case, having four voices shouted praise for one's food was never a bad feeling. The owner's expression slowly began to soften. Until...

"At least after eating that stuff across the street, anyway!"

And there it went.

"The food is delicious, and the prices are normal. I can see why the women and elders favor this place now. But still, all of the young men go to the other place. You'd think that this inn would be swarming with customers, but there don't seem to be many here at all," said Mile, perplexed.

Wearily, Reina explained.

"Mile, sometimes I wonder if that thing atop your shoulders is just there for show. Think about it. Locals who aren't hunters have their own homes, so there's no reason for them to eat out every single night. Think of the kinds of people who eat out every night in spite of not being a traveler or those who have no homes because they are always on the road sleeping at inns. Who would those people be? Young hunters! I mean, comparatively speaking, there are a lot more male hunters, aren't there?! Of course, people living in their own homes *do* eat out every now and then, but for the most part, these would still be young, single men, wouldn't they? Most women would rather cook for themselves, so they hardly ever eat out.

"In addition, most hunters who are already past their thirties would have gotten married ages ago—men and women alike. They have their own homes, spouses, and maybe even some children, so they have no reason to eat a sad, solitary meal in a place like this!"

For some reason, the mood in the room seemed to darken. Mile swore she could hear quiet sniffles here and there, but it was probably just her imagination—or so she wanted desperately to believe.

That was when the owner barged in.

"What're you tryin' to say?! Look at that! Now everyone's lost their appetites, and no one else is placing any orders! You're ruining my business!"

With no choice but to take responsibility for this turn of events, the Crimson Vow ordered yet another round of food...

After returning to their room, they held a discussion.

"I mean, there isn't really anything interesting about this place at all."

"Yeah, like, there aren't any juicy scandals or creepy conspiracies here or anything. So boring!"

"........."

Mile and Mavis thoroughly agreed with Reina's assessment, but they found they were not at all in agreement with Pauline's words, which came immediately after.

And then, Mile quietly asked, "If I recall, over at the Maiden's Prayer they said they were getting harassed by the Wild Bear, didn't they? However, as far as I've seen, the owner doesn't seem like the sort of person who would do a thing like that at all... Even if he is a bear."

"Huh..."

It was impossible to tell what sort of person someone was just from their appearance or from talking to them for a little while. It was normal for a swindler to be attractive in face and manner and to seem completely trustworthy. Nowhere in the world would you meet a con man with the face of a villain. Well, of course it was possible that somewhere out there was a con man who looked like a mustache-twirling hustler and just got by on their wits... At any rate, the owner of this inn did not seem like the type who was very good at concealing his true intentions, and even when he overheard them talking about the House of the Maiden's Prayer, he had never slipped a bad word in.

"After he's done cleaning up the kitchen and dining room, and finishes his preparations for tomorrow, let's ambush him!"

"Yeah!!!"

You shouldn't go meddling in other people's affairs, you say?

You shouldn't poke a bear just to see what will happen?

Don't worry about it! What's life if you aren't living it to the fullest?!

If you always hold back and never do anything that you want to do, then you'll die with regrets—and for Mile, one time was enough!

After killing a bit of time with their usual jibber-jabber, the Crimson Vow moved down to the dining room on the first floor. When they got to the bottom of the stairs, they found the lights in the dining room low, the washing and tidying complete, and the owner and his wife in the kitchen, putting the finishing touches on their preparations for the next day.

"Hm? Can we help you with something?" asked the owner, stepping out of the kitchen.

Mile leapt straight into it, asking, "Um, could we ask you all something about the House of the Maiden's Prayer?"

"What? Do you all have something to do with those girls? Or did someone put you up to this?"

The owner looked a bit frightened, and his wife, hearing the conversation, came rushing out of the kitchen.

"We've nothing to do with them, and no one put us up to this," said Reina bluntly. "We were merely curious about the situation."

"Seriously?"

The owner's shoulders slumped. However, he seemed to realize that if they truly had some ulterior motive, they would not have asked him so directly. Most likely, it was nothing more than childish curiosity. He began to lower his guard.

"It's not somethin' to go babbling to outsiders about. You'd best just leave things where they are," he said.

However, the four would not be deterred so easily.

"If you were to ask us whether we have anything to do with that establishment, we would tell you no, we absolutely do not," said Pauline. "However, if you were to ask us if we had no stake at all in this situation, nor any reason to require this information, then we would also have to say that you are wrong."

"What?"

The owner stared at her.

"What I'm saying is, we stayed there for a night and paid exorbitant prices for lodging and food. This matter has affected us, and we have every right to demand an explanation!"

Pauline was fuming now. The owner and his wife grimaced.

Here, Mile stepped in. "We would like to know about the House of the Maiden's Prayer, but there is something else that we would like to know before that!"

"Wh-what is it?"

"How is it you got yourself such a young and smokin' wife!"

"Sh-shut your mouth!"

After talking in circles for ages, the owner and his wife—perhaps simply because they were too tired to keep resisting—finally agreed to talk about the House of the Maiden's Prayer.

According to the owner's explanation, the situation was as follows:

For as long as the two inns had been in business here on this same road, they had always been rivals, but their competition was a friendly one. Because they were in the same business, they had the same worries and frustrations, and they always gave each other advice and helped one another out when times were tough. They had always gotten along well and been close friends, even during their parents' times, and their grandparents' times before that.

In their youths, the owner of the Wild Bear, Dyllus (the son of the Maiden's Prayer's owners), and Aila (third daughter of the owners of the local general store) were thick as thieves, all being close in age. Indeed, until they were all of marrying age...

"So then, Miss Aila of the general store became your wife..."

"No, that's not it." The owner immediately shot down Mile's conjecture.

"Well, that's where it seemed like the story was going! I mean, how could you manage to snag yourself a hottie like her without having made an impression on her while she was still an innocent child?!"

"Just how much sass is in those little mouths of yers?!"

Reina's exceptionally rude phrasing had pushed the owner to his limit.

"I met Lilieze in the forest while gathering food and firewood one day, back when my parents were still managing this inn. Our paths crossed when I came across her being attacked by a monster and risked my life to save her."

"Of course you would have met her in the forest! You are a bear, after all..." Mile chuckled.

"Shut up!"

"Ahh, how wonderful! Why, to your wife, you must be her knight in shining armor!" praised Mavis.

The owner scratched the bridge of his nose, blushing slightly.

"So, what kind of monster was it?" Mavis continued. "A goblin? A kobold? Don't tell me—was it an orc, or something even worse...?"

Suddenly, the owner averted his gaze, in a way that suggested he was not keen to answer. Seeing the suspicion on everyone's faces, his wife answered quietly from beside.

"Um, well, it was a ferocious monster known as a 'jackalope'... I wasn't really concerned about there being a jackalope nearby—I mean, it wasn't very big, and even if it had struck me with its horn it wouldn't have hurt much—but my husband here came rushing out, yelling, 'Watch out! That is a deadly, ferocious Poison Jackalope from Hell! Take cover!' and risked his life to save me from it..."

This was the scam of the century.

Mavis looked at the owner as though she were gazing upon a pile of muck.

Reina and Mile appeared utterly weary.

And Pauline wore a face that was almost congratulatory, seeming to convey a sense of, *Well played, sir...*

"From the looks of it, your wife is at least ten years younger than you! Just how old were you at the time, you bastard?! Th-that's... That's absolutely criminal!"

Mavis must have been deeply affected by the situation to use such strong language. She looked about ready to leap up and grab the owner by the throat. Quickly, his wife stepped in.

"It's all right, I understood the situation from the beginning. It would be one thing if I were a sheltered young maiden living in some sanctum in the capital, but there's no way that someone who grew up around here wouldn't already know about jackalopes. Honestly, I thought to myself, 'Ah, what an amusing and witty person, he wanted a chance to talk to me so badly...' I had no idea if he was joking or serious, but honestly I thought the fact that he would make up such a ridiculous excuse was pretty adorable."

"Wh-what?! You knew...?"

"Of course I did, you silly bear!"

The owner was stunned at this revelation, and his wife tittered to herself. The two of them stared deeply into one another's eyes, and...

"Gwaaaaaaaah!! You two save that for later, when we aren't here!" Reina screamed.

She hadn't the slightest interest in witnessing a pair of strangers' public display of affection. *Especially* if one of them was a bear.

Deep down, the other three wholeheartedly agreed.

"Anyway, this is all beside the point! After you went and got yourself a wife all on your own, those other two got close, right?"

The owner nodded.

"Even after we all married, we still remained friends. Lilieze became a part of our group, they had children, and we all lived happy lives... At least until five years ago, when Aila suddenly took ill from a plague and passed away. Me and Lilieze did what we could to help out with the children and lent a hand wherever else we could, but things were tough for them..."

".........."

The four girls were silent.

"And then last year, Dyllus, their father, passed away as well. The eldest daughter, Meliza, was only fifteen, and the youngest, Alile, was no more than seven. I can't believe that idiot..."

The owner trailed off, his expression one of regret and sadness.

"Of course, that wasn't all. After Aila died, there was no way that Dyllus could be expected to raise three young girls and also run a business on his own, so in addition to the young chef he had been employing up until then, he hired on an old bag from the neighborhood to work as a waitress-slash-bookkeeper. The oldest, Meliza, started helping out at the inn, while the middle daughter, Lafia, both worked and looked after her younger sister, Alile. They all made do somehow, but once Dyllus died, those girls were really in a bind.

"In order to keep the business that their parents left them going, and so that they could continue to live together as a family, the sisters steeled themselves through their sadness and started to drum up ways to keep the inn afloat. Until, that is, that bookkeeper made off with all of the inn's money and their savings, too. And *then*, while they were still in the middle of this new crisis, that chef who was working for 'em tried to get his hands on the girls so that he could make the inn his own. He went after all *three* of them..."

"Wh..."

Since yesterday, the Crimson Vow had been struck with shock after shock, but this was the biggest surprise of all.

He should've at least left it at only the oldest girl... they all thought—though of course that was not really the biggest problem here.

"The old lady was eventually caught, but they never got the money back, and the girls and all their loyal customers got together to drive that cad of a chef out. After that, the girls felt that they couldn't trust folks anymore and decided they were just gonna run the inn and dining hall all by themselves. Those girls did their damnedest, and everyone in town who knew their story did what they could to help out—even the merchants' guild gave them a loan to help keep the place afloat, which doesn't happen every day. Soon enough, those girls started to earn enough for them to live a normal life. But then..."

"But then?" Mile interjected.

The owner knitted his brows, and replied, "They got greedy."

"Ah..."

Suddenly, the Vows understood.

The sisters, no longer able to trust the adults around them, had decided to milk the help that had been extended to them for all it was worth. And then, they probably realized that they could use their status as sweet, tragic young girls as a selling point.

"Plenty of people tried to advise them, but they wouldn't take a word of it. Even me and Lilieze tried to talk to them, thinking they might listen since we'd been family friends for so long, but they just thought that we were trying to ruin the Maiden's Prayer or take them over, and they refused us. I mean, I can't blame them. They were betrayed by their trusted employees one after the other, but we'd known them since they were babies, so we were really kind of hurt..."

A sadness crept across the owner's face.

"After that, they apparently decided that we were their rivals. They started spreading rumors that we were obstructing their

business or sending in unsavory acquaintances to harass them
and other things like that... I mean, as far as obstructing them?
The only thing that's happened is that Meliza slept in late one
morning and by the time she got to the town market I had already bought up all the cheap, choice vegetables, and the like.
And there are always unsavory guys on the road, aren't there? At
those prices, you're gonna end up only getting guys who won't
complain about paying up to stay in a place staffed by cute girls—
guys who might get the wrong idea and act out of line, aren'tcha?
So really, this is all their own doing."

"Ah..."

The Crimson Vow expressed their condolences with their expressions alone.

"I mean, the crowds of overnighters and diners have always
been split between our two places, so that's no big deal. Besides,
in a little town like this, everyone already knows everyone else's
business. Even the way things are now, we aren't really bothered.
It's just..."

"Just?"

"In a year and a half, this'll all be over," said the owner, continuing to explain. "Everyone's got a lot of compassion for those
three girls, especially while they've still got Alile, who's only eight
years old, under their wings. They feel for Lafia, in particular,
who's only thirteen and working her hardest to take care of that
little girl. But in a year and a half, those girls will've had two more
birthdays."

"Oh..."

Indeed, after two more birthdays, the two girls, now thirteen and eight, would be fifteen and ten, respectively. At fifteen, you were considered an adult. And ten was the age at which most people took up a proper employment. At ten, you could officially register at the Hunters' Guild or take up an apprenticeship at a shop or workshop to receive instruction in craftsmanship. In other words, even if you were not yet an adult, you were recognized as a member of society and a true and proper worker.

The three sisters would all be of normal working age. No one would have any compassion for three adult sisters all working to run a business that they owned themselves. There was no reason for anyone to pay an exorbitant amount of money to a group of three adults who had a higher collective household income than they themselves might.

No longer would there be a place for the people who would pay high prices merely out of sympathy. Plus, any travelers would be wont to change establishments the moment they heard the inn's rates. If the Wild Bear Lodge were full, they would just keep walking on to the next town or simply plan to stop at another town the next time they were in the area. Most of the customers who stopped at the inn were regulars, anyway—merchants who passed through the town time and again or other travelers making round trips from the big city to their hometowns. Even now, the number of overnight guests at the Maiden's Prayer was already dwindling.

In other words, it was as the owner had said. The House of the Maiden's Prayer had only a year and a half to go.

Pauline handed down a ruthless sentence. "They're definitely going to go bankrupt. They'll probably still get guys coming through there with their eyes set on the oldest and the middle girl, but that won't be nearly enough to keep things running. Plus, if they only have customers like that, those guys will be at each other's throats, and whenever a new client shows up, they'll assume he's a rival and send him packing. As a result, fewer and fewer people will start coming by. Eventually, it'll become a haunt for only a few repeat customers, and soon the end will be upon them, without a doubt."

The owner nodded sadly in agreement. "We want to do something to help them, but they keep refusing us. If we tried to force help on them, they could call the authorities or have their regulars chase us out of town. At the very least it would provide them with public proof that we were interfering with their business. Of course, most of the people in town already know the situation, so it's not that big of a deal, but..."

"All those guys feel pretty good about themselves, thinking they're doin' those girls a favor, but not a one of them realizes that all they're doin' is tying the noose around those girls' necks themselves and ruining all their prospects for the future. They probably all think that they'll be able to get one of those girls and run the inn with their new wife and sisters-in-law, but they don't realize that by the time it comes to that, there won't even be an inn to run."

"........."

"Well, I guess we've solved the mystery, so let's get back to bed," said Pauline. "We'll head out to the next town first thing in the morning!"

"Huh?"

The owner and his wife were dumbfounded.

"Y-you're not gonna go talk to them for us...?"

Here was a group of girls who had followed the conversation with interest, understood the issues, and seemed to have a keen sense for business. Naturally, the owner and his wife had expected that they might be able to lend a hand and share their knowledge with the sisters. Therefore, they were somewhat bewildered by Pauline's abrupt speech.

"I mean, it's really none of our business. We were just curious as to how they could have so many customers at that inn despite charging such ridiculous prices. Now that the mystery has been thoroughly solved, there's no reason for us to remain in this town any longer. It's none of our concern if an inn that laughs in the face of fair business practices goes bankrupt, and you can't help someone who doesn't want to be helped, right? Factor in the reality that we stayed a night here in this inn, and they'll probably end up thinking that we're a bunch of rivals, too..."

Unable to refute Pauline's logic, the owner and his wife were silent. An unpleasant atmosphere filled the room.

"Hup!"

Mavis lightly smacked the top of Pauline's head.

"Eep!"

"You shouldn't be so cruel to someone who's in trouble."

"........."

Indeed, the girls were nothing but a group of children who had lost their parents and sought desperately to protect the business they had left behind. Pauline, of all people, could not overlook that fact. Perhaps her words came merely from a place of anger at seeing people stray from the scruples of an honest merchant, or perhaps she didn't want to make them waste any more time on this town for her sake. Which it was, Mavis and Reina didn't know. Only Mile took Pauline's words at face value.

"Are you sure about this?" asked Pauline.

"Do whatever you want. We aren't in a hurry, and it's not as though we'll run out of money if we don't take on another job straight away. The only reason we even prolonged our stay here in the first place was because this seemed like an interesting situation it might be fun to stick our noses into. We may as well see it through to the end. I mean, we can't just throw our hands up and run out just when things are gettin' good!" said Reina, grinning.

Pauline couldn't help but smile as well.

"Hee hee hee..."

Seeing that wicked grin, Mavis, the owner, and the owner's wife all felt their lips twitch up in the beginnings of smiles.

"Um, you can't just throw your hands up and run off in the middle of a job, either..." Mile muttered, but no one seemed to hear.

"So a-anyway, you'll talk to them? Do you have some good ideas, then?" asked the owner.

Pauline replied with a grin. "Of course, I do! If things go on the way they are, then that inn will be ruined in a year and a half, won't it? The way to guard against that is simple. To keep them from being ruined in a year and a half, we must ruin them now!"

"Whaaaaaaaaaaaaaaaaaat?!"

From Pauline's tone, it sounded as though she were making a perfectly fair suggestion. However, no one in the room could accept this...not even Mile.

"Wha...? But that won't solve anything!"

This seemed like a reasonable reply.

"Well, I mean, if they won't be persuaded, then the only choice is to physically drive them out. If we can't convince them that that inn is already devoid of any value, and that we aren't after their property or their money, then no matter what we say to them, it'll be useless. Therefore, what we have to do is drive them to the point just before total ruination. If we get them to a point of 'as good as ruined' or 'the end is just a matter of time now,' then I think they might be interested in listening to what we have to say."

The owner and his wife were silent.

It was up to Mavis to ask the obvious question.

"So what, precisely, is it that you intend to do to convince them to listen to your advice? I mean, brute force is obviously out of the question. If we go out of our way to ruin them, won't we just wind up with all their hatred and resentment coming our way—and drag this inn's reputation through the mud at the same time? Besides, they might end up calling their customer posse or the town guards on us..."

Naturally, Pauline was not one to overlook such a fundamental issue.

"The Lenny Gambit."

"Wh...?"

"If the Maiden's Prayer's selling point is 'three beautiful and tragic sisters,' then this inn just needs to provide exactly the same thing."

"Wha...?"

"You remember when Lenny had us work as waitresses, tending to the customers? We need to recreate that but an even more amped-up version. An inn where the rates are cheap and the food is good that's staffed by 'four tragic young beauties' who were driven from their home country. All the customers will be ours!"

"Whaaaaaaaaaaaaaaaaaaaat?!"

And so, the waking nightmare began.

"How odd..."

Meliza, the eldest of the three sisters running the House of the Maiden's Prayer, tipped her head.

"What's wrong, sister?" asked Lafia, the second sister, as she exited the kitchen.

"Mm, well, somehow it seems as though we don't have nearly as many customers as we did yesterday..."

Of course, Lafia had already noticed this. She cooked all of the food herself, so there was no way that she *couldn't* have noticed.

"Hmm... I think you're right, but this business always has its ups and downs, doesn't it? I don't think it's anything we need to worry about."

Meliza, the eldest, tended to worry and fret over every little thing, perhaps because she carried the burden of the inn passed down in their family for generations and of caring for her sisters.

This was the inevitable result of the position she had been put in, and every day it made her little chest ache... (This was not metaphorical—in relation to her age, she literally had a small chest.)

Meliza was sixteen years old. She was beautiful and personable. To put it gently, she was slender; to put it less gently, she was flat as a board. She served as waitress, bookkeeper, and receptionist. Her cooking ability could be scored in the negative digits.

The second sister, Lafia, ran the kitchen all by herself at the age of only thirteen. That said, her cooking ability was nothing beyond the reach of any typical thirteen-year-old girl. That was perfectly fine as far as many of their male customers were concerned. Those men probably went elsewhere when they wanted to eat some particularly good food—but when they wanted to delude themselves into thinking that they were being served a meal by their lover or daughter, they came here. If you considered it from that angle, then Lafia's cooking was perfect—even on the occasions when a dish came out entirely wrong.

Up until her parents died, Lafia had been an energetic, lively girl, but these days she was rather gloomy. She was of normal build and stature for her age, which was to say, she was around Reina's height. Naturally, her bust was larger than Reina's—and her elder sister's as well.

Because they were a bit worried about having Alile, the third sister, who was currently napping in their personal quarters, do things like carrying plates full of food, she was left in charge of collecting the dishes and cleaning the tables once the customers were done eating. In truth, although she had mainly been allowed to do so by her sisters so as not to feel left out, the task allowed her to unleash her true potential in drawing the sympathies of their customers. In fact, she played a key part in their scheme.

The three sisters of the House of the Maiden's Prayer were a perfect fighting unit. Indeed, like the Kisaki Sisters or the Yagisawa Sisters or the Kashimashi Girls, they were an indomitable trio.

And then, the following evening...

"Something is definitely going on. We've hardly had any customers come in for dinner and barely any overnight guests at all. Even the visitors who told us that they would be staying for a while have been checking out early... There is most certainly something afoot!"

Those who stand in the way of the House of the Maiden's Prayer will not be forgiven!

Meliza, who trusted no one since the events surrounding their father's passing, and would stop at nothing to defend her sisters and their inn, stood, her eyes flashing.

"Lafia, mind the place. I'm going out for a bit."

"Huh? Oh, yes, okay."

Lafia was startled at her sister's sudden change in demeanor, but since they had few customers at the moment, she and Alile would be more than able to manage the inn in her absence. Alile was eight years old, so at the very least she could tend to the finances, and of course, no one who came expressly to a place where the prices were so high would ever try to swindle them when it came to payment. Anyone who would bother with that would have gone to a cheaper, better establishment in the first place.

The thought should have been comforting, but it left Lafia a bit depressed...

The moment Meliza stepped outside, she headed straight across the street to the Wild Bear Lodge. There were of course other pubs and eateries around, but the Wild Bear was their number-one rival. As far as Meliza was concerned, that designation was an official one. Plus, given that they had been losing both their evening diners *and* their overnight guests, the Wild Bear was immediately suspect.

It took her all of twenty seconds to cross the way. Meliza stood in front of the entrance of the Wild Bear and carefully put her ear to the door.

"Yes, they wanted to force me into an unwanted engagement, so I flew from my home with nothing but the pocket change I had saved up, a single sword for my own protection, and the clothes on my back..."

"I was abused by my stepmother and her daughter, who were

certain to kill me in order to get me out of the way, so I fled, as quickly as I could..."

"My father, a peddler, was killed by bandits, and the hunters who took me in afterwards were all wiped out while on escort duty, leaving me completely alone..."

"Bandits murdered my father, and then the clerk who had hired those thieves stole my father's shop..."

"You've all been through such tragedy! But it's all right now! For as long as you're in this town, we'll protect you, so you don't have to worry anymore!"

"That's right! You can take it easy and keep working here for as long as you like!"

"But I mean, not forever, though! Just until they find themselves a good husband, right?"

"Y'ain't wrong! Wahahaha!"

"Ahahahahahaha!"

Raucous laughter exploded throughout the room.

Wh-what is going oooon?!?!

Meliza was certain that the male voices she heard from within were the regulars who, up until a few days ago, had come to the House of the Maiden's Prayer to eat almost every day.

Th-those traitors...

Stewing, Meliza carefully pushed at the door, opening it a crack so she could peek inside. What she spied there were the four girls who had stayed at the Maiden's Prayer just a few nights ago.

Th-those harpies... Grrrnngh...

They were using their own misfortunes as some kind of marketing stunt—could they sink any lower? Yet as Meliza ground her teeth in anger, something suddenly occurred to her.

That's exactly what we're doing.

The revelation stunned her.

They were cutting into the market share by doing the exact same thing that the Maiden's Prayer was doing—far more efficiently and successfully, at that.

"Miss Mile, another of those fried rock lizard dishes you brought out earlier, please!"

"Idiot! If you order that, she's gonna be stuck back in the kitchen!"

"Oh... But I mean, it's so good I'm just dyin' to eat more. Goes perfect with ale, don't it?"

"It does... Well, guess we've got no choice, then. Everyone who wants some more rock lizard, get yer orders in now! That'll make the prep easier for little Mile, yeah?"

"Ooh, then count me in!"

"Me two!"

"I want two servings!"

With the orders rolling in one after another, the girl called Mile, who looked even younger than Lafia, rushed back to the kitchen.

A girl who was younger than Lafia but a better chef.

A cheerful redhead the same age as Lafia, who was friendly with the guests.

A very...large-chested girl around the same age as her, who was carrying on complex exchanges with the customers who seemed to be merchants.

And a boyish beauty who was deep in conversation with the swordsmen hunters about the art of swordplay.

They didn't stand a chance.

In shock, Meliza gently shut the door and stumbled back to the House of the Maiden's Prayer, listlessly dragging her feet all the way.

She was still light-headed when she returned to the Maiden's Prayer, but she was no wilting maiden. She was a valkyrie who swore on her father's deathbed to manage this inn and protect her two sisters, even if it cost her her life. Her heart was not so fragile as to be broken by the likes of this.

She began to plan her counterattack at once.

"B-big sis! You can't do this..."

As Meliza moved to exit the inn later that evening, swearing to win back their customers, Lafia tried all that she could to dissuade her. Meliza would not be deterred.

"It's of no consequence to me. I *will* win our customers back!"

What Meliza was currently wearing was a garment that most adult women in this world would consider a "devilish," even "aberrant," length, showing off her knees as well as her cleavage. In other words, it left nothing to the imagination.

Such a garment would not be at all strange for a child or a girl who was still underage—or for a female hunter for whom ease of movement was key, a dancer, a waitress, or other such person. However, for an adult woman who was none of those things, such dress would clearly be frowned upon. And yet for Meliza, who would do whatever it took to defend her dear sisters, such considerations were little more than a trifle.

As she placed her hand on the door, there *was* a moment's hesitation, but it was no more than a second or two.

Then, she flung open the door, took a step outside, and immediately froze, her eyes wide.

"The last time! This is the last time I'm ever wearing this! I'm serious!"

Before her was the large-chested girl, red-faced and shouting.

On her top half, she wore a tight shirt, the hem pulled up by her bust so that her whole midriff was showing. From her in-seam down to her knees, her thighs were mostly bare. Meanwhile, the bottom garment dug in, leaving no mystery as to the shape of her rump.

Indeed, it was Pauline, along with her old friend: Mile's old gym uniform.

Is she a pervert?!?!

She couldn't do it.

No matter how firmly Meliza might have steeled herself, she could *never* bring herself to wear anything as scandalous as that.

She collapsed to the ground in defeat, cringing as the large-chested girl's angry shouts echoed through the street.

"Keep it down!"

It seemed that her thoughts voiced themselves all on their own. Rather loudly.

She slunk back to the Maiden's Prayer, gripping her skull. She was no match for a girl who would abandon all pride and dignity. Furthermore, setting such an example for her sisters was entirely out of the question. She would do literally anything to make her sisters happy, but dragging those same sisters' reputations through the mud to achieve that would be a rather stark confusion of ends and means.

There were only a scant number of customers in the building, including the elderly couple who often looked after Alile. Lafia alone would be more than enough to handle that crowd, so Meliza took her seat at the front counter to think.

As she contemplated the way they were managing the inn, she began to worry. Was it right to be running the inn that her parents, her grandparents, and her great-grandparents had cherished in such a way?

That said, in the long hiatus they took after her father's death, they had already used up most of his savings. Thanks to their former employee's embezzlement, all their working capital had vanished as well. The Merchants' Guild had extended them a loan, but saddled with debt, and understaffed with only a novice chef on hand, they had no choice but to stoop to underhanded means in order to compete with the Wild Bear Lodge.

As she thought about it now, Meliza had no idea if they had made the right decision. However, that was little more than hindsight at work. Back then, she'd assumed it was the best option.

In truth, this plan had served them quite well until now. They had paid back their loans and put away some savings in case of emergency, even if that amount was still modest. Upon reflection, she had no regrets. What she had to think about now was how to remediate things going forward.

Should they return their prices to the standard rates? Honestly, she had not expected to keep things as they were forever. Sooner or later, even the young men who were their regulars would get girlfriends and even get married. Her sisters would get older, and once they were of age, they would no longer be able to garner exorbitant sums merely out of sympathy.

That said, could they really compete with the Wild Bear on a level playing field, what with their amateur cooking? Especially now that their rivals had that shameless cow of a girl, that dreamy beauty, and those two girls around Lafia's age, who were maybe, sort of, just a little adorable? It would be a reckless battle, one with only the slimmest chance of victory...

Those girls, who seemed to be rookie hunters, even had a leg up when it came to making conversation with other hunters.

It was impossible. They were invincible in every way.

But if she did not do something, at this rate they were going to be facing poverty again. Though they had dutifully paid off all their debts, they could not expect to be offered another loan. The Merchants' Guild did not look favorably upon how they had been running the business, and the way things were, it was uncertain whether or not they would be able to repay another loan in full. If they got anything at all, it would never be at the low interest rate and with the lax terms that they had received previously. There was no doubt that had been a special case, granted to them out of compassion.

After the small handful of diners went home for the evening, Meliza locked up the doors and headed up to bed where she passed a tumultuous, sleepless night.

The next morning, past breakfast time, the last of the morning diners had vacated. After cleaning rooms and making beds, there would be nothing to do until it was time to begin the preparations for dinner.

And of course, when it was off hours at the House of the Maiden's Prayer, it would be off hours at the Wild Bear Lodge as well.

After thinking the whole night through, Meliza had come to a decision that morning, around dawn. Now, she resolved to do what she must.

Aside from the shopping, all of the preparations for meals were generally left to Lafia. Even if Meliza were to step in here, she would be of little help. Still, Lafia had plenty to do, and when Meliza told her sister that she was going out for a bit, Lafia thought little of it.

And so, Meliza arrived at the Wild Bear Lodge.

Naturally, the door was not locked, so she flung it open easily and burst inside.

"Huh...?"

The owner, his wife, and the Crimson Vow, who were all assembled in the empty dining hall, were stunned by her sudden entrance.

Glaring at them all, Meliza screamed, "I'm sorry! Please, have mercy on uuuuuuusss!!!"

And with that, she leapt into a practiced and splendid jumping dogeza.

Oh, thought Mile—frivolous as usual—*it looks like they do extreme apologies in this world, too...*

"Wh...?"

Though they were all surprised, the most shaken amongst them were the owner and Pauline.

"P-please stop that! Even if it was just to force you to listen to us, we were the ones who were using underhanded means!"

"Guh..." Meliza groaned. The man had no idea that his own words had just condemned the Maiden's Prayer's methods as "underhanded means," but she could see this clearly.

"P-please stop!" Pauline continued in turn. "We'd already prepared secondary and tertiary attack measures! You can't be surrendering already!"

Her plans had been spoiled.

Thank goodness! Thank goodness I decided to give up and surrender noooooow!!!

Though it was not warm inside, Meliza felt herself breaking into a sweat.

"Now then, why don't we go ahead and discuss this. Sound good, Miss Meliza?" asked Mile from her seat.

Meliza nodded.

Initially, Pauline was meant to be the moderator for this conference, but the moment she started talking, Meliza seemed to flinch, so it was decided that a change of plans was in order. Given their past relationship, and the strain that had been placed upon it these past months, they thought that it might be difficult for Meliza to talk to the owner and his wife one-on-one, so from the three remaining members of the Crimson Vow, who had no past connection with either side, they chose an intermediary. Of course, Mavis was clearly not suited to this sort of talk, and if Reina was in charge, then nothing would ever get settled. Pauline was already out, so by process of elimination that left Mile, who seemed as though she wouldn't hurt a fly, to serve as the chairman-slash-facilitator.

"Now then, Miss Meliza, what do you think of how the House of the Maiden's Prayer is being operated currently?"

Mile, who had little in the way of delicacy, cut straight to the chase.

"Y-yes, well, it's easy and profitable work, so I'd say it's going rather... Oh, who am I kidding? It's rather hopeless."

Seeing the looks of sorrow upon the owner and his wife's faces, and how Pauline's expression twisted in unease and scorn, Meliza quickly changed her tune. Even she herself had finally come to the realization that their current way of doing things was not an infinitely sustainable one. However, they were swiftly running out of time to return to a standard business model, and as it stood, if they were to drop their victim act and all that came with it now, they could never hope to compete with the Wild Bear with their amateurish cooking. Outside of the men who came in with their eyes set on the three sisters, they would lose all of their customers to the Wild Bear Lodge, and then they would only be three maidens, left without a prayer.

"So then, what do you intend to do from now on?" asked Mile.

"........."

Meliza was hard-pressed to answer. If there were an easy solution to this, she would already have found it.

It was then that Mavis cut in. "The problem is your food, isn't it? None of the other jobs at the inn should be a problem for you. In fact, it's work that should be easy for three young girls to do. So, hire a chef. Isn't that the obvious solution?"

"........."

Meliza was silent.

Just as the owner's story had suggested, Meliza was still opposed to the idea of hiring outsiders on.

"The owner here told us everything. You really don't trust anyone else with a part of your business, do you?" asked Mile.

Meliza hung her head.

"It's true..."

Just as the owner had said, the girl no longer had faith in others. She had no problem dealing with them as customers—as marks who she could squeeze for all they were worth—but she could not trust them with the shop's money. Plus, for the three sisters, whose memories still smarted at the near-assault by their former chef, being alone at the inn with a strange adult when all of the overnight guests were away was, understandably, out of the question.

"Is there not a single person who you all could trust enough to work alongside you?" Reina asked.

Meliza thought for a while, and then replied. "Hmm, well, I guess there's the people here, and Miss Celila from the market-place, and Lisaphy from the blacksmith's shop..."

Obviously, there was no way that either the owner or his wife could abandon this establishment. Running an inn and restaurant all alone was impossible, so naturally, they had to decline.

"Well then, what about Celila or Lisaphy?" asked Mile, but the owner interrupted.

"That's impossible."

"Auntie Celila is the chief of the marketplace. You'd never find her working at a place like this. Plus, I dunno what you would expect a lady who's already in her eighties to be able to do... And Lisaphy, on the other hand, is Alile's playmate—she's only eight years old. If we tried to drag her over there and make her work, her mother and father, the smiths, would have a fit. Plus it ain't like *she* can cook, either."

"........."

They were at a standstill. Everyone racked their brains, but nothing promising came to mind. The Crimson Vow were silent, but then, Meliza offered a proposal.

"U-um! You all seem good at cooking! How about you all come to the Maiden's Prayer?"

"Huh?"

Their confusion was resounding.

"Come on! I mean, you can make that fried rock lizard that the customers love so much, right?!" Meliza gestured at Mile, talking wildly. "If you came and worked in our kitchen and did the cooking, with Lafia helping you out, then that would solve everything... Yes, that's it! That's the only way!"

Mile stared blankly.

"I mean, it is a good plan..." The owner, his wife, and Mavis all nodded in admiration.

Even for ones as wary as the sisters, a girl of twelve or thirteen like Mile would be no problem. Plus, they wouldn't have to have Mile involved in anything regarding money—as long as she stayed absorbed in her cooking, the sisters' suspicions and anxieties would be eased.

"That *would* be perfect," said Reina decisively, "*if* Mile were free to simply cut off all ties with the rest of us like that."

A reasonable reply. It would not be an impossibility to stay for two or three weeks, perhaps, but who knew how many years it could take to raise a thirteen-year-old girl into a full-blown chef.

She could not stick around that long.

Plus, Mile was merely recreating the food of Earth via magic, something that could only be replicated through the most incredibly advanced methods of cooking in this world. She did not herself possess the skills to perfectly pare vegetables, nor slice radishes into thin circles, or perfectly fillet a fish so as not to disrupt the molecular structures.

Mile also tended to use a generous helping of all the spices and seasonings she had stored away in her inventory—without considering things like profit margins. That alone was reason enough to disqualify her from cooking as a profession.

In other words, if they were looking for a master chef to teach Lafia, Mile was not the one.

"Out of the question! I invoke my veto!" Mile immediately refused, not even stopping to entertain the thought. Obviously, she knew herself and her limitations.

"B-but..."

Just as Meliza began to sink into despair, the front door of the inn swung open.

"Father, we're home!!"

Two young men of around fifteen or sixteen walked in.

"Who are they?" the Crimson Vow asked.

The owner replied, "My sons. They've been off in the capital training as chefs since they were twelve years old. Learnin' a trade like cooking just by apprenticing at your parents' place ain't much of an education, so we usually send our kids off to work at other places to study. We told 'em, you boys work hard out there and don't come back 'til yer fifteen. I guess that was three years ago..."

"You suck, Papa Bear! Did you seriously forget your own sons' birthday? I bet you forgot you even *had* sons!"

"Well, that's our father for you... My, what are Meliza and these four lovely ladies doing here?"

The two brothers, who appeared to be fraternal twins, were both tall, handsome, and of stalwart build. Indeed, exactly the sort who would be quite popular amongst the girls of this world. The Vows glanced at Meliza to see her staring at the two, mouth hanging open.

And suddenly, Mile screamed, "Is this a *deus ex machinaaaaaaaaaaaaaaaaaaa*?!"

"Uh, day-oos... eggs... monkey-nah? What is that?" Reina repeated. Honestly, she was accustomed to hearing this sort of thing out of Mile, so she did not appear all that surprised. Mavis and Pauline were no different.

"It's *deus ex machina*! It's like in a play or something, when it's getting to the climax, and it looks like the heroes are never going to survive and suddenly some contraption representing a god gets lowered down from the ceiling on a rope, and the 'voice of god' magically settles everything!

"When a story's done right, it should be carefully plotted, progressing with the inevitability of cause and effect, with the conclusion being derived from the intentions and efforts of the cast of characters. You can't just have all the problems fixed by some 'convenient solution' just appearing out of nowhere without any build-up! That's heresy! It's garbage writing! Lord Tezuka would never allow such a thing!!!"

The other three desperately tried to soothe Mile, who was seething with anger.

"So, who's this Lord Tayzooka, anyway?"

While Mile continued to rage, Meliza popped back over to the Maiden's Prayer and retrieved Lafia and Alile. All of the previous night's guests had already left for the day, and they hadn't yet taken on any new customers for the evening, so it would be fine to lock the door and leave the place unattended for a bit.

For Mile, whose primary entertainment in her past life had been stories in the form of books and motion pictures, seeing a narrative resolved with something akin to a *deus ex machina*— including "it was all a dream"-type resolutions—was completely unforgivable. She continued to rant and rave the whole time until Meliza returned with her two sisters in tow.

"I... this *can't*..."

By the time Reina finally calmed Mile down, the three girls had already taken their seats.

"It really is unusual to see you get so worked up like this, Mile," said Reina.

"S-sorry. It's just, it feels like all the work we put in up until now was for nothing—like the universe is mocking us. It plunged my heart into an inky darkness... It's just like when Pauline realizes that she's a single gold coin short."

"This has nothing to do with me!" Pauline shouted.

"So... Are we all good, then?" asked Mavis.

The other three nodded.

Mile however, was still in a sour mood, and demanded, "Why did you all neglect to mention this important of a detail?!"

The owner scratched his head and replied, "Well, I mean, you never actually asked us about our sons, so..."

"There were no signs of them! We figured that maybe you couldn't have kids, or they had all died or something. We didn't press the issue! That's not a subject that you could expect *us* to bring up! Whatever. Come on and tell us about your sons, then."

Meliza and the two sons sat quietly, not daring to speak.

"Well, as you can see," the owner explained, "we've got two boys. They grew up alongside Meliza and her sisters, and when they turned ten, they took up work as chefs, or at least, as sous-chefs to learn the ropes. A guy we knew who was setting up a restaurant in the capital asked for them to come help once they turned twelve, so I let 'em go off to learn as apprentices. It wouldn't do 'em much good for us to send in two boys who didn't have anything to contribute, so those two year I taught them at least the minimum in terms of skills. We figured that once they'd gone off and mastered the basics, they could come back and I'd teach them all my special techniques. So, what's the deal then, you two? Learned everything you could? Yer tutors give you passing marks?"

"Obviously they did if we came back here! We'll show you the certificate from our master later. There's a letter for you too, Pops. But it's all the way at the bottom of my bag, so I'm not gettin' it out right now."

Hearing this, the owner nodded, the corners of his lips turning up into a smile. Truly, he would have liked to show a bit more joy at his sons' return, but now did not seem the appropriate time, so he restrained himself.

Then, Mile, who had been deep in thought about something or the other, suddenly screamed, "That's it, that's it, that's it! It's clobberin' time!"

The innkeepers on both sides appeared completely perplexed by this sudden interjection of unclear meaning, but the other three Vows simply looked tired, as though they were completely used to this sort of thing.

"Mile! What have we told you about saying weird, confusing things that only make sense in your head when there are other people around?!"

However, at this point, Mile was so worked up that she could not be swayed by Reina's words and turned to the owner, saying, "You need to explain to your sons everything that's been going on here. From the beginning."

It was true; his sons needed to know the details of the situation, and if they had any hope of proving to Meliza and her sisters that they bore no ill will towards them, it made more sense to do it while the girls were present.

Even if hearing their story told all over again might be a bit unpleasant for them.

At Mile's behest, the owner explained to his sons everything that had been going on. His sons' expressions at hearing this were ones of sadness and regret. It was a natural reaction—this was the first that they were learning of the death of the girls' father, who was like a second father to them, as well as all the hardships that the girls had gone through just to keep themselves and the inn alive, while the two sons were away, unknowing, unable to have done a single thing to help.

Still, they did not press their father as to why he never contacted them about the matter. Even if they had known, there was little that two young boys such as themselves could have done about it at the time. What good would two young men who had abandoned their training and their work prospects be to anyone? The two knew this, so they could not bring themselves to berate their father for keeping them in the dark, not wishing to put unrest into the hearts of his only sons.

"All right, now that you are all aware of the circumstances, it's time to start making some plans for the future!"

Finally, Mile began to unveil her scheme.

"Including the apprentices, all of the cooking staff is currently present, and I have an idea for a way we can utilize you all. Here is my plan: For the times of day when the dining halls are open, from preparation to close of kitchen, how about a staff exchange?"

"Huh?"

Voices of confusion rose throughout the room.

"What I'm saying is, you will take turns. During the times when the kitchen is active, the matron here and one of her sons will be in charge of cooking at the House of the Maiden's Prayer, with Meliza and Alile in charge of waitressing and bookkeeping. Meanwhile, Lafia will work at the Wild Bear Lodge, along with the owner and the other son. Both sons and Lafia can work as assistants to the matron and the owner respectively, while furthering the study of their craft. That way, both of the establishments will have proper food, as well as a young girl helping them out. This should lead to an even split amongst the customers, allowing both inns to thrive! And furthermore, both the sons and Miss Lafia will grow to be full-fledged chefs along the way..."

"Whoooooooooaa!!!"

"A-are you a genius?!?!"

Meliza was overjoyed. In their youths, the two sons of the Wild Bear, Elethen and Beist, had been the constant companions of the Maiden's Prayer sisters. And so, Meliza, who knew them as youthful but honest and hard-working, as well as kind and gentlemanly to each of the sisters, found their tall but boyish appearances rather charming. Up until the age of twelve, girls tend to grow faster than boys, so Meliza, who was a year their senior, had always been a fair bit taller than the boys until the day they left for the capital. Back in those days, she never saw them as anything more than two younger boys from the neighborhood of whom she and her sisters were fond. She certainly never acknowledged them as men.

Now, however, in the three years that they had been away, the two had grown tall, and their faces, though still childish, had taken on a rugged edge—in short, they were incredibly handsome.

They had appeared.

They had finally appeared.

The genuine article, two paragons, leagues beyond men like hunters, who were rarely so bright and might perish any day.

Furthermore, they were chefs, something that the Maiden's Prayer so desperately needed—chefs who would be honing their craft under the watchful eye of their skilled father and further polishing their skills by both of their parents' sides.

Finally.

Finallyfinallyfinallyfinallyfinallyfinallyfinally!!!

Meliza had grown so accustomed to a life of pessimism, but now her heart was singing.

"Hm, sounds like a pretty good idea to me. So then, I suppose I'll go to the Maiden's Prayer, while you stay here, brother?"

"Yeah. I am the older one, so I guess that makes sense... Works for me. That fine with you two? Mom, Pops?"

Suddenly on the spot, the owner thought for a moment, and then swiftly replied, "Yeah, I think that's for the best. This might actually be better than trying to teach you both at the same time, anyway... Lilieze and I can probably even switch places now and then. If that's good with you three girls, then I've got no complaints. What'cha think, Lilieze?"

The three girls and the owner's wife all nodded happily in agreement.

"All right then. It's a plan! We'll figure out the details of this all tomorrow, but tonight, we celebrate! After all of the evenin' diners have gone home, we're throwing you boys a proper welcome home party! Of course, you and your sisters are invited, too, Meliza!"

"Thank you!!" the three sisters replied in chorus, smiles on all their faces.

My, but which to choose...? Meliza pondered. *Elethen, the older, is rather rough around the edges, but he's strong and reliable. Beist, the younger, is slight and delicate, but so conscientious and ever so kind... Oh, but if I were to marry Elethen, I suppose that would make the Wild Bear Lodge our inheritance, which would leave Lafia the House of the Maiden's Prayer...*

As the sails of Meliza's dreams began to unfurl, she suddenly noticed something that poked a hole in them.

"Do you still remember our promise?" asked Lafia.

"Come on, how could I forget? Even if it was an accident, I saw what I saw, and I'm prepared to take responsibility," said Elethen.

"Ahaha..."

Their manner was most definitely a flirtatious one.

"Wh-what is going on?!"

Meliza was stunned at the pair. There seemed to already be some kind of deeper connection between them. And exactly what was it he had "seen"?!

She was shaken, but her sister appeared to be happy, so Meliza steeled herself and said nothing.

Well, that's fine, there's always Beist... I'll just take the second son as my husband! I mean, if you really think about it, between a wild child like Elethen and someone as gentle and thoughtful as Beist, there's only one obvious choice. Plus, Beist is the one who I'm going to be working alongside from now on. Indeed, Beist is th—

"Big brother, you were gone for so looong!! I thought I was gonna have to wait forever!" said Alile, clinging to Beist's leg.

"I'm sorry, I'm sorry! Will this make it up to you?" asked Beist, pulling a pendant from his pocket and draping it around Alile's neck.

Alile's cheeks went red.

"J...just what is going on heeeeeeeeeeeeeeeeeeeeeeeeeere?!?!"

Meliza's scream echoed throughout the building.

"Wh-wh-wh-whawhawhawhawha...?"

Meliza was trembling, her eyes bloodshot. The Wild Bear family was perplexed, but the Crimson Vow understood everything.

"Um," Mile asked the owner, "Do you have any other children?"

Meliza's expression was crystal clear, and Mile could easily guess at the circumstances.

"Well," said the owner, "We do have a daughter, but she's already married. As for sons, it's just these two."

"Ah..."

It was all over. This poor girl's dreams had been demolished in a matter of seconds. However, when one considered that Meliza had done everything she had done for the sake of her sisters' happiness—and that that dream looked as though it was about to come true—she ought to be a bit happier... So thought the Crimson Vow, though not a one of them would have been brave enough to say so to her face.

The two couples sidled up to one another.

The owner and his wife looked on obliviously.

And Meliza was frozen, seething with white-hot rage.

We gotta get outta heeeeere!!!!

The second evening bell rang, and all the diners went home, the overnight guests heading up to their respective rooms.

"We're here!"

Lafia entered, calling out in a cheerful voice, as Alile followed behind with a smile on her face. Meliza wobbled in third, a mask of death still on hers.

She was like a shell of her former self.

Now that her worries for the future of her sisters and their inn had been all but eliminated, she had lost all will to fight. The rosy future that she had only just begun to dream of had been snatched out of her hands in an instant. Furthermore, her sisters, only thirteen and eight, had soared past her, snagging two good men for themselves, and leaving only her, sixteen years old and all alone.

At this point, it would be fruitless to try and convince her otherwise.

For what had she struggled all this time? Apparently, her sisters had already had a happy future laid out for them from the start.

And as for her? What about her happiness?

"Nnnnnnnnngh..."

She could not cause her sisters worry, Meliza thought, but she also could not help the growl of resentment that escaped from her chest.

Her sisters, for their part, knew exactly how she was feeling. However, they would never relinquish the objects of their affection. Certainly not on this day, when they and their sweethearts had finally been reunited after three long years of waiting, when they had all sworn, on both sides, that their feelings would not change no matter how many days went by. Their eldest sister, who had looked down on the boys as nothing but a pair of squirts, treating them like children and not considering their future prospects, had brought this on herself.

Sorry, sis, the two thought. *And thank you for having such a lack of foresight!*

Indeed, had Meliza played the part of the "wonderful older sister," a beauty with a silver tongue, the two younger girls would have never stood a chance. This was all made possible thanks to their dunce of a sister.

Lafia and Alile thanked her, truly and deeply, from the bottom of their hearts.

A pair of grins spread across their faces. *Hehe.*

Waaaaaaah! They're scary! These two are seriously scary!! Seeing the sneers that the two girls wore, Mavis, Reina, and Pauline shuddered with fear... Though of course, what Pauline was most frightened by was their skill.

Seeing how Mile grinned blithely, not realizing that anything was amiss, the three found themselves, for once, just a little bit envious.

The only people in attendance at this homecoming party were the employees of both inns and the members of the Crimson Vow. After the owner said a few words, they all toasted, and then spent the evening in lively conversation while eating and drinking their fill. Of course, Elethen and Lafia, and Beist and Alile were surrounded by force fields of their own making—invisible walls with all the strength of a lattice-power barrier.

Atop the tables was the food that the owner and his wife had been preparing since the last call for evening dinner, along with plenty of ale for the boys, who were now full-fledged adults. As with many countries in this land, there was no minimum drinking age here, but Mile, Lafia, and Alile kept only to tea and diluted fruit juice. Meliza, however, drank and then drank some more. No one, including the owner and his wife, who seemed to have finally gotten a grasp on the situation, would have dared to stop her.

This was dangerous. Everyone, save for Meliza herself, and the four who were in their own little worlds, sensed this.

"Um," Mile ventured, "are there no other good men in this town? Say someone who's young and attractive, earns a good living, and would be interested in Miss Meliza?"

The owner, who looked as though he had all but given up, replied, "Well, there are..."

"Whaaaaaaaaat?!?!"

The four were shocked. What an unexpected reply!

"Y-you're saying there *is* someone like that?!"

Though they had heard it with their own ears, Mile and her three companions were half in disbelief.

"Meliza's never minded having hunters as customers, but she's always said things like, 'hunters are all just a bunch of broke losers,' and, 'it's a trade for ruffians who could die any day.' She always ruled them out as potential marriage partners from the get-go. But you yourselves should know that not *every* hunter is like that, right?"

It was not untrue that many hunters were guys who couldn't make it in any other job or people who schemed to claw their way to the top by strength and skill. In fact, this included even Mavis, who was striving to become a young, noble A-rank, and then a knight. These were the types of men whom Meliza would be keen to avoid.

However, there were also those who would someday be forced to follow in their parents' footsteps and assume a life of boredom, who worked as hunters to live a life of freedom while they could, and joined parties who only took on relatively safe jobs. Moreover, there were whole parties of veterans who were brought together by parents to look after youths. Colloquially, these were referred to as "young lord hunters" and "the hired help." Such arrangements were not especially numerous, but they were not so rare, either.

There were also those who were saving up money in order to open their own businesses and those who only did simple things like herb gathering once a week for the sake of their health and had other jobs for their primary income—hunters who only did the work as a hobby and other such anomalies.

Without knowing of such exceptional circumstances, Meliza was likely to eliminate any hunter from the pool of potential marriage candidates simply because they were hunters. Yet leaving these prejudices aside, who knew how many of the regulars at the Maiden's Prayer were honest, reliable, and attractive enough to catch the eye of the rather shallow Meliza?

"A-are there really guys around here like that?"

"Of course there are. Meliza herself probably doesn't even

know it, but there's a young man who works as a hunter and is the heir to his family's small, but successful shop, as well as a guy who calls himself a D-rank hunter but really only works one or two days a week to spend time with his hunter buddies. He spends the rest of the time tutoring the children of nobles. That's not to mention the guys who never have to worry about money and hunt just for sport, takin' on only jobs that excite them, and well—all sorts of others in various circumstances."

"........."

Now that they thought about it, the owner must be right.

No hunters who were strapped for coin and living payment to payment would have been able to afford to dine at the rather expensive Maiden's Prayer every day—staying all the way through both breakfast *and* dinner at that...

They were the sort of guys who you'd have to ask, "When do you ever work?"

"I-In that case..."

"Now that her two sisters have found men for themselves, Meliza's gonna be in a hurry to do so, too... Probably too much of a hurry," said the owner, throwing a glance Meliza's way as she continued to gulp ale.

"So if someone who was likely to give up their trade as a hunter and settle down after they get married found out..."

"Plus, Meliza's pretty popular. I'm sure there are plenty of guys who would be game to devote themselves to a non-hunting trade if they knew that they would get to court Meliza—and if she knew what those trades were, Meliza might be swayed also."

The owner looked to Meliza, who was still drinking like a fish, and the two couples, who were surrounded by force fields so impenetrable that not even alien invaders would have been able to disturb them. Just a few years ago, he never would have been able to fathom the idea of those girls and his own sons getting together. However, now that that reality had been thrust before his very eyes—along with the impossible tragedy of the eldest daughter having been skipped over in the process—a whirlwind of emotions swirled through the owner and his wife's minds...

"Is it my age? Is my age the problem? Or is it my chest? *Is something wrong with my chest?*"

The eldest of the party, Mavis, who, based on her age, would likely stop growing soon in a measure that was not her height, began to fret over the inadequacy of her bust.

Hearing this, Reina, who was perpetually enveloped by a feeling of inadequacy at the fact that both her height *and* bust seemed to have stopped developing, pulled the liquor bottle toward herself and filled her cup up to the top, chugging it down in a single swig— "R-Reina, you shouldn't drink so much!"—all the while glaring at Pauline, who was the one person who had no room to talk.

Mile, of course, was carefree as ever.

She still had plenty of time.

Her height and her bust were still blossoming. She had only just turned thirteen, after all.

Ignorance, it would seem, truly is bliss.

CHAPTER 44 |

A New Base

"WE SHOULD MAKE IT to the next town pretty soon," said Reina, hunched over a map. The Crimson Vow were taking a short break.

They were on a journey, so naturally, even they had a map on hand. Without one, they would find themselves lost very quickly. However, said map was nothing like the kind in use on modern-day Earth. It was a rough thing, much like the maps you might find in the guidebook of an RPG. Indeed, it was the sort of thing that marked only mountains and forests and rivers, and paid no regard to scale. Nevertheless, if one were to encounter a road with three forks or something of the kind, a map was still indispensable. It was the sort of world where taking a turn onto the wrong path could mean death, after all.

After somehow slogging through what they had begun to think of as "the celebration with delicious food but super bad vibes" at the Wild Bear Lodge, the Crimson Vow had booked it out of that town first thing in the morning. There was nothing left for them to do there, and even if they wanted to stay, they could not bear the atmosphere any longer. They could not handle having to watch the continued flirtations of the two young couples—or the grim and ghastly looks upon Meliza's face as she looked upon the same.

Plus, the discussion of the previous evening had quickly morphed into the tale of why not one of the four, cute as they were, had managed to find a boyfriend their age who was their equal. They all came from very different circumstances. There was Mavis, who was aiming to become an A-rank as quickly as possible. Reina hoped to be a B-rank. And Pauline wanted money. Still, they all had one thing in common: none of them had any time to waste on something so frivolous as men.

Only one amongst them, Mile, thought to herself now and then how nice it would be to make friends with some boy sooner or later. However, such a thing was impossible while they were on a journey such as this one. In any case, Reina was a horrible saboteur, even if Mile was never aware of it.

At any rate, though the owner and his wife had tried again and again that morning to offer them a monetary reward, the party refused, saying that they had no intention of profiting off a project that they had merely undertaken for the sake of amusement. With that, they bid farewell to the owner, his wife, their pitiful sons, Lafia and Alile (who looked somewhat relieved), and Meliza, who was still down in the dumps, before leaving the town behind.

"I really hope that Miss Meliza can be happy," said Mile.

"She'll be fine," Reina replied. "The owner and his wife said they'd find some men who suited Meliza and try to sway them into a proper career. She's a beautiful girl who comes with her own inn! I bet there are tons of guys who would love to get their hands on her. She'll have the pick of the litter. There's no need to worry!"

Somehow or the other, Reina and Mile had begun to grow fond of the girl, and together, they prayed for her happiness.

Why they felt such a kinship with her was unclear...

It was late that same afternoon.

Thanks to Mile's inventory, the Crimson Vow moved much quicker than most hunters, traveling over 40 kilometers a day on average. Most travelers could only make it thirty kilometers if they were feeling particularly sprightly, so needless to say the four were incredibly fast-paced for a group of young girls, rookie hunters or not.

It was mostly thanks to the inventory. Furthermore, they had healing and recovery magic on their side.

In any case, after arriving a bit early at the next town where they planned to stop for the night, they popped into the local guildhall as always, to make themselves known and check out the job and information boards. Then they headed to an inn to rent a room.

In this town, there was little difference between the inns. The rates differed very slightly, but the food and amenities were more or less the same, so it seemed that the choice was up to them.

This was how things usually were, anyway.

After picking a suitable inn and scarfing down dinner, they headed up to their room. Weary from a full day's travel, Mavis, Reina, and Pauline tidied themselves up with cleaning magic and then headed straight to bed,

Mile, as always, was burning the midnight oil.

Aside from the times they were camping out, the three other members of the Crimson Vow always got a full eight hours' sleep, while six hours was more than enough for Mile. Such had been her pattern even in her previous life.

And so, after erecting a magical cloak to keep the light from leaking out and disturbing her companions, Mile illuminated the area around her with a spell and withdrew from her inventory a ratty piece of paper, along with the ballpoint pen-like object that she had asked the nanomachines to make for her, and began to write.

In the beginning, she had attempted to use the quills that people in this world normally used for this purpose, but having to dip the quill in ink over and over again was such a bother, and when she had tried to create something like a fountain pen, the paper was so thin that the nib snagged it and ink spread everywhere. It was quite the disaster.

Next, she tried a pencil, the simplest and most reliable implement, but of course it dragged on the paper, and she kept having to erase things, so all it did was irritate her.

Mile had a rather short temper.

In truth, she was normally quite patient, but when it came to anything that interfered with her reading or writing, she morphed into a Mr. Hyde very quickly. This was the sort of girl she was.

And so, what she finally landed upon was something like a ballpoint pen.

Mile had instructed the nanomachines to make the item however they liked, but of course, that was a little bit outside of the rules, and they could not accept such an instruction. Fortunately, Mile herself knew enough about the basic function and construction of a ballpoint pen to guess that, given time, such an item might come to appear in this world even without the nanomachines' intervention. Thus, the instruction was not to make an item that couldn't exist in this world, but rather, to simply cut down on the time it would take for such a thing to be invented. As such, the nanomachines accepted the task as something that was within the bounds of Mile's knowledge and gave her order the okay.

It was always rather difficult to determine precisely where the limits lay...

All that aside, Mile now continued writing with her ballpoint pen-like object.

The fact that the tip of that pen was made from something like orichalcum or mithril was, again, of no great concern to the nanomachines. The paper was what was going to someone else, and it was not as though Mile had any plans for mass-production or putting the objects on the market. Even if she tried, it would be a wildly, absurdly expensive venture to undertake.

And so, around the stroke of midnight, Mile finally tucked herself into bed.

The next morning, once the Crimson Vow had finished eating breakfast, they packed up at the inn and headed over to the guild.

They had no intention of lingering in such an ordinary town as this one. Indeed, they planned to continue heading straight on to the capital of this kingdom. Just in case, however, they decided to stop in and check if there were any good jobs that would take them in the direction of the capital or any relevant bits of intel to be had.

It was normally quite rare to find jobs that were difficult, unusual, or even interesting in such a small town as this. Therefore, they deemed that it was best to ignore these small places and instead carry on to a bigger city, where they could stay a short while.

Sure enough, once they checked the board, they found that there were no interesting or good-paying jobs. The next merchant caravan bound for the capital was not leaving for several days yet and had already assembled its full escort.

"Well, guess that's it for us here, then," said Reina. "If we set out now..."

"Oh, wait a minute!" Mile interrupted. "I need to send something out. Give me a few moments, please."

With that, she pulled some sort of bundle out of the pack that she carried for those times when she wanted to appear as though she were a normal hunter.

"I'll just be a moment!"

She rushed over to the reception window. It was not the job acceptance and completion window that the four were so familiar with, but the request window, a place that was as good as foreign territory to them.

"Excuse me! I'd like to have this sent out, standard service. Certified delivery to the capital of Tils."

Such delivery requests were a standard service of the guild. Normally, if one needed to transport something from one town to another, you did it yourself, or else made a request to a merchant to do so by way of the Merchants' Guild. However, if it was an unusual item—a bulky package or something valuable—one could also go to the Hunters' Guild to make a standardized transport request. Even if it was a fair bit more expensive than hiring a merchant...

So, why would one contract the Hunters' Guild, despite the higher cost?

For one, it was overwhelmingly more secure.

Even if the Merchants' Guild were involved in the request process, for requests made through the guild, the individual who was transporting the item would still be a normal merchant. Among such people were those of poor character, and moreover, the possibility that even honest merchants would be attacked by bandits.

In the case of the Hunters' Guild's standard service, transporting guild documents was the carriers' main job, so even if they were attacked, there was little chance of them having much money to steal on their person. Plus, because they were carrying such important documents, they often had an escort of other skilled hunters in sufficient number to ward off attacks. Furthermore, assaulting an official guild convoy would make one an enemy of the Hunters' Guild throughout the land, meaning that a large-scale subjugation force would immediately be organized, regardless of cost or profit, extending to all of the neighboring lands.

This subjugation force would advance from the country where the incident occurred and from the neighboring lands on every side. It would capture any criminals it found, not stopping until every last one was dead. Anyone who picked a fight with the Hunters' Guild—anyone who underestimated their might—would not be allowed to get away. If the guild failed to retaliate, such assaults would happen again and again.

Don't mess with the Hunters' Guild.

They would spare no expense, no measure, to burn that message into the mind of every evildoer. This was the Hunters' Guild's way.

Finally, on top of hiring a number of skilled hunters as escorts, the guild transport had only one wagon, so its carrying capacity was limited. And because unlike a merchant's caravan, they valued speed over cargo volume, a guild transport rarely set out fully-laden.

They were fast, secure, and carried very little. Obviously, it would cost a premium to take advantage of such a service.

"Would you mind holding on a moment?"

As Mile handed the parcel over to the clerk, a voice called to her from behind. When Mile turned to look in the direction of the voice, she saw...

"A-an elf?"

Indeed, there stood a tall and slender middle-aged man, with long hair, a warm and gentle face...and pointed ears. No matter how you looked at him, this man was an elf—an elf among elves, even.

"W-whoooa! It's a real live elf! This is the first time I've ever seen one!"

Reina smacked Mile on her head.

"Did we or did we not spend several days with Dr. Clairia?!"

"Oh, I guess you're right..."

With Dr. Clairia's ears, inconspicuous as they were, mostly hidden behind her hair, Mile had completely neglected to recognize her as an elf in her memory.

"Wh-wh-wha-what can I help you with?!"

Though she had had no trouble talking to Dr. Clairia, Mile was suddenly stiff with nerves. The other three shared her sentiment wholly. Because Clairia's ears *had* been hidden, she looked like nothing more than a normal human; in fact, they had at first taken her for the guild master's daughter. So, even after they were made aware of the fact that she was an elf, it still did not really feel that way.

This particular gentleman, however, was far too elf-like.

"What?! Are you ladies acquainted with the young Miss Clairia?!" asked the elven gentleman—it would be rude to call someone who was middle-aged an "elder," after all. But then again, given that he was an elf, who knew how old he actually was? "When did you meet her and where?! Is she doing well?"

"Oh, yes, she seemed very well indeed. As for where we met her—wah!"

Mile's attempt at a reply was interrupted by Reina seizing her shoulder.

"You can't just give some strange man you've never met information about a lady! Especially not without her consent!"

"Ah..."

Indeed, the people of this world were surprisingly persnickety when it came to personal information. Hunters had always been incredibly tetchy about others looking into their pasts or their capabilities, and a lot of quarrels arose because of it, so at some point or other it had simply become an unspoken agreement that it was taboo to inquire into a hunter's personal information. Just as they maintained this practice amongst themselves, hunters often refrained from enquiring into other people's personal information as well, except when necessary to complete a job.

Obviously, needing to establish confidence in someone else when it came to contracts or hiring was another matter, but for the most part, the rule was, "If it doesn't have to do with work, you don't need to know about it." Slowly, this sentiment had begun to spread to the rest of the population as well.

Furthermore, most humans—the Crimson Vow included—knew little of the mysterious societies of the highly secretive elves.

Why would Dr. Clairia be living as a scholar alongside humans, when elves rarely resided with humans at all?

Why had she left her elven village?

What was her relationship like with her family and clansfolk?

Did she have any enemies?

Mile could certainly not go handing out information about the professor without knowing the answer to a single one of those questions—doing such a thing could mean revealing the current whereabouts of a victim on the run from some past danger to a stalker.

A dark feeling overcame Mile, who had been pursued herself many times in her previous life, and she unconsciously, reflexively, began chanting a spell of protection.

"O water, come forth and become shackles of ice to bind... *Gah!*"

Smack!

Reina's karate chop landed straight in the middle of Mile's forehead.

"Stop that!"

"Hold it, hold it! Hold it, I say! I am no one suspicious!" the elf protested.

"That's exactly what a suspicious person would say!"

"Then what exactly would you *like* me to say?!"

"'I'm a suspicious person?'"

"........."

The group sighed. Suddenly, they realized that they were surrounded by other hunters, hands on the hilts of their swords, gripping their staves with spells at the ready. Given that one of the party had begun a close-range combat spell in the middle of the guildhall, and it seemed as though a battle with the elf was about to unfold, this was an incredibly natural reaction.

"S-sorry everyone, we're fine! Nothing's going on here! J-just having a bit of a laugh with an old friend. Isn't that right, Uncle?!"

"Huh? Oh, yes, yes indeed, oh, uhm, you little prankster!"

The elf was momentarily perplexed at Mile's sudden change in attitude but quickly played along. Truly, with age came wisdom.

Tch...

Pfft...

Heheh...

The air, thick with tension, began to thin again. Everyone let their hands fall from their weapons, and, chuckling, returned to their original positions. Normally, the others would have been irritated at this clear misconduct, and even berated the Crimson Vow, but as one of the two parties was an elderly elf who seemed to be minding his manners, and the other was a cute, rather clueless-looking young girl, the veterans were happy to simply laugh it off.

Besides, most of the hunters had already had their eyes on this group from the moment they had entered, seeing as they were a party of four lovely girls they had never seen before. As a result, they were already aware of what was going on. In truth, they should have chided the girls so they'd know better next time, but there didn't truly appear to be a need for it.

Indeed, behind Mile stood the combat mage, red in the face and her fangs bared. "Honestly, Mile, what were you thinking, chanting a combat spell in the middle of the guildhall like that?!" Reina shouted. "If the other hunters had attacked us without asking questions first, it would have been entirely your fault! First off..."

After being thoroughly chewed out by Reina, Mile abandoned her delivery request for the moment, and the Crimson Vow, along with the elf, moved to the dining corner of the guildhall.

"So, what did you want to talk to us about?"

Through all the commotion, the tension that Mile felt toward the man had faded.

"Oh, right. Sorry. I heard earlier that you were sending something to the capital of Tils, so I was hoping that I might be able to hitch something on to your parcel..."

"Oh!"

Parcel hitching.

Even if you added a small letter or document to a parcel, the price of shipping would not change up to a certain size or weight. So one could combine shipments and still come up with the same price. Then, after breaking the seal, the person who received the original package could take the enclosed item and deliver it themselves or else forward it on via some other method.

The cost of forwarding something to another town would vary by country, but it still tended to be fairly expensive. However, as long as the item was destined for somewhere else within the

same capital, one could hire on one of the young children who hung around the guild as hopefuls, and the job would be completed with just a few half-silver spent. It was fortuitous to come across someone else who was sending a parcel to the very same city, so it was no surprise that the elven man hoped to get in on Mile's shipment.

"So, what do you say? Might I ask you to do this?"

"As long as you pay half of the shipping costs."

As far as Mile was concerned, there were no downsides. The destination of Mile's package would be the original one, so there was no risk, and she would not complain about getting someone else to shoulder half the cost.

"Oh, splendid! For the most part, our kind live rather self-sufficiently, so we don't have very much of what you humans use as currency. This is especially true for elders such as myself, who rarely make it out of the village. Now I'll be able to use the left-over money to buy a souvenir to take home!"

The elf seemed joyful. Mile smiled.

"So then, about Miss Clairia..."

As Mile unsealed her parcel to add the letter in and write a note about the addition, the gentleman turned to Reina, explaining, "I don't wish for you to tell me her place of residence or anything like that. I just wish to know if she is well in health and spirit, if that is no bother to you."

"Just what connection do you have with the professor?" Reina asked suspiciously.

The elven gentleman—whose name, it turned out, was

Elsatorc—replied, "I'm just an old fellow whose clan has ties to hers. Miss Clairia is very popular among the adults of the local clans. Everyone hopes for their children to grow up to be just like her—there are even portraits and dolls of the young miss in families' nurseries."

"Whoa..."

All four of the Crimson Vow, including Mile, still in the midst of her writing, looked stunned. While it was true that Dr. Clairia was particularly beautiful, her looks could not have stood out all that much amongst elves, who were beautiful by nature. Besides, she had left her village to live among humans, and personality-wise, she was no saint. Given the fact that she was doing a job so lofty that she could be called "Doctor," she was likely getting on in age. So, how she could possibly be so popular amongst other elves was wholly beyond them.

The dubious looks on their faces were plain to see, so Elsatorc explained further.

"We elves are rather solitary creatures by nature. Once our children reach forty or fifty years of age, they lose their fondness for their parents and soon leave home to live on their own, drifting further and further away from their families."

Fifty years! the four silently thought. *That's a really long time to be living at home!*

"However, no matter how old she got, Miss Clairia always stuck by her father. Everyone was so very jealous of him."

"Aha..."

Everyone thought back on the time they had fled with the

freed captives from the excavation site. Suddenly, they remembered something: Dr. Clairia's reaction, the way her cheeks reddened and her eyes shimmered when they mistook her for the guild master's daughter and told her, "Your father asked us to look after you."

"She really loves her father..." said Mavis.

"She's daddy's little girl, huh?" said Pauline.

A fondness shone on both their faces.

Mile, however, was once again compelled to shout a word that did not yet exist in this world: "Are you all a bunch of fathercons?!?!"

"What's a 'father-cone'?" asked Reina.

"Um, it's when a little girl is in love with her father to an abnormal degree."

"Ah." Reina was not so far off from that herself, and somehow or other, she understood.

"Well, anyway," said Elsatorc, "All I wanted to know is that she's happy and healthy. The next time I'm in touch with her parents' village, I'll let them know. Really, I have no doubt that girl sends her parents letters all the time, though I'd bet you she lies and says she's fine, even when she's sick or in trouble, so as not to worry them. I'm sure hearing it confirmed by a third party would put them at ease..."

The Crimson Vow accepted this explanation. They understood what he was saying, and there shouldn't be any problem with telling him how she was. It wasn't as though they had given up her location or anything. With that in mind, they told him only that she was doing well, careful to avoid offering any information about the ruins. Instead, they relayed an amusing story of a blunder that Dr. Clairia had relayed to them when they were sharing gossip—the time when she was standing in line at a festival, pretending to be a child so as to get free candy, and got to the front of the line to find that the one handing out the candy was a nun who recognized her and chased her away...and so forth.

In all the hubbub, Mile finally finished making the revisions to her letter, and she slipped the envelope she had received from Elsatorc in with the original two of differing sizes, then rewrapped the parcel. She handed the parcel over to the clerk and paid the delivery fee, then collected her share from Elsatorc, who thanked them over and over. Finally, the four of them left him, and the guild, behind.

With that, the parcel would be sent on to the next guildhall, then transferred again and again until it finally reached the capital of Tils, where it would be delivered to the one whose name was written on the parcel. The recipient could deal with the rest of it from there. Whether or not the recipient would follow the instructions written within was a matter of mutual trust, but Mile had full faith on that front.

The guild would never reveal from where the parcel had been sent. The fee had been paid in advance, and as soon as the package was opened, the guild would know for whom it was intended, so there was no trouble there. The sender was free to choose how much she revealed of her name and address.

With this, it was unlikely that a third party would ever

discover the Crimson Vow's current whereabouts. When it came to matters of secrecy, the guild could be trusted in full, and the letter itself had nothing in it but the bare essentials.

"All right now, on to the capital. Let's roll out!!" Mile called happily.

The other three smirked.

"Now that I think about it," she continued, guilelessly, "if elves normally live with their parents until they're forty or fifty, and Dr. Clairia is an exception to that rule, then just how old *is* the professor?"

"………"

Mavis, Reina, and Pauline were silent.

However, there was something that none of them yet realized, and that was what might come of the information that they had given to Elsatorc. Sure enough, they had told him nothing of Dr. Clairia's location. However, there *was* someone who *would* know where the professor was.

The next time that the clans made contact, Elsatorc sent on a letter addressed to Dr. Clairia's parents, along with various other documents. The professor's parents were overjoyed to receive this letter from the clan elder, and wrote about it in their reply to their daughter's next letter.

"Gaaaaaaaaaaaaaaah!!!"

Dr. Clairia's beloved father now knew about the bungled

candy fraud incident—an embarrassing blunder that Dr. Clairia didn't even like to think about. She writhed on her bed, clutching her father's letter, which suggested that she shouldn't "behave in such an unbecoming way."

"Grrrgh! How dare he cast such shame upon me—my own dear father! I won't forgive him. Or rather, I won't forgive *them*, those careless girls! I'll find them! I'm gonna find them!!!"

The professor continued to writhe on her bed, howling, before suddenly realizing that she was gripping the precious letter from her father so hard she was wrinkling it. Moving fast, she neatly smoothed it back out and placed it gently into her desk drawer.

"So how long do elves live, anyway? I've read a lot of books that mention them, but none of them ever seem to have an exact figure," said Mile.

Of course, Reina and Pauline—both commoners who had not read nearly as many books as Mile—could not be expected to reply. However, Mavis, the daughter of an influential count, who grew up surrounded by a father and brothers who favored her by talking of a great many things, knew much about the enigmas that were elves.

"The thing is, it's actually hard to accurately determine, and no one can say for certain. Most elves, though they have long life spans, don't usually die of old age, but of accidents, or illness, or fights with monsters. Plus, even among those who do succumb to old age, it seems that there's a huge range in the ages at which that happens.

"There are a lot of theories about this. Some say it's due to differences in magical power, or that it's decided by a roll of the dice at the Goddess's hand when they're born, and so forth... In addition, from the time elves are born until they're about fifteen or sixteen, they develop at the same rate as humans, but after that their development slows, and for about half of their lives they continue to appear as though they're between the ages of fifteen and thirty-five. After that, they go through a period of rapid aging again, and then they fade slowly into their twilight years.

"Actually, that means that Elsatorc, the man we were talking to before, is probably pretty old. With respect to Dr. Clairia, he wouldn't be a grandfather, or even a great-grandfather, but even some earlier generation than that."

"Fwah!"

Mile let out a gasp of admiration.

And then, she suddenly thought of another race that looked young for a very long time.

They're like saiyans!

After many nights of traveling and camping out, stopping now and then along the way to do some hunting and gathering, or exterminating monsters, the Crimson Vow finally arrived in Shaleiraz, the capital of the kingdom of Vanolark, through which they currently were traveling.

Vanolark was adjacent to Mile's home country, the kingdom of Brandel, in the direct opposite direction from Tils, the home country of the other three members of the Crimson Vow and the place where Mile had first become a hunter. Naturally, not a hint of any rumors about some party of rookie C-rank hunters from another land would have made it this far. Therefore, they decided to make a home of this capital for a little while, not as a party who had made something of a name for themselves by standing out a little too much, but instead, as just another bunch of no-name rookies. That would be their objective, at least for the moment.

Back in the capital of Tils, they had become a little *too* well known, thanks to the graduation exam. Having a reputation that was a bit beyond one's station could only be a barrier to leading an honest life.

"First off, we find an inn. We'll be staying there for some time, so we better pick a good one. After we book our room, we pop in at the guild, let them know we'll be around for a little while, and gather some information. And then, for dinner, we feast! To celebrate the start of the third chapter of the legend of the Crimson Vow!"

"Yeah!!!"

"Wait," asked Mile, "What were chapters one and two?"

Reina smiled at this naive question and replied, as though the answer were obvious, "Our meeting at the Hunters' Prep School was Chapter One, and our adventures in the capital of the kingdom of Tils were Chapter Two. Somewhere around Chapter Ten, we save the kingdom from danger and become S-rank hunters!"

"........."

✧◆✧

"This is the place!"

The Crimson Vow stood before an inn. Indeed, it was the inn where they had chosen to stay while they were in this city.

At first, they had stopped by the guild to ask for recommendations, but they had been met with refusal, and the explanation that, if the guild recommended any one specific inn, this would be seen as favoritism and a disruption of fair trade. It was annoying, but it made sense. In a small town, they could expect to get information in the event that the town's two inns were clearly divided into one for the wealthy and one for the common man—or if there was important background knowledge that would safeguard them against unfortunate happenings. However, in a large place with many inns, one had to choose for oneself.

Now that they thought about it, in the town where they had found the House of the Maiden's Prayer and the Wild Bear Lodge, both inns had been meant for commoners, and yet the opinions of the guild staff had been incredibly split, which had been quite a problem.

Probably what had happened when they asked was that the people there thought they were being helpful to some strange little girls who didn't know the way of things in that town. They decided not to dwell on it.

At any rate, the four of them went around to a number of inns, examining the exteriors to see if they were clean and well maintained, checking any rates posted outside, and paying attention to the sort of people who were entering and leaving. After careful consideration, they made their decision. If this inn turned out to be a dud, they would simply reflect on their failure of judgment and use the experience to help guide them next time.

Plus, they weren't taking on a monthly contract this time, so if it was a dud, they could simply change inns the next day.

Ka-cling!

"Welcome!"

As the four of them entered the inn, they were greeted by the chime of the doorbell as well as the cheerful voice of the young girl at the front desk.

Why was it always a young girl at the front desk of inns?

Well, the answer was obvious.

In this world, the death rate for children was particularly high, so everyone had a lot of them. Well, actually, the death rate was high for people of *all* ages, but children were, of course, most susceptible to illness and accidents. So when one had both boys and girls, which of the four major job types—jobs requiring strength, dirty jobs, dangerous jobs, and jobs where you dealt with customers—were the girls most likely to be directed toward?

It was barely even worth thinking about.

The only time you *didn't* see a girl at the front desk was at inns that were staffed only by one family, when that family had no young daughters of their own.

When hiring someone for the job, of course one would hire a young girl, preferably one who was not yet of age. That way you could pay them less. Of course, there was, well, *that*... which should go without saying.

And so, it was no surprise that at this inn, as with most inns, the one at the front desk was a young girl.

"W-we've gotta stay here! For a while! In fact, why don't we live here forever?!"

Mile tugged on Reina's arm, her eyes glinting.

"Wh-what's gotten into you?"

What had gotten into her was this: The girl at the front desk of this inn was a very young girl of five or six. And atop this girl's head were a pair of ears.

Er, well, every human in the world has two ears on their head. However, this little girl's ears were not on either side of her face but on the very top of her head.

Indeed, she was what the youth might refer to as a "catgirl."

"A-a beastgirl..." said three of the Crimson Vow.

"We're in luck!"

One voice stood out—and you should already know by now whose it was...

"Sorry, did my daughter do something?"

Hearing what sounded like a quarrel, a man suddenly came rushing out of the kitchen, flustered. Given that he had referred to the girl as his daughter, he was likely the manager of this inn. In other words, the owner.

With a beastperson as the receptionist, it was probably not rare for guests to try and pick a fight. He was probably used to such a thing.

However, judging from his looks, the owner appeared to be a normal human. Was his wife a beastwoman, then? Or did he have one somewhere in his bloodline?

Sure enough, the beast blood in the young girl appeared to be weak. The beastfolk they had met in the forest were a lot more bestial, with a layer of fluffy fur, but this girl appeared to be mostly human. Except, of course, for the ears.

What about a tail? Did she have a tail? Mile couldn't help but wonder.

"Ah, no, everything's fine. This one here is just kind of a beast-folk enthusiast..." said Reina.

"B-beastfolk enthusiast?"

The owner appeared to be in disbelief.

Indeed, the fact that Mile was something of an anthro-lover was a well known fact amongst the Crimson Vow. They had heard from her, again and again, just how terribly splendid beast-eared girls were. Again and *again*, to the point of fatigue...

"U-uhm, can I touch them?" asked Mile, a peculiar glint in her eyes.

Reflexively, the owner moved to stand between her and the counter. Perhaps sensing danger, he stepped forward to tend to the reception duties himself.

"So, were you looking to lodge at this inn?"

"Yes. We wanted a four-person room for an indefinite stay. Might you have any rooms available?"

Glancing Mile's way, the owner looked ready to refuse, but after several seconds of internal conflict, finally he squeaked out, "U-unfortunately, we do..."

"........."

"Have some decency, Mile! Keep a handle on those weird desires! You made us look ridiculous out there!"

The moment they entered their room, Reina immediately began laying into her teammate.

"B-but she had cat ears! *Cat ears!*"

"There were people with cat ears at the ruins, too!"

"Th-that was different! Those things on the tops of stinky old men's heads were different! They may have looked the same, but they were completely different!!!" Mile protested desperately, bristling at Reina's assertion.

Unable to understand why Mile had gotten so terribly worked up, Mavis and Pauline stood slack-jawed.

"Hang on, I'm going downstairs. Be back in a minute!"

Barely a few moments had passed since they entered their room on the second floor, but now, for some reason, Mile was heading back down to the first.

"........."

There was no point in stopping her. Seeing how she kept fidgeting, she would be useless in any further discussions. They would have to give up on going by the guild today. Having come to that conclusion, they decided to let Mile do as she pleased.

Mile's heart was pounding with joy, but she crept down to the first floor, walking silently so that the owner would not take notice of her, and took a seat at the table closest to the front desk. She then removed from her inventory some jerky, some dried sardines, some milk...and some *catnip*.

This was just unfair! Mile was playing dirty!

In her previous life, too, Mile had always kept some fish sausages and Baby Star ramen in her bag, just in case she should run into a cat or a pigeon. (Baby Star ramen is very popular with pigeons, you see.) So of course, she would never go about unprepared in this world, either.

In her storage, she had jerky and dried sardines that were low in sodium; milk that was nutrient-rich and free of lactose, which cats could not properly digest; and a small sprig from a catnip-like plant that she had spotted one day while in the midst of a gathering request. All of these she had stored away in the inventory for safekeeping.

Jerky and sardines that were meant for humans were too salty for cats, and the cow's milk that was drunk by humans did not have enough nutrition for the little creatures either—plus they got diarrhea from the lactose, and under the wrong circumstances, they might perish. Mile would never allow herself such a misstep, yet the catnip was still rather dangerous.

Catnip affected a cat's central nervous system, so in some very rare cases, their breathing could become over-labored, which too could lead to death. Yet as long as it was only used in small amounts under observation, there wasn't a huge danger of that, at least.

And so, Mile looked over to the front desk and the girl who stood there, and began to wave at her, sprig of catnip in hand.

Twitch.

The young girl's ears perked up in Mile's direction.

Sway sway.

Twitch twitch.

Sway sway sway...

Twitch twitch twitch...

Sw—

Grab!

"Gyahh!"

"Just what do you think you're doing?"

The owner stood behind Mile gripping her by the head, an expression of pure anger on his face.

"I, uh, well I was...!"

Mile panicked.

"My daughter is not a cat! Catnip has no effect on her!"

"So you've tried it, then?"

"Er..."

It would seem that he had.

Well, there *were*, in fact, many cases where catnip had no effect on a kitten or female cat to begin with...

After an extended discussion with the owner, Mile somehow managed to get across the fact that she harbored no ill intentions. That said, he still refused to believe that she had anything but a wicked heart. However, Mile could not even bring herself to accept that.

"So you don't hate people with beast blood—in fact you adore them. But still, what the hell were you thinking? Are you stupid?"

"Are you really one to say that?!"

"I, uh, well..."

Indeed, as Mile implied, he certainly was not one to talk.

Finally, after Mile promised the owner three things—one, that she not give the girl so many snacks that it would interfere with her eating three square meals; two, that she was forbidden to use catnip or any other suspicious items on her; and three, that Mile not interfere with her work—she was granted permission to play with his daughter, little Faleel.

Still, when Mile requested that, at the second evening bell, after Faleel finished her work at the front desk-slash-dinner register, she come up to their room to play until she got sleepy, the owner screamed, "Then when am *I* gonna get to play with her?!"

It was a reasonable objection.

"You really brought her up, huh?" Reina asked wearily.

After her discussion with the owner, Mile had returned to the room, and the four discussed their upcoming plans. Afterwards, they returned to the first floor and ate dinner. Mile waited with baited breath, and when the second evening bell finally rang, she swept Faleel up princess-style and carried her back up to their room.

At the moment, the owner was busy cleaning up the kitchen and getting started on the next day's preparations. As soon as he finished, he would come up to collect his daughter.

Mile hugged Faleel from behind, sitting the girl on her knee. And then she began scratching behind her ears, just at the base.

"Bwah, that tickles..."

Faleel was in turmoil.

"Stop that!"

Crack!

The side of Reina's hand smacked down upon the crown of Mile's head.

"M-my turn next!" Mavis cut in from beside her.

Naturally, Mavis, the youngest of her family, who was always one-sidedly doted upon by her elder brothers, had aspirations... of spoiling and cherishing a little brother or sister of her own, that is.

"Wh-what about my turn?" Pauline asked, fidgeting. She was nostalgic for the days when her little brother was young and she had to look after him while their parents were busy at the shop.

"You all, I swear..."

With a weary face, Reina rebuked all three of them.

"Obviously, it's *my* turn next!"

About an hour after the second evening bell rang, the owner came up to the girls' room to collect his daughter.

"Wha…"

He knocked and opened the door, then stopped, his eyes wide in shock at what he saw inside. It was Faleel, playing with the Crimson Vow, rolling around laughing.

"I-Is that really my shy little daughter?"

Indeed, those who patronized the inn never discriminated against or bullied little Faleel, whose beast lineage was quite clear. Anyone who might be keen to do would flee the inn the moment they saw her sitting at the desk—or if they were to make a fuss about it, the owner would chase them off. Nonetheless, the girl maintained a rather reserved manner, very unlike the overly familia…er, not thinking of guests as gues…ahem, um, *friendly* sort of manner that little Lenny had with her customers.

Of course, Lenny was ten years old, while Faleel was only six. She had few topics to make conversation about, most jokes went over her head, and so forth.

At any rate, until now, the owner had never seen Faleel even smile, let alone roll with laughter, around anyone who wasn't her family. Come to think about it, though she *was* a shy girl, he could not recall ever having seen her laughing so joyfully before, even around her own family.

"………"

Though working at the inn did keep him busy, perhaps there was a problem here.

The owner hung his head in shame.

Didn't I Say
to Make My Abilities
Average in the
Next Life?!

CHAPTER 45

A Suspicious Request

THE NEXT MORNING, when the girls descended to the first floor for breakfast, the owner was nowhere to be seen. He was most likely away in the kitchen, leaving little Faleel to tidy the room and set the tables, along with two slightly older boys.

Wait, he has three children? I wonder if his wife is off in the kitchen, too.

Mile pondered this as she looked at the three children but then noticed something strange: both of the boys appeared to be normal humans.

Hm?

All four girls were curious about this, but while the family was busy running around with breakfast preparations, they wouldn't have time to be answering any questions. Unlike during dinnertime, the guests who were present for breakfast would all be showing up rather quickly within a brief time frame. Even if the menu was fairly truncated compared to the dinner spread, they would still be quite busy. It would go against common sense to try and take up an employee's time with frivolous things during a rush like this. Instead, the common etiquette for any diner would be to eat quickly so that his or her table could be freed up for others.

Thinking this, the Crimson Vow sat quietly, all their attention on their meals. However...

Huh?

Mile tilted her head yet again. Just now, she had caught a glimpse of a woman in the kitchen. More than likely, she was the owner's wife—in other words, Faleel's mother. However, yet again, this woman appeared to be nothing more than a normal human. Of course, she had only caught a glimpse, so perhaps Mile had missed something. Perhaps Faleel's features were merely some atavistic, recessive trait—or there was some other peculiar circumstance at work. However, whatever that might be, as nothing more than a group of overnight guests, it was really none of their business to comment on.

Mile pretended that she hadn't seen anything and silently returned to her meal.

After eating, the Crimson Vow popped back up to their room, strapped on their dummy packs, and then left the room behind, completely empty.

They did, of course, intend to stay at this inn again tonight, but depending on the job they took, there was a possibility that they might end up leaving the city for a short while. Should that happen, they would not wish to leave anything outstanding, and so, they decided to settle up the bill for now as well.

"We'd like to pay now, please," said Reina at the desk.

"Huh? Big sisters, you're leavin' already?!"

Faleel was startled by the request, and a look of sadness spread across her face, but Mavis quickly explained.

"No, no, it's just that we might have to go far away for a job, so we just want to take care of our bill now. If there aren't any good jobs, or there aren't any jobs that need us to go away overnight, then we'll be right back here tonight! Even if we have to go far away, we'll definitely come back after."

Hearing this, Faleel looked relieved. Apparently, she was quite enamored of them.

All according to my plan...

As Mile silently gloated, feeling as powerful as the god of a brand-new world, she happened to look over to the inn's guest register, which lay atop the desk. In the blank space beside their four names, there appeared to be some manner of childish scrawl. Perhaps it was Faleel's notes for her own personal reference.

What might she have written? Suddenly burning with curiosity, Mile read along to see...

Mayvis: Shes tol but shes got no chest. Probly a elf.

Rena: Shes got fangz. Shes probly got sum beestfok blood in her. Just lik me.

Poline: I sens evil on her. Probly a deemon.

Miel: Shes a skwirt. Probly a dworf.

H-how rude!

Did she think they were some kind of all-star cast of non-humans?! Mile seethed internally, but of course, she could not reveal such a reaction to a child of only six years old.

That said, if Reina or Pauline were to see this, things were sure to get out of hand. Mile casually flipped the page of the register to one that did not have their names written upon it.

Still, her analysis of Pauline was spot on! A beastperson's intuition is a fearsome thing!

Once the bill was settled, the Crimson Vow headed to the local capital branch of the Hunters' Guild.

"We are the C-rank hunting party the Crimson Vow, registered in the capital of Tils Kingdom. We are currently journeying in order to gain new experiences, and we will be stationing ourselves in this city for a short period. We look forward to working with you all," Mavis explained at the reception window, introducing the group.

"Oh, my, my! Thank you! How courteous," the clerk replied, smiling wide. "My name is Felicia. I'm the receptionist. The city of Shaleiraz welcomes you! If you desire, I can have one of our representatives give you information about this city, as well as the monsters and gathering spots in the surrounding areas. Would you like that?"

"Will it cost us?" asked Pauline.

"Ah, no. We provide information as well as local maps and other materials to anyone who has come from afar and will be operating here for some time, free of charge. It is part of our sworn duty as guild employees to provide for the security of our hunters and safeguard against any unnecessary trouble."

There was no sense looking a gift horse in the mouth. The four girls replied as one, "Please and thank you!"

As the Crimson Vow sat at a nearby conference table receiving their information from the representative, a number of glances were cast their way.

There was a slender beauty, of around seventeen or eighteen;

A busty beauty of around sixteen or seventeen;

And two cute little girls of around twelve or thirteen...

And among them were two highly valuable mages.

Normally, to have a C-rank party with that sort of composition, at least three of the members would have to be C-ranks—or else, if the two youngest were perhaps still D-ranks, then at least one, if not both, of the two who were of age would be B-rank. In a country such as this, which had nothing like the Hunters' Prep School, a girl of twelve or thirteen who was a C-rank was almost unheard of. Honestly, even in Tils, which did have such a school, the sight was rare. For a young person to attain such a rank, she would have to have some manner of extraordinary skill or some special abilities, such as outstanding magic genius or the like...

A beautiful girl under twenty who was already at a B-rank was an even more improbable sight. Even with as much strength and renown as the Roaring Mithrils had, only their leader, Gren, had yet to rise above a B-rank. It was not a rank that some little girl could attain easily.

In other words, this was a group of beautiful young women, youthful in body but with the strength of hunters much their senior, with special abilities and no man in sight. Such myths were sung of in the bawdy epics of troubadours across the land, with titles like, "The Ballad of a Man's Wet Dream."

Most of the hunters who were based in the capital of Tils had been present at the graduation exam. Therefore, they were already aware that the Crimson Vow had incredibly exceptional abilities for rookies. As a result, no one of lesser ability ever dared make a pass at them, and no one of greater ability tried to tangle with them either.

Plus, they all feared what rebuke might come from their betters should anyone dare lay a hand upon the girls.

Their betters. Including higher-ranking hunters, the guild's upper management, or the Crown...

And so, it had been tacitly decided that all the hunters would watch over them.

Yet here in a foreign land, where such details were known to none, the Crimson Vow appeared a tasty morsel indeed. And now, the all-male parties who were present here in this, the capital branch of the Hunters' Guild of the Kingdom of Vanolark, sat biding their time, waiting for the appropriate to time to speak to the Crimson Vow, silently keeping an eye on the competition.

After the guild employee finally finished giving the girls the rundown on the area, the Crimson Vow stood and moved to check the current entries on the information board. This would have been a prime opportunity, but what they were doing was an incredibly crucial task for hunters, so much so that interrupting them now would leave a horrible first impression. The men continued to wait, no one yet daring to call out to them.

After they were through with the information board, the Crimson Vow moved to check the job board. When they had decided upon a job and were moving to the reception window to further discuss it—*that* would be the moment to strike. That would be when the men could offer advice or pointers, or propose they accompany the group to the hunting grounds, as it was their first time in an unfamiliar place—or some other excuse.

Most of the parties who were aiming for the Crimson Vow came to the same conclusion at once. And because they all knew that the others knew what they knew, a fierce and silent war broke out...

"Oh!"

Just then, Mile suddenly raised her voice.

"What's up?" asked Reina.

Mile pointed to a single card that was pinned to the board.

Investigation request. Reports of a group conducting suspicious activities at Golem Ridge. Members to be captured or executed pending results of the investigation.

The four looked at the request and then looked at one another. In the back of all their minds floated the images of the beastmen operating at the ruins. News of the investigation into the beastmen had yet to make it this far, apparently. It would probably take time for those in the palace to investigate and discuss what was to be conveyed to other kingdoms.

And so, Reina tugged the posting from the board.

"Are you sure?" Mile asked.

Reina shrugged her shoulders.

"You want to do it, don't you? Even if it wasn't our main goal, this was one of the points of this whole journey for you, wasn't it? I mean, this might not even have anything to do with that other incident at all. Even if it did, well, we already know that beastfolk are no big thing. And if one of *those* shows up again, I get the feeling that we can just bring up the names of those guys from last time in order to get them to sit down and have a conversation. Anyway, I doubt that anything that coincidental would happen here."

Mavis and Pauline nodded in agreement.

This was perhaps a little overly optimistic. The last incident had been settled neatly, but there was no guarantee that things would go so smoothly the next time. Regardless, Mile wanted desperately to take this job and continue her investigation. She nodded as well.

The pay was fairly decent, but given that the level of danger could not be easily predicted and there was no guarantee that the hunters would necessarily encounter their targets, the job seemed to have been posted there for some time without anyone choosing to take it on. Seeing that the Crimson Vow intended to accept this job, the other hunters, who had been waiting to speak to them, were confused. In their confusion, they lost their chance to talk to the girls entirely.

Things don't always go the way one hopes they will.

This was also true of the Crimson Vow, who assumed that the individuals they might encounter this time would also be beastmen. They had already forgotten what the elder dragons had said—namely, that they were going to check in on the beastmen *and* demons who they had investigating on their behalf across the land.

"Huh? Um, this is the job you wish to take, then?" Felicia, the clerk, asked as Mavis handed her the job slip, confusion clear upon her face.

"Um, it is. Yes?"

"I would really recommend choosing differently..."

Not this again!

This was the third time now. The four were growing weary.

"We are already fully aware that there's a chance that this job has been left as a 'red mark' job, that the level of danger is unclear, and that it's possible we might turn up empty-handed, with a failure mark. One member of our party is still underage, but we are a full-fledged C-rank party, so there is no need to worry about us. Should we happen to fail, the blame lies solely on our shoulders," said Reina.

As there was nothing that Felicia could do, she reluctantly processed the request. Even she was aware of what it meant that the Crimson Vow were C-ranks at such a young age. And she knew how many other parties would have set their sights on them, as well. Of course, what had put the glint in those men's eyes was

not just that the Crimson Vow had the ability of C-rankers, but also that they were a group of beautiful young girls. Had they merely been a C-rank level and nothing else, there would be much less excitement from the hunters. Yet as it stood, most of the parties who were currently present were practically drooling.

Furthermore, their young ages meant that, even if they had talent, they would still be lacking in experience, which should have put their abilities at a firmly middling level. To become C-ranks so young, things must have been going quite favorably for them, so it was likely they had become rather conceited. This was the primary reason that talented hunters often died early deaths.

In other words, the chances of the girls successfully completing a job that so many other hunters had avoided was slim. This was Felicia's logical conclusion.

They were a group of cute young girls—a rarity amongst hunters—and they were polite and courteous to the guild staff. It would weigh terribly on her conscience to have them travel all the way to this kingdom only to have get wiped out on their very first job there. With this in mind, Felicia shot a wild look at the local hunters, who had all neglected to take on this job that the Crimson Vow had just accepted. It was a look that said, "Do something!"

There was no hunter in this capital who was foolish enough to defy Felicia's command. Swiftly, one five-man party jumped into the fray.

"You girls have a moment? You all just arrived in this kingdom, didn't you? I can't say I applaud the choice to take on a dangerous job in an unfamiliar territory with so many uncertainties. What do you say? Why don't you pick another job? Or, if you *really* want to do it, why don't we tag along with you?"

The young man smiled, a sparkle in the flash of his pearly whites.

The Defenders of the Covenant were a crack team of five beautiful young men, known to those at this branch as the Pretty Boy Party, but they were more than just a set of pretty faces. They were fairly skilled for a group of men still in their twenties, and except when it came to matters involving women, they were fairly sincere. As the party's name suggested, they were men who kept their promises.

The other parties were stomping mad that this lot—of all people—had jumped out ahead of them, but it was their own faults for hesitating to make the proposal themselves.

Indeed, the proposal that the Defenders had made was a right and just one. Felicia nodded heartily, satisfied. At least, until the Crimson Vow replied.

"We don't need any extra burdens."

"I'm pretty sure you all wouldn't be able to keep up with us..."

"That'd make our cuts of the pay go down!"

"Ahaha..."

"Wha...?"

The leader of the Defenders was speechless at their replies. Felicia was slack-jawed as well.

"Y-you're being a bit hasty there, aren't you?" the leader

managed to get out, still forcing a grin, though his cheeks were twitching.

However, as far as the Crimson Vow were concerned, their affairs were very clearly none of his business. Just as they said, the men would be nothing but a burden, and besides, they had certain battle techniques that they were not prepared to reveal to others.

They did not enjoy making fools of other hunters, but if they did not assert themselves now, more and more parties would try to come cozying up to them later on. So, reluctantly, the Crimson Vow decided to make this into a demonstration.

As always, Reina gave the direction.

"Mavis, do the thing."

"On it. Excuse me, could someone please take out a copper coin and toss it up in the air?" Mavis asked, urging the others around her to move away and clear the space for safety's sake.

"Sure, I'll do it," one of the hunters offered, intrigued.

And so, the coin was thrown.

Shing!

Swish!

Snap.

There, before everyone's eyes, were two freshly cut halves of a copper coin atop Mavis's outstretched palm.

Yes, once again, it was the copper-cutting trick.

She cut the coin, snatched it with her left hand, then sheathed her sword with her right. She had practiced this so very many times that it was no longer even useful as a training device and had been relegated to nothing more than a party trick.

"Wha...?"

The hunters and the guild staff were wide-eyed in shock. The leader of the Defenders of the Covenant was wide-eyed as well, but he was yet undeterred.

"A-are you a B-rank?" he stammered. "Well, even if you have one B-ranker, the rest of your party is still made up of only a mage and two underage D-rankers. You won't be able to get enough done. You need to team up with us—we've got a full front line."

Mavis cocked her head, confused.

"I honestly have no idea what you're talking about. Everyone in this party is a C-rank, and if you wanted to know who among us was the weakest, I... No, never mind."

Even though Mavis herself was the one who was about to say it, she was a little bit depressed at the prospect.

Reina then placed her next order.

"Mile!"

"Okay! Pardon me, another coin, please!"

At Mile's request, the hunter who had thrown the previous coin pulled out another from his purse.

Shing!

Swsh!

Snap.

Just as in the previous display, Mile snatched back, and then held out her left hand.

Unlike the last time, the coin atop her palm was cleaved not in two parts but into four.

"........."

This time, even the leader could not speak.

All of the frontline fighters in the building were completely silent, but from somewhere in the room, someone who sounded like a backline mage raised their voice.

"Might we see the mages' skills, too?"

While the coin-cutting trick was nothing more than a simple demonstration, when you watched a mage use magic, it revealed a number of things about the range of their skills. Even if you faked it a bit, anyone watching could make a fair guess at your abilities based on your specialty, your casting speed, and your efficiency. It was probably only an urban legend that you could determine a tank's effectiveness from watching it fire a single round, but there had to be at least a grain of truth to it.

And so, in response to that question, Pauline replied as follows:

"We could certainly show you, but if we do, could we request that any ruined buildings be restored or any deceased persons brought back from the dead? We can destroy things on our own, but unfortunately we can't restore anything or resurrect anyone."

There was not a being alive who could do such a thing—except perhaps the gods.

"........."

At this, the mages in the room fell silent, too.

"Now then, if you'll excuse us," Pauline said to Felicia, tipping her head slightly, and the Crimson Vow, having finished their job-acceptance paperwork, left the guildhall behind.

When Felicia finally returned to her senses, she looked toward the B-rank party, the Silver Fangs, who had been sitting at a table in the corner watching the commotion, and flicked her chin.

Signal received, the five men slowly stood.

There were two swordsmen, one lancer, and two mages. Every one of them, front line to back, wore bright silver breastplates atop their leather armor, which was clearly how the party got its name. Seeing that they were B-rank, they were financially stable, and all of them were in what could be said to be the prime of their lives, so they had no interest in clamoring after some little girls. And so, they had merely sat and watched the preceding circus with a smile—even if they, too, were stunned at the copper-cutting display.

But now, at that chin signal from "No-Hope Felicia," one that clearly said, "Follow them," they hurriedly stood.

"No-Hope."

This was a shortened version of, "Anyone she glares at better abandon all hope." Not even the Silver Fangs would be so bold as to defy a signal from her. Not in the slightest.

The Silver Fangs, who had already been thinking of going away for a while, had made all their necessary preparations and simply popped into the guild one last time to give their regards before heading out. Therefore, they were ready to leave at a moment's notice. Felicia knew this, of course, and it was why she had chosen them.

The Silver Fangs left the guildhall in a hurry, and soon enough the Crimson Vow were in their sights. They appeared to be standing around chatting about something—and the Silver Fangs, who had overheard their conversation in the guildhall earlier, decided against approaching them directly, instead choosing to follow at an appropriate distance.

"All right, time for our 'Sahnik Spied' move! Let's go!"

"Okay!"

At Reina's call, the other three crowed in reply, and all four switched into the high-speed mode that Mile had introduced to the group, the so-called "Sonic Speed."

First, Reina, Mavis, and Pauline all dropped their swords and staves, along with the dummy packs that they carried, and placed them in front of Mile. Mile stored these away, along with her own sword and pack, and in exchange, produced a set of small flasks, handing one to each of them.

Indeed, with each of them carrying the minimum amount possible, they could move much faster. Even if they should suddenly be faced by robbers, it would not take Mile more than a second to retrieve everyone's gear from storage and hand it over. Anyway, the staves actually had nothing to do with casting spells. As long as they were walking on a road with good visibility, there was no increase in danger.

"Now, onward to Golem Ridge! Crimson Vow, roll out!"

"Oh, they're walking now. What were they just doin'?"

"Who knows? C'mon, let's follow 'em!"

And so, the Silver Fangs began following the Crimson Vow, leaving a wide gap between them. Still, as soon as they started walking, the men noticed something peculiar.

"Th-they're fast!"

"We can't keep up with them at this rate!"

"Th-there's no way a bunch of little girls can keep up this pace! They've probably just temporarily sped up for some reason. I'm sure they'll slow down soon."

The Silver Fangs were optimistic about this, but soon enough, one of them noticed something else.

"Say, is it just my imagination, or are they not carrying anything?"

Because the Fangs were traveling at a distance that would keep them from being discovered—or at least allow them plausible deniability if the girls did notice them, they could not clearly make out the details of the party. Yet now that he mentioned it, it did appear that they weren't holding anything at all.

"I'm pretty sure they all had packs on when they left the guild, didn't they?"

"Yeah... Plus, there's no way anyone could just go up to Golem Ridge empty-handed."

".........."

No matter how long they walked, the Crimson Vow's pace did not appear to slacken.

Even if they were in the prime of their lives, there was no way that a group of men, burdened down with gear and weapons, food and water, medicine, camping materials, and so forth, could ever hope to keep up such a pace on foot. And yet that was the pace of these four speedy young girls, who wore nothing more than a single tiny flask at each of their waists...

The Silver Fangs. The silver breastplates that each of them wore were the party's namesake.

This armor that they all wore was not only for the sake of granting them stronger protection, but also served as a proud mark of the party's unity. At the moment, however, that proud mark was nothing but a burden.

That beautiful, gleaming silver armor was rather heavy.

Truthfully, this was the reason that most hunters wore only leather armor. Even knowing this, it was party policy for each of the Silver Fangs, from the frontline fighters to the backline mages, to wear their silver breastplates. This policy favored protection over ease of movement, and it was perhaps due to this that they had all lived to become B-ranks, so perhaps it was not such a bad choice after all. On the contrary, it was the optimal choice for this party.

Now, however, they were finally seeing the downside.

"This is hopeless. Sorry, you all go ahead. I'll catch up with you when those girls stop to take a break..."

One of the mages dropped out.

Then the second mage dropped out.

"Sorry guys, just go on without me. When those girls make

camp for the night, come back up to the main road and wait for us to catch up."

Typically, mages did not have the stamina of frontline fighters to begin with. Unlike the mages of other parties, the mages of the Silver Fang were stalwart in battle, thanks to those silver breastplates; however, the burden of their armor became enormous when they tried to move fully laden.

"Damn it, they aren't slowing down at all," the leader grumbled, some time after the two mages had dropped out.

Just then, the Crimson Vow broke into a run.

"Wha?!?!"

The distance between the two groups widened in the blink of an eye.

"I can't do it, I can't keep up! This is it for me!"

"Idiot! If we go back with our tails between our legs like this, Felicia will... Well, you know! *That!* It's *that* I'm talking about! There's a reason she's called 'No-Hope Felicia'!"

"In that case, please, leader, you go after them! And once they've settled on a campground, please come back and let us know."

".........."

It was then that the Silver Fangs finally understood what the swordswoman who seemed to be the leader of the Crimson Vow had said:

"You'd never be able to keep up with us..."

That was not just some empty boast meant to make a fool of the other hunters but an expression of an honest fact.

"Think we've lost 'em, Mile?"

"Huh?"

"The other party that was following us. That's what it was, wasn't it? If there wasn't something like that, you wouldn't have suddenly said, 'Why don't we jog for a bit?'—would you?"

"Ahaha!"

Reina's guess was dead-on. Mile laughed and scratched her head.

"I'm tired. Can we go back to walking now?" wailed Pauline, who had the least stamina of all of them.

Mile figured it was probably fine now, so she allowed them to return to a normal pace.

"So this is the place..."

Thanks to the map that was provided to them by the guild staff and some directions from a helpful traveler they met along the way, the Crimson Vow arrived at the mountainous area known as Golem Ridge around sunset the next day.

For most normal hunters, the journey would have taken a bit longer, but if they did not arrive by sunset, then they would have had to make camp for yet another night and not arrived until the next morning. It was only a half day's difference in time, but the difference between getting started on their job in the afternoon when they were already weary and getting started bright and early in the morning after a full night's sleep was immense.

"Let's take it easy tonight so we can be ready for tomorrow. First, let's start getting dinner ready..."

"And then it's story time!"

What exactly had Mile so excited for those folktales of hers this time?

The Wolf Boy
Once upon a time, there was a young wolf boy named Ken...

The Ant and the Grasshopper
Grasshopper: "Would you mind sharing some food with me? Even a little will help."

Ant: "Uh, sorry Grasshopper, but this is all for me."

Grasshopper: "Aw c'mon, Ant..."

The Little Matchgirl
"That's it! If I'm going to freeze to death anyway, I might as well use this little match to set the whole town ablaze!"

"........."

As tonight's Japanese folktales drew to a close, all four girls were overtaken by sleepiness.

The next morning, the Crimson Vow used magic to draw some hot water and had a simple breakfast. Mile packed away the tent, still erected, and they were ready to roll out several times faster than any normal hunting party would be. Their destination was the peaks of the mountains. Naturally so, as the other hunters' reports of suspicious people had come from parties who were heading up toward the summit.

Even if they came up empty-handed, they could still go home with the same things that those other hunters were likely after—AKA rock lizards and herbs that grew only on the summits of rocky mountains, such as the elusive "rocky mountain summit grass."

They could have at least put a little bit more thought into that name, Mile grumbled internally.

"About 30 meters ahead, in the two o'clock position! There's one rock lizard, medium size!" Mile reported.

Reina was swift with the command.

"Let's get it! Mavis, Mile, get ready for an ambush! Pauline, get your freezing magic ready and then hold!"

"Roger!"

After their first experience hunting that large rock lizard, they had since acquired many others, all stored away in Mile's inventory. That way, even if they ended a job without catching one, they would not end up taking any demerits.

After dealing cleanly with the rock lizard, they continued

to head for the summit. That was when Mile reported, "At the 12:30 position—huh...? R-rock golems! Three of them! That's right, now that I think about it, based on our past encounters I should've expected there would be golems around, since wherever there are rock lizards..."

"Huh?"

The other three stared blankly at her.

Very timidly, Mavis asked, "M-Mile, do you have any idea what the name of this place is?"

"Huh? Of course I do..."

"Then say it!" Reina said with a scowl, rubbing her temples.

"Okay. I'm pretty sure it was Golem Ridge... Ah."

The other three were struck by a terrible fatigue before the battle could even begin.

Ker-blam!

Wham!

Ka-smack!

It was over.

The three golems rolled onto the rock face, their legs obliterated. As they tried to drag themselves along with their arms, Mile and Mavis pierced the golems through the heads with their swords, and the creatures ceased to move.

"I knew it. If you destroy the parts of their heads that are in charge of their sight and hearing, they stop moving. But why? It doesn't seem like that should count as a vital area for them."

Mile stared at their lifeless bodies, her head cocked, but the other three appeared wholly uninterested.

"What are you doing? Let's go already!"

"C-coming!"

The Crimson Vow proceeded toward the summit, slaying rock lizards and rock golems along the way, but soon Mile began to feel a sense of unease.

"Are we being watched?" she asked.

Reina nodded. Mavis and Pauline, whose senses were not so sharp, stared blankly.

"That's strange. According to the guild's information, the suspicious parties were split up into several groups, all keeping hidden and working in separate areas. As soon as the hunters encountered them, they ran away. They didn't say anything about lookouts."

"Maybe they've gotten farther along in whatever they're doing, and the circumstances have changed?" Mile suggested.

"Why is it only at times like this that you show a bit of smarts?!" Reina shouted.

Mavis and Pauline nodded in agreement.

"Th-that's rude! Even at the prep school, my marks on our class assignments were better than all of yours, weren't they?!"

"That's right, come to think of it."

Mavis and Pauline looked as though they could not believe it. Seeing their expressions, Mile puffed out her cheeks.

"*I'm* the one who can't believe *you* guys!"

Somehow, Pauline managed to calm Mile down, and they returned to their conversation.

"Well, nothing's going to come of all this if we continue on this way. So, shall I do it?"

"Please do," Reina confirmed.

Carefully Mile retrieved her slingshot from her inventory, moving in such a way that anyone watching might think that she was pulling it from her pocket. Of course, there was a mismatch between the size of her pocket and the size of the slingshot, but, well, one couldn't think too hard about that.

She gripped a metal pellet, likewise drawn from her "pocket," and fired a quick shot. These were not the pebbles that she normally used for this purpose but specially made metal slugs. Most pebbles were oblong, which meant that their firing accuracy was lower, and there was a chance that they might explode on impact, which could cause quite the disaster. The metal pellets would not miss their mark and were guaranteed to sink in or pierce through their target.

Fwip!

"Gaaaaah!!"

It hit.

Apparently, the metal slug had pierced its target.

Really, being pierced through was not such a bad thing—far better than the alternative of having something lodged in your body. If there was a metal pellet lodged in your flesh, you would have to dig deep to wrench it out again.

Naturally, she had not struck any vitals.

On the surface, it would seem as though the Crimson Vow had taken the preemptive strike, but in this world, if you were following someone at a close distance undercover, observing them, it was likely that you were planning a surprise attack, so you could not complain if you were attacked in return. Being struck by a surprise attack would put one at a huge disadvantage, so it was only natural that the Crimson Vow might counter with all they had the moment they caught wind of such a thing. Anyone who subscribed to daft philosophies like, "If you aren't attacked, then there's no need to counterattack," or "No attacks until you can justify a legitimate self-defense," would soon perish here. The ones who abandoned such foolishness lived on.

Therefore, it went without saying which of these two opinions was most prevalent in this world. Dead men could tell no tales, after all.

Anyway, what if their followers were only scouting without any intent of violence? Well, scouting undercover was malicious enough, so it was fine to knock out or capture them.

"Now to bring them in for questioning…"

"Don't move a muscle!"

"Frame!"

"Wha…?! A magic barrier?!"

Hearing the sudden, commanding voice from behind, Reina immediately shot off a fire spell, but the suspicious person quickly countered, putting up a wall of magic in defense. Unlike ice javelins, which were made of tangible, materialized ice, fire spells could be deflected with magic.

The man, who appeared to be some sort of leader, had just managed to get the magical barrier up in time before shouting,

"Wh-what's the big idea?! Why would you just attack us like that?!"

The group of suspects was made up of four men, the same number as the Crimson Vow. All four of them were wearing hoods. At first glance, they appeared to be human, but two protrusions atop each of their heads made their hoods stand up at points.

Those are beast ears, aren't they?! That's way too conspicuous!

Among the beastmen they had encountered at the excavation site, the majority were far more fuzzy in appearance, but that did not mean that there could not be those among them who appeared mostly human. The Crimson Vow, who had just recently seen little Faleel at the inn, would not be so easily fooled.

Likely, the beastfolk had chosen from those of mixed blood for this cover operation, sending out those individuals whose human traits were more predominant so that the humans would not suspect their true nature.

"What are you talking about? Isn't it obvious?! You were lurking at a close range, scouting us out, so that you could launch a surprise attack. Shouting, 'Don't move!' is as good as saying, 'We're about to capture you!' isn't it? Who do you think would just stand there and obey? If you like, why don't you come along with us to the capital and report to the authorities? We wouldn't mind that all."

"Er..."

The man who appeared to be their leader was lost for words.

"Now, why don't you go ahead and tell us why it was that you were planning to attack us? Be honest. If you don't, you'll be executed as bandits."

"What?! Why would you call us bandits?! Humans are such cretins..."

"Shut up, you idiot!"

The leader frantically tried to stop his companion's reply to Reina's needling, but it was already too late. He had already as good as confessed that they were not humans. Though, honestly, the state of their hoods had given them away from the start.

"My," said Mile, "I've heard an exchange just like this before. We've already encountered cohorts of yours investigating some ruins in another kingdom, so we know the whole story. Plus, your hoods are sticking up. We've found you out, and you must be hot under there. Why don't you go ahead and take those off?"

"Y-you bastards! Just how much do you know?!"

The leader, already resigned to the fact that their cover had been blown from the get-go, lowered his hood. Seeing this, the other three lowered their hoods as well. With their ears covered, it was more difficult to hear, and of course, Mile thought, the continuous pressure on those ears had to be uncomfortable. But then...

What appeared from under their lowered hoods was a pair each of... horns. *Horns.* HORNS!

"Th-they're cowmen!" Mile exclaimed unconsciously.

At this, the four men all screamed at once. "We're demooooooooooooooooons!!! We aren't beastmeeeeeeen!!!"

"Huh?"

"Huhh??"

"Huuuuuuuuuuhh???"

They had heard that demons and beastmen were on friendly terms, but apparently demons could not abide being mistaken for their allies. Interracial relations are such complicated things...

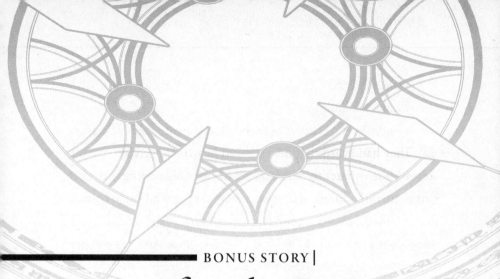

After the Rain

"Looks like the rain's finally stopped," said Mile.

"Thank goodness," Reina replied.

"It's been three days now. Hopefully, we can finally go out and get some work done tomorrow."

"But it's still gonna be all damp and muddy out in the woods. Why don't we stick to jobs in town for the next few days?" said Pauline, a bit peevishly.

"What are you talking about?! There are plenty of parties who go out and work in the rain. Pauline, you're too soft! As a C-rank hunter, you need to have a bit more discipline."

"Oh, yes, you're right, I'm just soooooo awful!"

Perhaps as a result of being cooped up in the inn for three whole days with nothing to do, an unprecedented aura of discontent had begun to emanate from Pauline.

"Now now, that all depends on what's on the job board, anyway…"

With Mile, the calmest of them all, as the rare voice of reason, the room settled down.

In her previous life, Mile had always been the indoors type, so being stuck in the inn with no amusements was no huge bother for her. Therefore, her mood had deteriorated little, and she had not grown so grouchy as her friends. As long as Mile had a paper and pen—and in fact, even without those, as long as she had her imagination—she could enjoy herself no matter how many days went by. She truly was an easygoing girl.

A rainbow…?

Mile clambered up to the roof, which was finally dry. She lay on her back looking up at the sky, pierced by the light of the sun, renewed after the storms.

It's been thirteen and a half years since I was reincarnated. So, three and a half years since my reawakening…

She thought of the walks that she and her sister used to take with their family just after the rain had let up. Back then, too, there were the most beautiful rainbows…

Her sister, her father, her mother… Were they all doing well?

Well, with someone as steadfast as her sister there, she needn't worry.

Mile smiled as she thought this, yet for some reason, even though the rain had stopped, there were streams running down her cheeks.

There's a rainbow, huh?

As Reina stood out in the yard, looking up, she thought of a time long ago.

She had been traveling with her father, waiting out the rain with their cart parked beneath a big tree. The rain had stopped and the sun came out again, and then, above them appeared a beautiful rainbow.

Then, too, there was the grand, sky-spanning rainbow that she had witnessed from the top of a mountain while traveling with the Crimson Lightning...

For a long time, she had thought that, even if she were to see a rainbow once more, never again would she feel the emotion—the happiness—that she did back then.

But now, for some reason, she felt that perhaps that was not such an impossibility.

Why would she feel that way?

Somehow, she knew the answer, but she fooled herself into thinking that she didn't.

Without Reina herself even realizing it, the corners of her mouth tugged at her cheeks, just a little.

A rainbow...?

When she was still very little, the sight of her elder brothers, forging themselves into knights, dazzled her.

And when they finally rose into the knightly ranks, she wanted to be just like them.

On the day of her eldest brother's promotion ceremony, after the rain, a beautiful rainbow spread across the sky...

And she swore a vow upon that rainbow. That one day, without fail, she too would become a knight.

The rainbow swiftly faded away, but the feelings she felt on that day and the vow that she had made—those things would never vanish. That seed of brilliance had taken root deep inside her and would only continue to grow.

She could do it.

As long as her friends were there beside her, Mavis von Austien could seize that rainbow.

All the female guests at the inn who saw the brilliant smile upon her face stiffened, their cheeks going red, but that was none of Mavis's concern.

Finally, the three of them returned to their room.

"Oh? Pauline, you haven't been outside? There's a lovely rainbow out there."

"Looking at a rainbow isn't going to make me any money. Instead of wasting time on that, I could be counting my coins..."

Reina and Mavis could only shrug at this ridiculous reply.

"Oh, that's right," said Mile. "In my country, there was an old tale that was passed down saying that there's a pot of gold buried at the end of every rainbow, at least according to—wah!"

Before she could even finish her sentence, Pauline grabbed Mile by the shoulders, staring at her with wide, bloodshot eyes.

"Let's go! What are you all waiting for? Hurry up and get ready to leave! You've got a shovel, right?!"

"Ah, ok, that's—wait just a..."

"........."

Surely, any "pot of gold at the rainbow's end" was not something that one could possibly hope to grasp. The moment you thought you had seized it, it would slip through your fingers and disappear.

Even knowing she was by no means a fool, upon seeing how Pauline's eyes had instantly clouded with greed, Reina and Mavis could only shrug, having already grasped the truth from Mile's description.

It was the same as always. Every. Single. Time.

"A rainbow then, is it? I wonder if somewhere out there, she's looking up at this rainbow, too..."

"I'm sure she is. Adele always loved seeing rainbows, after all."

"Yep. I bet you that right now, Adele's saying something like, 'I wonder if Marcela and the others are seeing this rainbow, too.'"

"Hehe. I'm sure you're right. I'm certain of it."

Didn't I Say
to Make My Abilities
Average in the
——— Next Life?!

Afterword

HI EVERYONE, FUNA here. Long time no see.

I present to you Volume 5 of the *Didn't I Say to Make My Abilities Average in the Next Life?!* light novel series.

The Crimson Vow have left the kingdom of Brandel behind and are continuing on their journey of self-improvement.

They are reunited with an old town and some old friends. Along the way, they encounter some new places, some new acquaintances, and a cute little catgirl. And, just at the end, perhaps some new enemies?

What does tomorrow hold in store for the Crimson Vow?

It is thanks to all of you that this series has been able to continue on for five whole volumes.

This is Volume 5! Volume 5! That's halfway to Volume 10!! (Obviously.)

It's been one year now since the publication of Volume 1 and my true authorial debut. I wonder if I'll get my promotion from "greenhorn" to "novice" soon.

Last month, the momentous one-year anniversary of the start of my career as a novelist, it was miraculously announced that one of my previous works will be published as well.

On June 2nd, K Ranobe Books, Kodansha's brand-new label for titles that were originally published as web novels on Shosetsuka ni Narou, will be publishing my *Shousetsu* debut, *Living on Potion Requests!* as one of their very first offerings—and on July 2nd, another of my debut projects, *Working in a Fantasy World to Save Up 80,000 Gold for My Retirement* (serialized the same time as *Potion Requests*) will be published by them as well.

In addition, both titles will be receiving manga adaptations, to be serialized in the web comic magazine, *Wednesday Sirius* (http://seiga.nicovideo.jp/manga/official/w_sirius/).

Because this series was so swiftly noticed by the folks on high, and because of its publication, these two other titles, which were from my origins, and which I had thought would only vanish into the depths of my memory, will now be making it to print as well. These two series, which I thought were nothing more than a foundation, boosters one and two on the lunar rocket that shot *Abilities Average* up into the sky, destined themselves to sink beneath the waves, forgotten.

But instead, here they are, showing right up alongside *Average*, saying, "Eheh, finally made it!" and "Sorry to keep you!"

Gosh, I'm so moved. I'm gonna cry!

...Ah, yes, right, this is the afterword for *Average*, isn't it, not for *Potion Requests*. A totally different publisher, you say? My apologies.

Well, anyway, it really feels like I'm used to the pace of a real novelist at this point, and now that I'll be continuing my previously unfinished and abandoned works along with the current one—all three at once—I will continue from my frantic first year as a novelist on to an even more hectic second year, I'm certain.

I mean, I truly am grateful.

I'm really not complaining, not at all.

Anyway, expect to see some new enemies and a new battle in Volume 6 (if it comes out)!

Please look forward to it!

And please, look forward to the reprints of this series, as well as its manga, as well as the publication of *Potion Requests* and *80,000*, along with their serialized manga versions, too.

Of course, as always, the manga version of *Average* can be found in the web serial, *Earth Star Comics* (http://comic-earthstar.jp/).

And finally, to the chief editor; to Akata Itsuki, the illustrator; to Yamakami Yoichi, the cover designer; to everyone involved in the proofreading, editing, printing, binding, distribution, and selling of this book; to all the reviewers on Shousetsuka ni Narou who gave me their impressions, guidance, suggestions, and advice; and most of all, to everyone who's read my stories, both in print and online, I thank you all from the bottom of my heart.

Thank you so very much.

Please continue to enjoy this novel and the manga from here on out.

With all of your powers combined, I'm sure we'll see it through to the next novel.

And then, I'll be one step closer to my dream...

—FUNA

Didn't I Say
to Make My Abilities
Average in the
Next Life?!———

AFTERWORD?

ITSUKI
AKATA